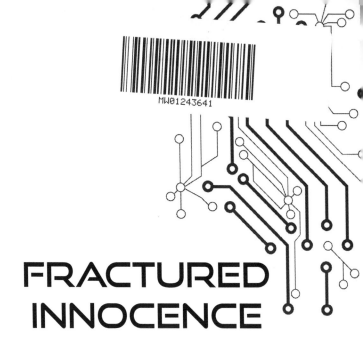

MW01243641

FRACTURED INNOCENCE

JULIA CRANE

Fractured Innocence
Copyright 2013 by Julia Crane

Published by Valknut Press
Clarksville, TN

ISBN-10:162411055X
ISBN-13:978-1-62411-055-9

"Freak of Nature" edited by Claire Teter
Cover art by Eden Crane Design
Formatted by Eden Crane Design

To my street team!
You have no idea how
much your support
means to me.

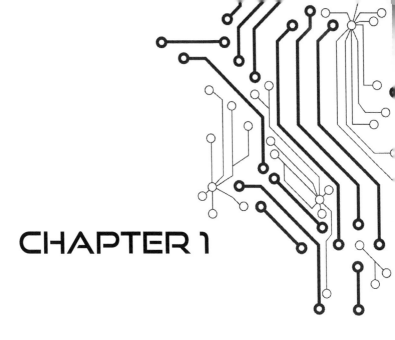

CHAPTER 1

Kaitlyn unwrapped the towel from around her head and dropped it into the hamper. Her dark hair tumbled down her shoulders.

Lucas gazed at her from the doorway. She loved the way he watched her so intently. It made her feel special. Wanted. Loved.

There'd been a time in the not so distant past when she was lonely and ached for any human connection. She'd been terrified of showing even a hint of emotion, knowing she would be reduced to even more of a robot and less of a person if she did. Fear had caused her to hide away what little human elements were left of her, tightly guarding herself by placing a protective wall around her.

Thankfully, those days were behind her. For the most part anyway. In the back of her mind, there was always the knowledge that IFICS still held all of the cards.

She paused. It still surprised her how easily

slang terms slid into her mind since the latest upgrades. *Held all the cards.* At least that phrase somewhat made sense, if one knew what poker was. Many phrases or sayings offended her sense of logic.

Kaitlyn crossed the room and opened the dresser. She stepped into her underwear and then into her black pants, pulling them over her hips. She clasped her bra and pulled the long-sleeved black shirt over her head. Sighing, she tugged at the sleeves to make sure all of her robotics were hidden from the human eye. On the compound, she could walk around freely and not have to hide what she was, but today they were leaving the compound.

She felt oddly exposed in the long-sleeved T-shirt. She had to move carefully so the sleeves didn't ride up her arms and reveal what was underneath—the parts of her body that made her not quite human.

Kaitlyn caught a glimpse of Lucas in the mirror and processed the creases in his forehead as concern. "It's going to be fine, Lucas."

"I know." He mumbled, raking his hand through his dark hair, making it even more tousled than usual. It was a nervous habit of his that she loved so much. "I'm just worried. This is your first *real time* mission. I'm a little distressed, that's all. So many things could go wrong."

Kaitlyn turned and met his gaze. Just the way she was taught. "Dr. Chambers told me I need to take your fears seriously, but you more than anyone know I can take care of myself. You helped program me, remember? There really is nothing to worry about."

"I guess." Lucas hesitated and then continued. "I know it doesn't make any sense, but a big part of me wishes I was going with you instead of Erik. There I said it." He gave her a half smile, and his cheeks flushed.

Kaitlyn inspected Lucas as he crossed the room. Her eyes roamed his bare broad shoulders and rippling stomach. The plaid pajama bottoms clung to his muscular thighs. Reluctantly, she tore her gaze away from his body and forced herself to look back towards his troubled face.

His clear blue eyes had never left her face. He came to a stop mere inches from her. She could feel the heat radiating from his body. She wished she knew how to put his mind at ease. She could tell by his elevated heart rate he was upset.

"Erik is a capable partner. You really don't need to worry. If anything happened to me, he would complete the mission."

Lucas's body tensed, and he took a physical step backwards. He looked as though she had punched him in the stomach. *Not good.*

He swallowed. "Jesus, Kaitlyn, I'm not worried about the mission. I'm concerned about *you*. It would kill me if anything happened to you."

She tilted her head and looked at him puzzled. "You would not die, Lucas. Your heart would continue to beat."

Lucas slipped his arms around her waist and pulled her towards him. His eyes bore into hers, making her feel weak in the knees. "It would feel like I died."

She laced her arms around his neck and pressed her body to his. Often her mind did not understand the human emotions, but her body did. Every fiber of her being wanted to be close to him. Comfort him. "I guess I'll just have to be extra careful."

He lowered his head, while Kaitlyn tilted her face upward. His lips pressed warmly against hers. She loved the way she felt in Lucas's presence. He made her feel alive—human. Her hand dropped to his chest to feel his familiar heartbeat. Her sensors could tell her his beats per minute, but deep down she knew the elevated rate was because of her nearness. It was exhilarating to know she had such control of his body. She was astonished by the power a simple touch had; it was completely fascinating.

A stroke of her hand made him shiver and her own desire spiraled wildly. Where Lucas was concerned her emotions ran freely. It was the rest of the world she had trouble with.

His hand slid from her waist to her ribcage, drifting slowly upward until his hand cupped her breast. Kaitlyn sighed. Less than an hour ago, they had been entangled in each other's arms. Her body still tingled from the feel of his bare flesh on hers.

"We could crawl back in bed," he whispered.

Reluctantly, she pulled away. "I can't be late, Lucas."

He touched her cheek gently, and a sad smile crossed his face. "You can't blame me for trying."

"I'll be back soon. It really shouldn't take very long." Her mind had already switched to the mission at hand. An image of the target, Vance Dasvoik, flashed in her mind with a bull's-eye on his head. Thirty-four years old, wavy dark hair streaked with gray, olive skin, cleft chin and unusual honey colored eyes. He looked normal, but he was by all accounts a very dangerous man. One that she would take pleasure in destroying.

"Not soon enough." Lucas ran his hand over his face. "But, you're right. We need to get to Harrington's office. He'll be pissed if we're late. I gotta throw on some clothes."

"I'll be downstairs." Kate grabbed her bag off the floor and trotted down the steps.

She wasn't looking forward to the changes she had to undergo this morning. Her teal-colored, robotic parts would be replaced with skin-colored pieces. She had argued with Harrington about it, but he insisted she needed to be able to blend in. In case anything went wrong.

Kaitlyn wanted Dasvoik to see exactly what was coming for him. To see the fear in his eyes when he saw a half human raining hell down on him.

Professor Adams had argued that she was showing vanity, and that was not the way she was programmed, which quickly shut down her own arguments. The last thing she wanted was more changes to her programming.

In the end, Harrington agreed to leave the parts on her back visible, as long as she never exposed herself in public.

Over the last several months, IFICS had accepted the glitches in her programming and was willing to work around them. No matter how robotic they made her, there was a human element that had to be dealt with. To say it was a learning process was an understatement.

She started out staying with Lucas in his

apartment off the compound, but she kept bringing too much attention to herself. Accidental eavesdropping on their neighbors revealed they thought she was some sort of freak, despite her attempts to emulate human behavior.

She wasn't ready to be in the real world. As much as it pained her to admit it, Harrington had been right about her forever being stuck between the world of humans and computers.

Kaitlyn pulled on her boots and took a final glance around their small home. Domino, their cat, rubbed her head against her leg, purring. Kaitlyn leaned down to scratch behind the cat's ears. She would miss the stone cottage and the cat. But mainly she would miss waking up with Lucas by her side.

After several months of cognitive behavioral therapy, Kaitlyn was finally allowed to live with Lucas. Of course, there had been a catch. They had to reside on the compound. Thankfully, as part of the compromise, they had their own house that was separated from the main buildings. No cameras and white walls that had marked her first few months as a laboratory experiment, before anyone realized that she was still human on the inside.

Another plus was their home was not too far away from where her good friend, Quess, lived with her grandparents, and there'd be no neighbors to gossip about how strange she was.

Harrington insisted he needed her nearby in case anyone tried to breach the compound. Even though she knew he had top of the line security and highly trained guards. Lucas explained to her that Harrington had been appealing to the ego they knew lingered from her human body.

Kaitlyn's appreciation for Harrington's brilliant mind increased tenfold. That man had a grasp of human nature that she would never possess.

As leery as she was about living on the compound in the beginning, it had quickly grown on her. She had the best of both worlds now.

Where was Quess? She should have already been there to say goodbye.

As if on cue, the doorbell rang.

Kaitlyn tugged the door open. Quess beamed up at her. Her copper curls peaked out from the green knit hat on her head. Her usually pale face was red from the cold.

"It's freezing out there. Let me in!" Quess laughed.

Right. Kaitlyn still forgot little things like that. She stepped aside and Quess crossed into the room until she was in front of the heater and held her hands over the vent.

"Are you excited?" Quess asked, her eyes dancing.

Kaitlyn returned the smile. Besides Lucas, Quess was the only other person Kaitlyn felt she could be herself around. She leaned in and whispered, "Probably too excited. Don't tell your grandfather."

Quess gave her a look. "As if I would tell him anything. You know better than that."

That was true. She really did trust Quess. She'd kept her secret—the fact that she still had human feelings—for a long time.

"How long will you be gone?"

"I really don't know. In theory, it should be a

quick mission. But Erik says nothing ever goes as planned."

"Erik is hot." Quess bit her lip and giggled.

"Is he?" Kaitlyn asked. She'd never thought of him that way before. Quess was always going on about boys.

"You're blind if you don't see that." Quess walked over to lean against the couch. "But I know you only have eyes for Lucas."

"That's true." Kaitlyn smiled.

Lucas came down the stairs. He was dressed in jeans and a dark sweater. His hair was disheveled as usual. "Did I hear my name? What are you girls talking about?" He looked at Quess and back at Kaitlyn.

"Erik's hotness." Quess grinned.

Lucas frowned. "Quess, you're like what, fourteen? I think he's a bit old for you."

"Fifteen now, I didn't say I wanted to date him. I just said he was hot. Cause he totally is."

Kaitlyn liked having Quess around, but today she was eager to get to work. "We need to get going."

"Geesh, just kick me out why don't you," Quess said.

"You were supposed to be here earlier." Kaitlyn reminded her.

"I know. I slept in. It's hard to get out of bed in this cold weather."

She wasn't sure what getting out of bed had to do with the weather, but she seldom knew what Quess was talking about. The girl was like an enigmatic puzzle that Kaitlyn was always trying to solve.

Quess crossed the room and threw her arms

around Kaitlyn. Kaitlyn froze, and then patted the girl on the back as Quess squeezed her tightly. This was not normal. Kaitlyn pulled back and looked down and was surprised to see tears in Quess's eyes.

"What's wrong?" Kaitlyn asked, alarmed.

Quess wiped her eyes with the back of her sleeve. "Nothing. Don't mind me. I'm just going to miss you. That's all. I know you'll be fine."

"I will be fine. You and Lucas are worrying over nothing." Quess's tears were making her uncomfortable.

Kaitlyn pulled back and looked at Lucas as he shrugged into his jacket.

"If we leave now we'll still be a few minutes early as long as we walk at a 5.5 mph pace. It's only twelve point thirty-three seconds from the cottage."

Quess snorted, and Kaitlyn turned to see if she was all right.

Waving them away, Quess said, "Hurry up and get out of here. I'll lock up and feed Domino while you're gone."

"I should be home in time." Lucas wrapped a scarf around his neck.

Quess shrugged. "If you say so."

"Are you ready?" Kaitlyn asked, meeting Lucas's eyes.

"Let's get it over with. The sooner you go, the quicker you'll get back to me." He grabbed a hat and pulled it over his ears before opening the door for Kaitlyn. She brushed past him, and he inhaled her clean scent.

She stopped and turned. "Bye, Quess."

The girl lifted her hand in farewell, then

picked up Domino in her arms before dropping into a chair.

Thirty-seven degrees outside. Kaitlyn's processor kicked in and regulated her body temperature. With haste, they made their way across the sprawling compound. A light sheen of frost coated the grass. The trees were mostly bare and the sky dreary and overcast. Lucas shivered beside her.

"I hate the cold." He mumbled, rubbing his hands together.

Kaitlyn grabbed his hand and interlaced her fingers through his. Her body heat radiated from her to him. He squeezed her hand.

"I think I envy that gift the most."

Kaitlyn tilted her head. "Gift?"

"Upgrade, gift, ability, whatever you want to call it. I'd love to never have to worry about being too hot or too cold."

It was hard for Kaitlyn not to think of herself as a freak. So when Lucas said things like 'gift' it threw her off. "It's normal to me so I don't know any different. I can't even remember what it felt like to be hot or cold." Kaitlyn saw the main building up ahead. She couldn't wait to get started. Finally, she would be able to use her *gifts.*

They stepped into the large reception area with charcoal-colored carpeting, light gray walls and black leather chairs placed around the room. The secretary sat behind a large onyx desk, appearing aloof, in her navy pantsuit, under the soft lighting.

Kaitlyn strode past the woman without so much as a wave. Lucas hurried behind her mumbling sorry to the woman. What he had to be sorry about, she had no idea. Maybe he knocked something over. No, she would have heard it.

"Kate, you should have stopped at the reception desk."

"We have an appointment. It's an unnecessary waste of time."

Lucas sighed. "The secretary should buzz Harrington and let him know we are here."

She looked at him blankly. "He knows what time we'll be here. This is not a surprise visit."

"Okay." He held up his hands in mock surrender. "You're probably right."

Kaitlyn pushed through the door to his office. Harrington looked up from behind a large mahogany desk. His dark hair was as perfectly styled as his handmade suit. His sharp blue-grey eyes, ruggedly handsome face and broad shoulders gave him a further imposing look. Harrington raised an eyebrow but didn't say anything. As usual, he commanded the room by his appearance alone.

Sometimes Kaitlyn wondered what was the driving force behind Harrington's focused intensity. She had grown to know and care about him over the past several months, but she still didn't understand him.

"We're a few minutes early," Lucas explained.

"I see that. Well since you're here, have a seat and we'll wait for Erik."

Kaitlyn sat down and stared straight ahead. She filtered through the noises: steady tick of the clock, the whirl of the electronics, the rustle of papers as Harrington continued to read the file in front of him, and Lucas's steady breathing.

A few minutes later, she heard Erik talk to the secretary outside, before he came through the door. He took a seat on the other side of Kaitlyn. She didn't look up or acknowledge him.

Harrington stood up and hit a button on his keyboard. Seemingly out of nowhere, a large computer screen appeared behind him. "Now that we have everyone, I want you to look over these photos. This is what you are going to find. You got a glimpse in the target folder."

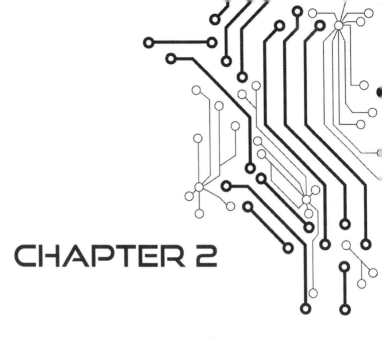

CHAPTER 2

Slowly, Harrington slid his fingertips across the screen, flipping through the images. He paused at the most heartbreaking ones—the close-ups. Rows and rows of cages filled with naked, filthy girls, and a few young men. Some of them were very young, maybe only eight or nine, but the majority appeared to be teenagers. They were without a doubt terrified. Harrington pinched and expanded one of the faces of a pretty, dark-skinned girl with frightened brown eyes. He left it there and sat back in his seat to face them.

"Bastard," Erik mumbled under his breath, his eyes locked on the screen.

Lucas's jaw tightened as he looked at the images. "That sonofabitch!"

"This is outrageous," Kaitlyn said, unable to believe what she was looking at. She knew the facts over two point four million people across the world were victims of human trafficking, eighty percent of them were exploited as sexual slaves. Somehow seeing the images blown up made the statistics more real.

"Remember, you're not on a rescue mission. You are there to detain or remove Vance and get the hell out of there. Human traffickers like him are cunning, dangerous and hard to catch. We'll send in a rescue team afterwards."

Kaitlyn nodded once. In and out—as discreetly and expeditiously as possible. The mission should be quick and easy. She tore her eyes away from the images. *Caged like animals.*

Erik leaned forward, his gaze upon Harrington. "These things never go as planned, and there's only the two of us. We'll have no backup?"

Harrington sat back with his fingers forming a teepee, tapping his lips. "Second thoughts, Erik?"

"No. Of course not," Kaitlyn said hurriedly, not waiting for Erik's reply. There was no way they were backing out now.

Erik glanced at Kaitlyn and then relaxed in his chair. "No, sir. I just wanted to make sure I was clear on the particulars."

"As you know, you will be in constant contact with Lucas and myself. If you get in a bind and need to be extracted, there will be a team on stand by."

"Who sent you the photos?" Lucas asked.

"We have an inside man. And before you ask, no he will not be of help to you once you board the ship. His identity is to remain a secret. It took a very long time to get a man embedded in Dasvoik's operation. He may come in handy later."

"When are we leaving?" Kaitlyn asked. She was

anxious to get started. With a quick glance back at the monitor, she thought about what Harrington said, about it not being a rescue mission. If there was any way possible she knew she would help them escape, regardless of Harrington's orders.

"We'll be flying on our private jet to the isolation facility. From there we will get more information."

"And where exactly is that?" Erik asked with a slight tilt of his head.

"Undisclosed location," Harrington said, firmly closing the conversation.

"Will Lucas be going?" Kaitlyn asked. This was the first she'd heard of an isolation facility. She had wrongly assumed they were going straight to Croatia.

"Yes. Myself, Lucas and Professor Adams will all be joining you."

Kaitlyn kept her face neutral, but she was relieved to know he would be joining them. She wondered if Quess already knew and that's why she offered to feed the cat.

"Olivia would like to see you before we depart," Harrington said, glancing at Kaitlyn, before he picked up the papers spread out on his desk, and neatly placed them back in the folder.

"Fine." Kaitlyn wasn't sure what she thought of Dr. Chambers. She knew the woman wanted to help her, but she was still apprehensive when it came to their sessions. Why did she need to see her right before they left? It would only delay their departure. But Kaitlyn knew better than to argue with Harrington.

She stood up and slipped out the door, effortlessly making her way down the long hallway towards Dr. Chambers' office. She could hear Lucas and Erik's footsteps echo behind her on the marble floor. It occurred to her that she hadn't said goodbye to Harrington.

Dr. Chambers' office sat off to the left at the end of the long hallway. Kaitlyn actually enjoyed being in the main office building on the compound. It was full of color, a stark contrast to the laboratory where she spent most of her time, where everything was sterile and stark white.

It occurred to her that footsteps no longer echoed behind her. Lucas and Erik must have veered off at the main entrance.

Absently, her hand touched the mocha colored wall, and she paused to take in one of the unusual abstract paintings. The splatters of colors spoke to her for some reason. It was almost as if she could feel the despair of the artist.

She shook her head and wondered where that thought had come from. Perhaps the artist had been jubilant when he or she put the paint to paper. Kaitlyn couldn't begin to know what was on someone else's mind, let alone someone she had never met. She couldn't evaluate their social cues or speak directly to the artist.

Why had her mind wandered down this path?

She dropped her hand and continued down the hallway. The silence enveloped her and sent a wave of calmness through her. Knowing that she was about to embark on a mission that would put an end to an evil man filled her with a sense of peace. A kind of peace she had not known since the day she woke up and noticed the teal plastic on her arms. Kaitlyn cringed, recalling the distressing day she realized she'd been turned into a cyborg. The day her life crashed down around her.

She didn't like to think of the countless hours she'd spent in the hospital bed, and later in the lab, constantly hiding the fact that she was terrified, alone and full of despair. Lucas and Quess were the only people who treated her like she had at least once been a human being. Their kindness had meant the world to her, even though she could not acknowledge her feelings.

Of course, when the opportunity presented itself, Kaitlyn escaped the confines of the compound, only to find herself even more alone and frightened. Faced with her past, Kaitlyn realized her old life had ended and decided to embrace the second chance at life that a cruel twist of fate had presented to her. A chance to make a difference.

Harrington had crossed every moral line when taking advantage of Kaitlyn's passing. No one understood why she still possessed certain feelings and emotions. Quess believed that they made the exchange so quickly after her death that her soul still lingered. A teenage girl was the only one to come up with anything even remotely plausible as an explanation.

Whatever the reason, Kaitlyn was grateful. Secretly, she relished the idea that her soul might still be intact.

The large wooden double doors loomed up ahead.

Hopefully, the session would go quickly. Her processors kicked up and quickly leveled out as the realization hit her that it was finally time.

Something good had to come out of her

transformation. If she could help others, it was well worth the loss of her old life. It thrilled her beyond belief that she was inching closer to putting her skills to good use. All of the hours of training had not been in vain.

But, first she had to get through this meeting with Dr. Olivia Chambers.

Kaitlyn walked into the waiting area. A cursory glance told her the secretary was not at her desk, or anywhere in the immediate area, so she proceeded to enter the doctor's office without knocking and closed the door behind her. She was immediately accosted by the floral sent of the doctor's perfume, Shalini, nine hundred dollars a bottle. The doctor, like Harrington, had expensive taste.

Dr. Chambers looked up from behind her desk, her fingers pausing over the keyboard. Her dark brown hair was down today, in loose curls around her face. For some reason, the look made her appear less abrasive. Usually, she wore her hair up in a bun and out of her face. Kaitlyn briefly wondered if changing her hairstyle might make her less robotic. She pushed the thought aside, because she often wore her hair down.

"Good morning, Kaitlyn. It's wonderful to see you, but what did you forget?"

Steps faltering, Kaitlyn did a quick scan of her mind, trying to comprehend what she'd done wrong this time. She'd only been in the room two point two seconds. There was no secretary. Dr. Chambers had requested to see her. Whatever she had done wrong completely escaped her, which was quite frustrating.

It always bothered her when she didn't live up

to the doctor's expectations. She looked forward to the praise Dr. Chambers gave her each time she learned a new nuance of human behavior. Kaitlyn found she pushed herself harder to try to impress Dr. Chambers, but there were consistently minuscule things she couldn't seem to grasp. It was as if her mind rebelled by telling her they were not important enough to retain. Which was absurd, since her brain was filled with innumerable pieces of useless information. She could speak several languages fluently, and yet she continued to remain socially awkward. It hardly seemed fair.

"I'm not sure. What did I forget?"

"You have to knock before you enter the room. If you do not, it's considered invading someone's privacy."

Kaitlyn filed the comment away and nodded her head in understanding. Often, it felt like she would never learn all the rules of society. She'd made the same mistake in Harrington's office. Lucas tried to warn her, but she had not listened. Perhaps it was because privacy was new to her. Everything she'd previously done was monitored by cameras. Her data was always readily available for Lucas and Professor Adams to read. The only privacy she'd had was a small corner of her mind that she had managed to keep to herself even after all of the upgrades and operations.

"Sorry." She didn't feel sorry, but at least she knew that was the proper response. Keeping up human appearances was exhausting. It had been easier when she pretended to be robotic at all times. However, her ability to blend in as a human was one of the things that made her such a valuable asset, which meant she would have to keep trying to improve.

"Please, have a seat." Dr. Chambers nodded her head towards the seat.

Kaitlyn lowered herself into the leather seat. She sat ramrod straight as her eyes scanned the room. Degrees hung on the wall displaying the doctor's impressive academic accomplishments: Stanford, Columbia and a medical degree from Harvard.

Bookshelves lined the back wall, filled mostly with non-fiction titles.

A vase of tiger lilies sat on the edge of the desk, and for the first time Kaitlyn wondered if the doctor was married. She didn't wear a wedding band, but that did not really confirm or deny her marital status.

"You can relax in here, Kaitlyn."

That was the good doctor's way of reminding Kaitlyn that she was being too stiff. Too robotic. Kaitlyn rolled her shoulders and relaxed her posture. She couldn't help but wonder if any of this would one day be second nature to her. *Probably not.*

Dr. Chambers entwined her fingers together and set them on her desk. Her complete attention focused on Kaitlyn. It made her uncomfortable. Dr. Chambers spoke to her as a person, but deep down Kaitlyn still felt like a science experiment. As if she was always on display with everyone waiting for her to mess up.

"What would you like to talk about today?"

Kaitlyn frowned, looked at Dr. Chambers, and didn't try to hide her frustration. Her hands clenched and she consciously relaxed them. "You asked to see me. If it were up to me, I would be on the plane right now."

"I see. So you feel like I am delaying your mission?"

"Yes." *Clearly.*

"Your flight will not be leaving for a few hours. I assure you, Kaitlyn. I would never waste your time. I know you are playing a vital role in this company. I'm only here to help you."

Kaitlyn just stared at her. She wasn't sure what her response was supposed to be. *Thank you*? *I'm sorry*? Neither of them seemed to fit the situation, so she said nothing. She was also annoyed Harrington didn't mention the delay. They were supposed to be leaving at six in the morning.

After a short beat of silence, Dr. Chambers closed her laptop and pushed it aside. "How do you feel about the mission?"

"How do I feel about killing someone who sells children into slavery?"

"I notice you say kill and not detain?"

"I don't plan on letting him live." Kaitlyn crossed her leg over her knee. As the doctor's eyes glanced down, a small smile tugged at her lips. She always approved when Kaitlyn adopted mannerisms she had drilled into her head over the last few months. Kaitlyn made a conscious effort, because she knew the doctor's approval or disapproval could sideline the mission.

"I'm afraid that is not the correct answer. You are tasked to detain Mr. Dasvoik and only use deadly force if your or Erik's life is in jeopardy."

"I'm not programmed that way. Vance Dasvoik

is my target and I am to destroy him."

"I see. Perhaps Harrington will have to make some changes to your coding." Dr. Chambers paused and leaned back in her chair. "After this mission, of course. I've seen the photos, and I happen to agree with you, Kate. But if you were ever detained, you cannot admit this."

"If I were detained, Lucas would have to shut me down."

"Yes, I guess he would. How does this make you feel?"

"I knew the risks when I agreed to come back to IFICS." Her chest tightened at the thought, but she would not show nor tell the doctor.

"Of course, but it must bother you on some level?"

Kaitlyn looked away. "It will not happen. I am more than capable of completing this mission."

"I hope you're right for all of our sakes. It's very risky sending you out."

"Dasvoik needs to be stopped. I can stop him."

"Yes, I believe you can. Thank you for stopping by to see me, Kaitlyn. I just wanted to make sure you didn't have any second thoughts."

"None." Kaitlyn pushed her chair back and stood up. Just as she was about to open the door, she turned and said, "Goodbye, Dr. Chambers."

The doctor smiled. "You've made great progress. I will see you when you return."

Kaitlyn nodded and walked into the hallway.

What an odd exchange.

"Kaitlyn."

Kaitlyn pivoted on her foot in the direction of Dr. Chambers, who was now standing in the doorway.

"You need to go to the laboratory for a final check up."

"I know. I am heading in that direction now," Kaitlyn said. She caught herself before she rolled her eyes. Obviously, she needed to go to the laboratory.

"Oh, okay." Chambers paused and tucked a strand of hair behind her ear. "Kaitlyn, please be careful."

Startled by the obvious concern in the woman's voice, Kaitlyn scanned her face to see if the feeling was legitimate. She noticed the crease between her brows and the slight frown on her lips. Like Lucas, she was honestly concerned for her wellbeing. The realization resonated somewhere deep within.

"Thank you for your concern," Kaitlyn said before continuing down the hallway. Many thoughts raced through her head. But at the forefront of her mind was the stirring of acceptance. IFICS was starting to feel like her new family, even though images of her old life still haunted her dreams. The chance at a second life looked better every day.

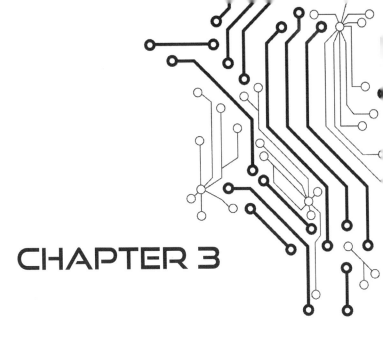

CHAPTER 3

Aaliyah's heart sped up when Noah pulled her close. She inhaled deeply. He smelled of soap and spice. How in the world she'd gotten lucky enough to catch his attention was beyond her, but she thanked her lucky stars every night. And every morning she prayed for one more day to be with him. Even if it really were just one more day, she'd still consider herself to be the luckiest girl on the planet. Scratch that, luckiest girl in the *universe.*

Only seventeen-years-old and already blessed with the kind of love people write books, movies and songs about. God was smiling down at her, that much was clear. As a thank you, she would be grateful and gracious to everyone she crossed paths with in her lifetime. It was the least she could do.

"You're gorgeous," Noah murmured into her

mass of curly hair.

Heat rushed to her face. Would she ever get used to his compliments? She hoped not. Vanity was a sin. But it felt so good to hear the words from his beautiful mouth.

His pale fingers trailed down her mocha arm. She loved seeing the contrast. It always sent a thrill through her body.

"I wish you didn't have to pick your brother up tonight," Noah said, tangling his hand in her hair while gliding his thumb on the nape of her neck. "We never get enough time together."

Aaliyah sighed. She also wished she didn't have to pick him up, but Darrius was her brother—her responsibility. Besides it wouldn't take *that* long to get him.

"I could meet you afterwards?" Aaliyah said with a trace of hope in her voice.

Noah pulled away and stared sadly into her eyes. "I wish I could, but I have to study for a test tomorrow."

Her shoulders slumped. Of course he had to study. He went to a prestigious private school where he was preparing to go off to some Ivy League school like his parents. At times like this, she was reminded of the vast difference between them. And it was much deeper than skin color. Aaliyah came from South Africa. They once had money and now had nothing, and Noah was born with a silver spoon. The saying *wrong side of the tracks* was an understatement in regards to her. Yet another reason Noah's affection awed her. He was so sincere and wonderful.

It had been mere coincidence that they ever crossed paths. Her mother made and sold tribal pottery as a side business. One of the many wonders of America. The ability to make money doing something you loved to do. Noah's mother had heard about the pottery from a friend and contacted her mom via the phone. Fate.

Since Aaliyah's mother's English was poor, she sent her daughter to deliver the requested piece. Her lips turned up at the memory of Noah opening the door. One glance had caused her heart to fall clear down to her toes. He was the most beautiful boy she had ever laid eyes on. Pale skin, freckles, green eyes and black shaggy hair that fell over his eyes. Perfection.

"Wow." He'd said, and stood staring at her with the same look of wonder that she knew was on her own face.

Speak. She stood there like a tongue-tied fool. The memory still made her grin.

"I'm supposed to drop this off to your mother." She'd held the vase out with hands trembling.

"Where are you from? Your accent. I've never heard it before."

"South Africa."

"Your eyes..."

That was everyone's reaction to her. She had unusual eyes compared to the rest of her. Her blue-green eyes were a stark contrast to her dark face, high cheekbones and full lips. Her mother's face.

"My grandfather was German and my father, well I'm not sure what he was." Her voice trailed off. Talking about her father made her uncomfortable. Her mother never said much about him. All she knew was the relationship was short and she never got the chance to tell him she was pregnant. A photographer passing through town.

She knew she was an anomaly. In the village, they looked at her like she was a witch child. She'd grown used to the stares and the whispers, but here in America, she *sorta* blended in. This was one of the many things she had grown to love about the States.

Aaliyah realized she was still holding the vase and standing outside the doorway. The boy was still staring at her.

He cleared his throat as he stepped back, letting her pass him and enter the enormous house. A large chandelier hung in the open living room off to the left. She'd been awed by the rainbow colors reflecting off the light. Even today she could recall the feeling of longing to run her hand on the grand piano and wondering if the boy played. She'd later learned he played the piano as if his fingers were made of magic.

And then he uttered the words that changed her life forever.

"Will you go to the movies with me tonight?"

Thankfully, she didn't drop the vase. The request came out of nowhere. It was hard to breathe let alone speak. "The movies? With you?"

"I know it's sudden, but I'm afraid if I don't ask now, I'll never see you again."

"Oh." Aaliyah wasn't sure what to say. This perfect boy wanted to see her again? She nodded her head. He was quite right. He probably never would see her again. "I would like that."

"Where can I pick you up?"

"I don't live in a nice neighborhood." She wasn't embarrassed by their apartment, but felt she should warn him. The crime rate was high and not the safest part of the city.

"I don't care. What's your address?"

Aaliyah rattled off the address, her heart racing a mile a minute. They had been inseparable since that day. She had never believed in love at first sight, but it was instant for both of them. His parents did not approved at first, but they had come to accept her. Even like her.

"Where did you go? Daydreaming again?" Noah laughed, wrapping his arms around her.

"I was thinking about the day we met."

"I think about that day often. One of the best days of my life." Noah's lips met hers. His lips were soft and he tasted like cola and mint. She was breathless when they finally pulled away. She always got lost in his kisses. It wasn't natural to be this happy. Was it? She didn't care. As long as it lasted she would enjoy it.

"I should go," Aaliyah said looking at the massive wooden clock on the wall. "I need to hurry to catch the bus."

"I wish you'd let me drive you home."

"It's too far away. And like you said you have a test tomorrow. You can drop me off at the bus station."

A short while later, Aaliyah hopped off the bus and hustled to get home quickly. The sun was dipping below the horizon. If she hurried, she would have just enough time to drop off her bag, check on her mamma and be a few minutes early to pick up Darrius.

More than anything, she hated to be late.

It was freezing out. She rubbed her hands

together, wishing for the third time that she'd worn gloves as she made her way into the shabby apartment building. One good thing about the cold was that it kept the bad seeds from hanging out in front of the building. She hated the way they teased her. They often grabbed her school bag or yelled out crude things. Disgusting.

Ignoring the ratty elevator, she ran up the five flights of stairs and down the dingy hallway with the warped, drooping ceiling. An old woman passed her with a little white dog on a leash. Aaliyah said hello, but the lady didn't bother to look up let alone reply. Most people in the building kept to themselves.

Not exactly a friendly bunch.

As she opened the door, Aaliyah was met with the smell of cigarette smoke and sandalwood incense. It really bothered her that Darrius's father would not quit smoking.

Inside wasn't much warmer than outside, but at least inside there wasn't the freezing wind that cut through the bones. Her mother sat on the floor, hunched over, working on a clay vase. She looked up and smiled when Aaliyah walked through the door. "Hoe was jou dag liewe?"

"The usual. Pretty boring." With a thud she dropped her bag on the floor. The books weighed a ton. It felt good to get the weight off her shoulders.

Her mother refused to talk in English at home. Aaliyah loved her native tongue, Afrikaans, but really wished her mother would try harder to learn English. She wasn't always around to help translate.

"Hoekom is jy so laat? Het jy weer daai seun

gesien?"

Aaliyah looked down at the stained carpet that might have once been a pretty peach color. "I'm not late, and if by that boy you mean Noah then yes, mamma, I was with him."

Her mamma gave her a slight smile, before her focus went back to the clay in her hands.

"I'm running to get Darrius."

"Moenie vergeet om melk en brood terug te bring nie," her mamma said without looking up.

"All right. I'll stop at the store on the way back." She wasn't even sure she had enough money to buy milk and bread. Aaliyah shut the door and ran back down the stairs and out into the cold air. By now, the sun was fully set. She didn't really like walking in the dark, but what could she do? It wasn't as if they could afford to get a second car.

The misty streetlights were almost useless. The pale yellow light did nothing to illuminate the sidewalk other than to cast creepy shadows on the ground. The tree branches looked like they wanted to reach out and grab her. Aaliyah picked up her pace. The school was only five blocks away.

Occasionally, a car would drive by with loud music, startling her. *Stop being such a baby.*

To get her mind of the fear of being alone in the dark, she thought about her and Noah, schoolwork, and wondered what they were having for dinner. Before she knew it, the school appeared ahead. She was early as usual. She never wanted Darrius to be the last kid waiting.

As soon as she entered the gym, she went over to the little stand that always had coffee, tea and hot chocolate for the parents. She poured herself a styrofoam cup of black tea. The heat felt amazing after being out in the cold.

Standing on the sidelines, she watched as the kids ran up and down the court, kicking the ball back and forth in a fast-paced game of soccer. It seemed like a senseless sport to her, but Darrius loved it. As long as he was happy, that was what mattered. Oh, how she loved that little boy!

The coach blew his whistle, and the kids gathered around to receive their after practice pep talk. Aaliyah was glad to be inside; her toes were starting to thaw. She sure wasn't in a rush to get back out in the cold evening air. Tipping back her head, she swallowed the last of tea and tossed the cup into the garbage can.

Darrius ran over to her with a lopsided grin. "Did you see me get that goal?"

"I saw! Now get changed so we can get out of here."

She watched while one of the boys fell in step beside him as they went into the locker room. It made her heart swell to see him so happy with friends.

A few minutes later, he ran across the gym floor and stopped just short of her. She almost gave him a hug, but she knew he would not be happy if she did. He was at the age where it was no longer cool to have his sister hug him in public.

"Do you have any homework?" Aaliyah asked as she shouldered her brother's backpack. They headed outside. The night seemed colder after the warmth of the gym.

"Yeah, just some math. Nothing major." Darrius pulled his hat down lower over his ears as the frigid air hit them, causing his teeth to chatter.

"We'll be home soon. I'll make you some soup to warm you up."

"Tomato soup?"

"Sure. We gotta stop and get bread. Maybe we can have grilled cheese sandwiches too."

"My favorite."

"Everything is your favorite." Aaliyah chuckled.

"Wanna race?" Darrius grinned.

"If you dare," Aaliyah replied. If they ran they would get home quicker. Not to mention it would help warm them up.

Without waiting Darrius took off and Aaliyah let him stay a few steps ahead. He was fast, but she was faster. She'd let him think he was going to win.

A horn blared and their steps faltered as they looked over their shoulders. A black sedan slowed and the window rolled down.

"Excuse me. We're lost. Could you tell us how to get out of the neighborhood?"

Aaliyah slowed to a stop, looked at the older man and then back at Darrius. The man seemed harmless enough, and it was a confusing neighborhood.

She hesitated, and then called Darrius to her. They walked towards the car. Aaliyah was careful to stay a safe distance, but close enough that they could still hear her. Something about the man's gaze – cold, direct and unblinking – was creeping her out. Even in a neighborhood known for its crime, he was more sinister than anyone she'd run across.

With her arm around her brother protectively,

she started to give directions. The back door opened, and the hair on the back of her neck stood on end. Her instincts screamed at her to run, but she was rooted in place. Frozen in fear.

A large man grabbed her from behind. She pushed Darrius forward.

"Run," she yelled.

Her brother looked at her, his big brown eyes filled with fear before he took off in a sprint. He didn't make it very far. Another large man stepped out of the car and chased him down. He threw him over his shoulder while her brother kicked and screamed.

Something pricked her neck; it felt like a bee sting. The ground swam before her.

Dear God, no! This can't be hap—. Her body went limp and her world black.

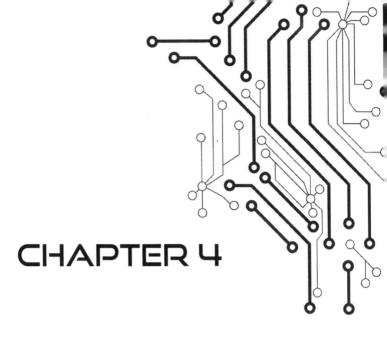

CHAPTER 4

Lucas hit the recline button and stretched out his legs, settling in for the flight. There was plenty of room for his long frame. Nothing but the best for IFICS. As usual, Harrington hadn't spared any expense. Everything the man did was top of the line. Even without the extra perks, Lucas would be forever grateful that Harrington had decided to take him under his wing, drastically changing the path of his life. If it weren't for him, Lucas would be a researcher or intern desperately trying to claw his way to the top, along with every other wannabe scientist. Harrington claimed he saw himself in Lucas and wanted him to reach his full potential.

Not only was Lucas a scientist, but he had a love and brilliant knack for computer programming. The combination was invaluable when it came to Harrington's vision, which was basically to bring the world kicking and screaming into the next era of technology. Kaitlyn was just a small part of IFICS. Harrington continued to make medical advances left and right. Unfortunately, most had not seen the light of day, mainly due to all the red tape from the government. In order to side step some of the roadblocks, Harrington maintained facilities all over the world in countries where the rules were not so strict. But mainly Harrington just did whatever the hell he wanted and kept his findings to himself.

Needless to say, Dr. Harrington had opened Lucas's eyes to a wonderful world of possibilities that he'd only read about in science-fiction books or dreamed about with his wild imagination. To say IFICS was cutting edge was like saying the iPhone was just a phone. A gross understatement.

Without a doubt, the greatest thing by far was meeting Kaitlyn.

He reached over and grabbed her hand and absently traced a circle on her palm. She entwined her long, graceful fingers with his.

He'd never been one to form attachments with women, so he'd been confused and surprised when Kaitlyn completely knocked the socks off him. From the moment her grey eyes met his, he felt himself spinning out of control with a longing so deep it consumed him. Until that moment, he had never needed anyone. Now he couldn't imagine his life without her.

The fact that she returned his feelings was inconceivable in more ways than one. Technically, it shouldn't be possible. Her feelings for him defied science and logic. This was one instance where his scientific brain said the hell with logic. His feelings for Kaitlyn had only grown stronger over the last several months. It was not always easy; she still struggled with integrating with society, but when they were alone—being together was as natural as breathing.

As if she could sense his thoughts, Kaitlyn leaned over and whispered in his ear. "I'm so glad you were able to come."

"I feel the same." He squeezed her hand, and Kaitlyn gave him a private smile, one she reserved for only him. As usual, the gesture caused his heart to thud against his chest like a jackhammer.

A shadow fell over him. Lucas looked up to see a slender blonde holding a tray with drinks. He smiled appreciatively at her.

Obviously, someone had put in his or her request beforehand. He could tell by the unusual assortments on the tray. Yet another fringe benefit of flying on a private jet. Lucas snagged the root beer float and handed it to Kaitlyn. Ever since they had recoded the sense of taste back into Kaitlyn's processor, she'd had an insatiable sweet tooth. Lucas thought it was adorable. Technically, she could live without food or sleep. Thankfully the extra calories didn't seem to interfere with anything. Her body quickly burned them off. If the world became aware that a chip could be implanted and obesity could be wiped out forever, the demand would be staggering. The invention would cause a drastic reduction in diabetes, heart attacks, high blood pressure and many more life threatening diseases. The life expectancy would increase, which Lucas believed was the main fear held by people in power. If people lived longer, it would cost the government astronomically. And a drastic cut in illnesses meant a loss of funds for the medical field. Millions, probably billions, lost in pharmaceuticals.

Without a doubt, their find would be the biggest medical miracle since penicillin, but unfortunately altering humans in such a way was a *very* gray area to say the least.

It was frowned upon by the government and forbidden by religious sectors. However, Harrington truly believed it was only a matter of time before such things were no longer considered taboo. Dr. Harrington loved to bask in his own glory, so it surprised Lucas that he didn't push the issue more. Go to the media. Something. But Harrington said he was content to use the knowledge behind the scenes in the meantime.

Kaitlyn nudged Lucas's arm, and he looked up startled. Lost in thought, he'd forgotten the stewardess was still there. "I'll return with snacks in about an hour. If that's ok?"

Lucas nodded and watched as she made her way towards Erik and Harrington. Professor Adams' head was flopped to the side and he was snoring loudly with his mouth agape, a prime example of the problems that faced the world. Adams could easily extend his life with the help of their advances; the nano-bots alone would make a world of difference, but Adams would rather age naturally. Fear for his eternal soul or something like that. Lucas found this hypocritical, since God was the one that blessed Adams with a mind that was able to come up with such wonders. It could be argued that by not using his talents to extend his own life, perhaps he was going against God's wishes.

He pinched his nose trying to banish the deep

thoughts. If he let himself, he could get lost in the complexities of such a conundrum.

Curiously, his eyes drifted back towards the stewardess. Harrington flirted shamelessly and Erik barely acknowledged the woman when he reached for his large glass of orange juice. He rarely acknowledged anyone. The phrase *cold as ice* came to mind. Erik was by all counts a loner. And yet women seemed completely fascinated by him. Even Quess. The blonde attempted to make small talk with Erik, and he just gave her a look and went back to the folder he'd been leafing through since they took off. Probably trying to commit to memory the layout of the cargo ship. Kaitlyn already had the information uploaded.

It amazed him that, even with Harrington, who was wealthy, handsome and powerful sitting there, it was Erik's attention the woman was after. It boggled his logical mind. Sure, he had the aura of danger that some would find appealing, but appearance wise, it didn't make sense. His face was not a handsome one. His nose was crooked from being broken too many times, his eyes were hard, and his mouth was always set with determination. His hair was cropped short and a dull brown. A large, jagged scar started at his temple and came close to his mouth. Lucas had tried to find out where he'd gotten the scar, but came up empty. When he asked Erik outright, he replied the information was classified, only making him all the more curious.

Women turned into a flustered mess around the guy. Lucas glanced at Kate. She smiled back at him with the straw still in her mouth. His heart rate increased exponentially. It was him she looked at that way, not Erik. He had to constantly remind himself of that fact when jealously crept in. Kaitlyn and Erik spent so much time together it was hard for him to see their bond strengthen. He was fearful he was going to lose her.

Even knowing it was a foolish, emotional thought, it had kept him up late at night more than once.

Several hours later, the pilot came over the speakers, announcing they were about to make their descent and requested they fasten their seatbelts. Lucas checked his watch. The flight had taken almost four hours and he had no idea where they were landing. Obviously, Harrington was playing it really close to his vest. Knowing Harrington, it was for no other reason than the fact that he loved the cloak and dagger aspect of his latest project.

After he buckled up, Lucas reached again for Kaitlyn's hand, lightly stroking his thumb on the smooth skin of her delicate wrist.

The landing gear thudded into position and Lucas's heart constricted. The moment he both dreaded and looked forward to was quickly approaching. The scientist in him was eager to see Kaitlyn in action, but the male part of him loathed putting her in direct danger. Seeing the one he loved walking into a potentially deadly situation scared the hell out of him. Rightly so.

He felt this way, even though he knew without a doubt she was more than equipped. She could run circles around the most seasoned soldier, even Erik, who was the best they could come up with. A quintessential warrior by all counts.

The former Marine Recon member was head and shoulders above his peers, but Kaitlyn was a super soldier. That knowledge did very little to quell the protective nature that she brought out in Lucas, which was laughable, when he thought about it. He was a scientist, not a soldier. No matter how much time he put in at the gym or on the range, he would never be in Kaitlyn's or Erik's league.

He really needed to pull himself together, because this was the first of many missions to come. He couldn't let his emotions rule him, or Harrington would pull him off the team in a heartbeat. Somehow, he needed to find a way to compartmentalize his feelings for Kaitlyn and focus on the objective of the mission.

The plane lightly touched down. Kaitlyn removed her hand from his, and her eyes bore straight ahead. The transformation in Kate was mesmerizing. Even her posture changed. She was now one hundred percent focused on the task at hand.

As she was programmed to be.

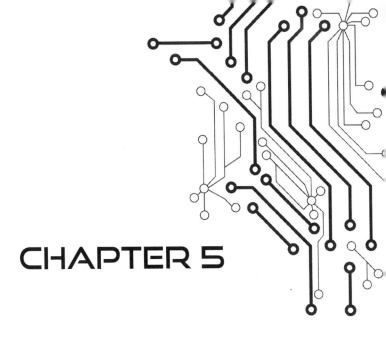

CHAPTER 5

A sharp pain pierced her head when Aaliyah woke, and her throat was so very dry. Goodness, she was thirsty. She tried to lick her lips, but her mouth wouldn't cooperate.

Her eyelids felt *so* heavy. When she tried to open them, nothing happened. The room spun, even with her eyes closed. A sour taste filled her mouth; she had to fight off the nausea.

Where was she? She tried hard to focus, but she couldn't think, her mind was jumbled. Groggy. Had she caught the flu? Malaria? What in the world was going on? So many questions raced in her head. She must be sick. Even her skin was cold and clammy.

Couldn't see.

As she came more in tune with her senses, the distinct odor of mold and lemons made her nostrils flare. The air felt heavy and stale. From the unfamiliar stench alone, she knew she wasn't home. The ground beneath her was hard and cold. Why didn't she have any covers on her? Why would she wake up somewhere other than her bed?

Aaliyah kept telling herself she was okay. No need to be frightened. Again and again, she repeated that to herself. Despite the words, she began to feel the faint twinge of anxiety and fear as she felt the emptiness around her.

She tried to move her limbs, but her muscles wouldn't cooperate. Couldn't move. Was she dead? No, her head wouldn't hurt if she were in heaven. *Would it?*

A door slammed shut, pain radiated throughout her throbbing head. Desperately she tried to grab the sides of her head with her hands, but they wouldn't move. Saliva filled her mouth. Another wave of nausea washed over her.

What in the world was going on? Why couldn't she pry open her eyes?

"When she wakes up, we'll bring her to Mr. Dasvoik. I think he'll be more than pleased with this juicy little morsel. I wouldn't mind a taste myself."

"Get your mind right. Dasvoik would slice you open if you touched his prize."

"I know, I know. But that doesn't stop me from fantasizing."

"Jesus, we have bigger things to worry about. Such as the boy. He's too young. They should have let him go. I don't know what the hell they were thinking."

"I'm sure they can find someone who wants him." The man paused, and she heard more shuffling. "For a good price."

The boy? Good price? Her heart pounded so rapidly she could scarcely breathe. Her eyes flew open, but she had to fight to keep her heavy lids from closing. Everything came rushing back to her. The car, the men and Darrius running. Her heart ached when she remembered that he didn't make it very far. They were talking about her Darrius.

This couldn't be reality. Had they really been abducted?

No! No! No! Please let this be a dream. A nightmare. Please let me wake up and find myself in my own bed. Things like this didn't happen, not to her. Not to her brother! Certainly not in America.

Her family didn't have money, so she knew this wasn't about ransom.

Without moving, she scanned the room trying to gain her bearings. She was curled up on the floor in the corner of a small room. Her body ached. She tried to straighten her legs out, but they remained bent. She couldn't even push herself up to sit.

The walls were white and lined by metal filing cabinets. A large wooden desk sat off to the left with a computer. No windows. No pictures or paintings on the wall. Nothing personal whatsoever.

Her eyes continued to dart around the room, finally settling on the men. They were large, wore dark suits and looked scary. One was tall with a hook-shaped nose and curly blond hair. The other was short but muscular with a bald head.

They were not the same men from the car.

Desperately, she tried to fight the panic that rose in her chest once she realized her brother was not in the room with them. Where was he? At least she knew he was alive from their comments. Too young? For what? So many questions and no answers. Maybe if she could figure out where they were, they could escape.

"Well, lookie here. Sleeping Beauty is finally awake," the tall man said. His voice was deep, and he talked with a slow Southern drawl.

"It's about damn time." The short one's voice was clipped and high pitched. They were both Americans.

She tried to speak, but no sound came out. Obviously, she'd been drugged. The thought pissed her off. She hated drugs. The only medicine she would take were the herbal remedies her mother made.

Oh, dear God. Her mother must be panicked by now. How long had they been gone? Too long. Had her mamma called the cops? Was anyone looking for them? Probably not. Her parents didn't trust the police. The milk. She'd never even made it to the store. What an absurd thought at a time like this.

Noah!

The bald man yanked her arm, pulling her up to sitting, but her limp body slid back down.

"She needs more time for the drug to wear off." The taller man stared down at her.

With a sharp glance at the tall man, he snapped. "Obviously, jackass."

"We'll come back in twenty minutes. She

should be good and ready by then."

Why couldn't she speak? She wanted to yell and beg them to bring Darrius to her. But it was useless. The door banged shut leaving her alone in the terrible silence. Her mind was wide awake, but the rest of her body was not cooperating. She was virtually paralyzed and scared out of her mind.

Think! There has to be a way out of this.

Once again, she scanned the dimly lit room, praying for some kind of sign that would tell her their location. *Anything.* If only she could get up and search the desk. She couldn't even crawl. She was alone and helpless. Terrified.

She must have dozed off, because next thing she knew the door opened and shut again.

"Rise and shine." A loud voice boomed through the room. "We've got places to go and people to see."

Slowly, she wiggled her toes and realized she wasn't wearing shoes. She looked down and saw she was wearing a gown. The type worn in hospitals. A whimper escaped when she realized she wasn't wearing any undergarments. Had these men seen her naked? A shiver ran down her spine as if she'd been touched by pure evil.

They roughly yanked her arms, pulling her to standing. Her legs felt like jello; it took her a moment to be able to put weight on them. Her feet ached with pins and needles as the blood reached them.

"Where's my brother?" she demanded. Her voice sounded thick and groggy to her own ears, but at least she could speak.

"Don't worry, the little brat is fine. That little

bastard bit me." The bald guy scowled.

Good for you Darrius. "Let me see him. I need to make sure he's ok."

Both men laughed.

"I'm afraid you may never see him again."

Her knees buckled. She could hear herself breathing in shallow little gasps, the only sound filling the room. This couldn't be happening. A nightmare? It had to be, because nothing else made sense.

"You're hurting me." Her tone was defiant.

"Now we wouldn't want that would we?" The taller man chuckled.

"We'll leave that pleasure to Dasvoik." The crude bald man raked his eyes down her body, sighing. "Unfortunately." He tightened his grip on her arm. "Maybe he'll get sick of you and loan you out."

Who is Dasvoik? Something told her she really didn't want to find out. *Loan her out?*

They dragged her down a long hallway. It seemed to go on forever. She concentrated hard to try and dampen the fear crawling inside of her. The walls were painted a subdued grey. The carpet was thin and beige, and the walls were bare. Nothing was giving her a clue to their location. They could be anywhere.

Eventually, they stopped in front of a wooden door and one of the men rapped loudly.

"Come in."

The door opened and she was pulled through. Not quite as rough as when they were in the hallway. When she looked up, she met the unusual golden eyes of an older man. Mid-thirties if she had to guess. He had olive skin and a face that was only found on models. Too pretty to be real. He didn't look scary. Maybe he could help her get out of this terrible situation. It had to be a horrible mistake.

His eyes trailed down her body and back up to her eyes. Aaliyah trembled beneath his intent gaze.

After a long moment, he set his pen down and walked around the front of his desk.

"You were not exaggerating. She *is* exquisite." He murmured. "And pure. What a wonderful combination."

His hand came up and touched the side of her face. She flinched and pulled back.

"Never! Pull away from me. Do you understand?"

Aaliyah froze. She didn't know how to respond. So she said nothing.

"I asked you a question." His thumb ran over her lips and they quivered beneath his touch. No one other than Noah had ever touched her in such an intimate way. It took all of her self-control not to recoil again. She raised her chin a notch. "I want to see my brother."

The man's eyebrow arched. "Do you now?"

"Yes." She jutted her chin out and straightened her spine. Hoping it would conceal the fear that was racing through her. Her mamma always said people saw what you showed them. If she feigned confidence, they believed it to be true, even if she was shaking in her shoes.

"And what would you do to see your brother?" His hand dropped from her lips. "Anything?"

Would she do anything to see her brother? To make sure he was alive? She knew she would.

He was her flesh and blood—her responsibility. But she wouldn't give the man the satisfaction of answering him.

"You have spirit." He sat back against the desk, watching her intently as a slow smile spread across his face. "I like that. I will take great pleasure in breaking you in."

The two men beside her remained quiet. The room seemed to grow smaller as the fear began to swallow her. She was not naive; she knew what he meant by breaking her in. The thought of him touching her made her legs buckle. The grips on her arms tightened, steadying her.

"Take her to my room," the man demanded. "Strip her gown and tie her to the bed. I will come to her when I'm ready."

What? "Please don't," she whispered as tears trailed down her cheeks. She tried to stop the tears, but they just kept coming.

"If you're a good girl. I *may* let you see your brother." He titled his head dismissing the men, and they dragged her limp body out of the room.

Aaliyah began praying out loud. In a frantic, hushed voice.

"Shut up!" the tall one yelled at her. She didn't listen. Surely, God would not allow that vile man to touch her!

They only went a few feet down the hall before they entered another room. It was large. In the middle of the room, against the wall, sat a king-sized bed with bright red sheets, red curtains, a Persian rug and a tall wooden dresser. There was also a large black mirror hanging above the bed.

The short one untied the back of her gown, his hand trailed down her bare back, she jerked away. He grabbed her bottom and kneaded it with his disgusting hands. Without thinking, she threw her head back knocking him in the chin. He swore and the larger man laughed.

"Feisty, Dasvoik will be happy."

"Shut up and get the rope." He rubbed his chin.

"Can't handle her?" The large man grinned.

"I just don't want to have to hurt her and have the boss man to answer to," he grumbled.

A sense of hope washed over her. Maybe the man with the golden eyes didn't intend to hurt her? No, he made it clear what he wanted from her. If he didn't want to hurt her, he wouldn't have her bound to the bed. Tied up, she wouldn't have a chance to escape. If she could just get away from the two of them before that happened.

When the taller man turned his back, she kneed the shorter one in the crotch; he went down to one knee howling. The larger man looked at her, shaking his head.

"It will go much easier for you if you don't fight it," he advised.

How could she not fight for her life? Her innocence? She was not weak. Frightened beyond belief, she would still not give up without a fight. The taller man circled around her, as her chest heaved up and down. She reached for the door, but he was faster. He grabbed her wrist and jerked it behind her back applying pressure, causing her to cry out in pain.

"Nice try, but there is no way out once the boss has his eyes on you. Be a good girl, and it will soon be over. The more you fight it, the more painful it will be. If you're lucky, he'll grow bored of you quickly."

Was that pity in his voice? He pushed her forward stopping in front of the dresser. He opened one of the drawers, her eyes widened in surprise and fear. There were so many vile objects. Knives, ropes, chains, whips, and things her mind could not register. Her eyes glazed over. The room spun, and her body swayed.

When her eyes fluttered open, she was tied to the bed. *Naked.* Her legs were splayed open, the air cool against her skin. The only person who had seen her completely naked was her mother. And now who knew how many eyes had seen her body? She couldn't even cover herself.

She pulled her arms and kicked her legs, screaming as loud as she could. The ropes were so tight she barely moved. She jerked her hips trying to turn over and a loud chuckle filled the room. Her face flushed with humiliation and fear.

"Now that's what I like to see."

The figure came closer, casting a shadow across her, but she didn't have to see him to know it was the man with the golden eyes. His voice was unmistakable. Smooth as honey, just like the color of his eyes. Could evil really sound and look like him?

She would soon know the answer to that question.

"Such beauty," he murmured. When he climbed on the bed, it moved from the weight of him. Her heart raced, and tears flowed freely down her face. She shook her head but couldn't get the words out. She was too scared.

"Now, now. Don't be afraid, my little flower. You're mine, and I take care of what belongs to me. Do you understand?"

A wail escaped her throat when his skin touched hers.

"Purity is so rare these days, let alone in someone as beautiful as yourself. How old are you my dear?" His hot fingers ran up her cold inner thigh. Her legs clenched. Her whole body tightened.

"I asked you a question."

She couldn't speak. Wouldn't respond. She wasn't going to give the monster anything. It was her only defense. As pathetic as that was.

"Ah, the hard way, of course." His voiced dripped of sweetness. Like he was enjoying himself. "I would have been disappointed if not. Would you like me to bring your brother in to watch?"

"No, please, no!" She thrashed her head side to side. She would rather die than have her brother see her spread out like this. He was just a little boy.

"Again, I ask. How old are you?"

"Seventeen," she cried out.

"Now that's much better. It wasn't so hard, was it, love?" His disgusting fingers wouldn't stop touching her.

Wasn't so hard? Was this man for real? She was tied to a bedpost and about to be raped. No, there was nothing hard about *that*. She spit in his face.

His hand stopped moving, and his eyes narrowed. He pulled his hand away, and wiped the spit off his face.

"Oh, petal, that was a very naughty thing to

do."

Aaliyah shrank back at his tone.

He stood up. She couldn't see him from the angle she was at on the bed but she could hear the movements. The sound of his zipper going down terrified her. He kicked his shoes off, a moment before his clothing hit the floor in a soft rustle. In all her life, she had never been so afraid. And then his feet padded across the floor as he walked away.

The drawer creaked open. Her mind went back to all the objects she had seen there. She screamed. Her breathing became labored, and sweat covered her body. Fear made the situation surreal.

He rummaged through the drawers. What was he getting? Her body shuddered. He slammed the drawer shut. His footsteps were quiet as he approached her.

She squeezed her eyes closed. Aaliyah could hear her own breathing, shallow and ragged in the silence.

"Look at me. I'm not going to tell you again to obey me. Your brother is close by. Close enough to hear your screams."

Her eyes snapped open, her mind abruptly clear. He stood above her staring down at her. All she could see was his muscular chest. He was strong, and he could bring her pain. How did she go from walking down the street to being tied to a bed?

"Lift your head."

She hesitated only for a second before obeying.

Her lips parted to scream, but he covered her mouth with duct tape. She felt like she couldn't breathe, even though she knew she could breathe through her nose. Her heart hammered against her rib cage. She prayed for strength to make it through what she knew to be unavoidable.

"This could have been so much easier. If you would have just cooperated," he said in a soothing voice that made her feel like she was the crazy one.

She trembled uncontrollably. Despite the tape, she still tried to scream through the gag.

"If you displease me, I will remove the tape, and your brother will hear you. You don't want that now, do you?"

She shook her head violently.

"See, I can be nice when I want to be." An evil smile spread across his face.

Terror gripped her.

And then came the pain.

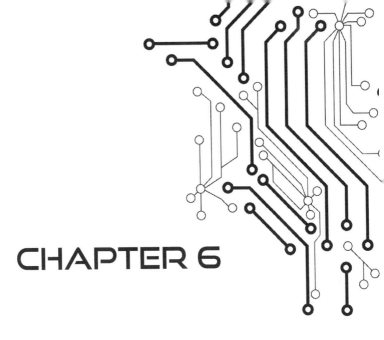

CHAPTER 6

Kaitlyn had no idea why Harrington insisted on keeping their location a secret. Her internal GPS immediately notified her when they landed in Eastport, Maine. The computer side of her brain gave her a quick breakdown of their location.

Population: thirteen hundred and fifty.

Temperature: twenty-seven degrees.

Local time: twelve thirty-seven.

Eastport's claim to fame: being the most eastern city in the United States. Images of the picturesque costal town flashed across her internal screen. Eastport appeared to be a beautiful location, but they were not there to sightsee.

A smile crossed her face, as Lucas glanced out the window of the plane. He swore under his breath, when he saw a foot of snow blanketed the ground. Kaitlyn's gaze dropped to his mouth. Memories of his lips on hers made her want to wrap her arms around him, but this was not the time or place.

"Good thing I brought my Gortex jacket," he mumbled. He stood up, pulled his bags from the overhead compartment, and slipped on his jacket.

He was so cute when he was annoyed.

Erik deplaned first. They had become accustomed to thinking of Harrington as their principal, meaning they always guarded his safety first. Kaitlyn went after Harrington, with Lucas and Adams following close behind.

A rush of excitement hit her as she stepped into the cold afternoon. Perfect snowflakes floated softly around them. The ground was slick with ice.

Slowly, she scanned the area. Kaitlyn counted three heat sources in the small airport. From the size and shape, plus heart rate, she deduced that they were humans.

Two large men stood waiting in front of a white van. They were dressed in khaki pants and black Arcteryx jackets commonly worn by Special Forces operators. Her sensors zeroed in. The targeting screen that was part of her internal weapon's system placed a bull's-eye on both of them, picking them up as potential threats.

Harrington held up his hand. "Relax, Kaitlyn. They are our escorts, not a threat."

She acknowledged his comment with a curt nod, but her body remained on high alert. Outsiders made her nervous. And the two men were clearly powerful and without a doubt deadly. Knuckle draggers, as Erik liked to call men in their field.

Harrington should have had a car waiting so they could drive themselves to the undisclosed location. The five of them strode across the tarmac, black cases in hand. Lucas was on one side of her and Erik on the other. They were two men she trusted with her life and both of whom she would freely give her own life for.

Once they were a few feet away from the men at the van, Erik increased his pace. Kaitlyn felt everything kick into high gear. What was going on? Did Erik sense something she had missed? Not a possibility.

"Kaitlyn," Harrington said with a trace of amusement. "It's fine."

Erik dropped his bag, reached his hand out to shake the other man's hand and then pulled him into a tight embrace. Kaitlyn tried to make sense of the situation. She turned to Lucas with a questioning gaze, and he shrugged.

After pulling away, Erik turned towards them with a rare smile on his face. "My old teammate, Ace. He saved my ass on more than one occasion."

It was strange to see Erik show such obvious affection. Kaitlyn was surprised to feel a twinge of jealousy. Erik was *her* partner.

Ace clapped his hand on Erik's shoulder, giving him a warm smile. "Erik returned the favor in kind. I believe we're even now, but who's counting."

Kaitlyn took in Erik's old teammate. Blond hair, blue eyes, chiseled features, six foot three, two hundred and twenty-three pounds. Heart rate a steady sixty-three beats per minute. With his relaxed posture, he no longer came across as a threat on her internal screen. But Kaitlyn wasn't sure she liked the man.

The other hulk of a man silently slipped around and slid open the side door. Moving with the grace of an athlete, he was almost the same height and weight as Ace. He appeared older. His dark hair was graying at the temples, but he was no less formidable. His posture was ramrod straight, head on a swivel, eyes alert. He was on guard. She wasn't sure she could say the same about Erik and Ace.

The older stranger's face did not reveal any thoughts or emotions. His eyes were calm and alert, his manor professional. He did not bother to inform them of his name, which met with Kaitlyn's approval, as she did not think it was necessary to do so.

"It's cold as hell. Can we get moving?" Lucas shifted on his feet, and his breath misted in the air.

Kaitlyn gave Lucas a weary look. *Cold as hell* was one of those sayings that made absolutely no literal sense, but now was not the time to bring up that fact.

They piled into the van, the three of them getting in the back while Harrington and Adams sat in the middle row. Kaitlyn looked at Erik, seeking to understand his sudden transformation. She didn't care for the way Erik's face had softened after seeing his old friend. It made her uneasy.

As if hearing her unstated question, Erik spoke. "We go way back. I had no idea Ace had been contracted out for the security detail."

"Thick as thieves." Ace turned and grinned.

A quick scan told her *thick as thieves* meant

they were loyal and as close knit as a family. Kaitlyn briefly wondered if there was anyone in her life with whom the saying would apply. Of course there was Lucas. He knew her better than anyone, and perhaps Quess. But maybe not. The saying seemed to indicate something deeper then friendship, but not quite the same thing as love. Language could be very complex.

Harrington glanced over his shoulder at Erik, arching an eyebrow. "He came highly recommended. When I noticed his background was very similar to yours, I did some cross-references. As a trusted teammate of yours, I felt secure in hiring him for this detail. It's as simple as that."

Erik seemed to accept the explanation. His relaxed posture was quickly replaced with the serious demeanor Kaitlyn had grown accustomed to. Hopefully, there would be no more lapses once the mission went live. It suddenly occurred to Kaitlyn that she also changed when in Lucas's company. She would have to be aware of that and not make the same mistake Erik had made. Letting her guard down was not an option. The mission and her job meant too much to her. For the first time, she wondered if it was wise to have Lucas so closely involved.

With a quick glance at his strong profile, she pushed the thought out of her mind. At the end of the day, no one knew her programming better than Lucas and in truth, no one else was capable of the job. Not even Adams. Much of her coding was specially designed by Lucas's incredible mind. Adams was more an overseer.

Their tires spun on the ice as they took off

down the narrow unpaved driveway, and Kaitlyn wondered where their next destination would be. More importantly, she wanted to know when they would be heading to Croatia. But she wasn't about to discuss details with the two unknown entities in the van.

Kaitlyn gazed out the window. They turned down a freshly plowed, rural road. Snow banks nearly four feet high lined the roads, and the van's tires crunched on the packed snow. Several buildings were scattered around, including a small general store and pizza shop. The snow-filled trees were quite breathtaking.

She could feel the heat from both Erik's and Lucas' muscular thighs pressed against hers. She found herself distracted by the unique bond she had to each of the men.

What in the world was wrong with her? She needed to focus; her total concentration was needed. She could not allow anyone—or anything—to distract her from the most important job of her life. Her entire reputation, and that of IFICS, could be built or destroyed during this mission.

Her attention went back to the scenery blurring past her. Small picturesque homes littered the landscape. A few children played outside, making snowmen. It wasn't long before they were in the middle of nowhere. The only things surrounding them were snow, trees and the occasional animal. Regardless of the cold, the sun shone brightly, glaring off the snow, but the tinted windows, along with polarized lenses that slid across her irises, caused her to be unaffected. Lucas squinted his eyes, and Erik pulled out a pair of sunglasses from his bag.

They drove over the man-made causeway, and her sensors alerted her they had left the city limits of Eastport. They were traveling through an Indian reservation, and soon would cross into Perry, Maine.

"We're about to pass the only store for miles. Do you need me to pull over?" Ace asked.

"No. The house is fully stocked," Harrington replied.

"Roger." Ace flicked on the blinker.

They traveled another seventeen minutes down a narrow winding side road before turning into a hidden gravel driveway, which had been recently plowed.

Tree branches scraped across the van. Enormous trees in a mile deep forest provided adequate coverage. A huge colonial with a wraparound porch sat off in the distance. She thought it was an unusual location, but what did she know? Harrington was the brains behind the planning, while she just followed orders.

Ace and his sidekick went in first to make sure the building was secure. When they came out, they walked the perimeter. Kaitlyn could have told them the place was empty, but she knew not to draw attention to her *extra* abilities. Once they had the all clear, they grabbed their gear and climbed up the stairs, kicking the snow off their shoes before taking them off in the mudroom. The screen door opened quietly, only to bang loudly behind them.

Kaitlyn took in her surrounding, instantly loving the large, open floor plan. Dark hardwood floors glowed softly, reflecting the midday light. A huge stone fireplace took up almost the whole side of one wall. A gun rack hung above the fireplace. She was surprised to find the rack empty. The furniture was sparse. An old worn couch draped with a red plaid blanket, two rocking chairs, and an oval, braided rug covered the floor in front of the fireplace. The house gave off a peaceful vibe.

The idea fascinated her. How could inanimate objects give off a vibe?

Harrington tore off his jacket, draped it on the coat rack and loosened his tie. "Kaitlyn, I would like to give you a quick tour of the place."

She nodded and went to his side. Without being told, she knew what he really wanted her to do—sweep for listening devices. It was one of the many protocols they had set in place on the rare occasions they left the compound. She was a virtual bug detector and would be able to detect any unauthorized radio frequencies as low as 15 kilohertz. Transmitters could use AC power lines or even telephone lines to carry signals. Technology was quite incredible, she had to admit. Thankfully, because of her, IFICS was head and shoulders above the rest, even in the clandestine world. Where others had to use special devices, Kaitlyn's sensors were all programmed inside of her.

Quickly, they went through each of the rooms. As she suspected, the place was clean.

"Is this your place?" Kaitlyn asked. There was nothing that gave away the fact that Harrington had ever lived there before, but he seemed at ease as they moved through the rooms. A calmness came over him and he appeared nostalgic in certain areas of the old house. She noticed the way he ran his hand over the woodwork. More than once, she caught a strange look of longing in his eye.

"Very astute of you. I used to come here as a boy. I've added a few additions to make it more user-friendly. Outside you'll find a gymnasium with everything you will need for training. There is also a shooting range indoors and out."

"Sounds promising," Kaitlyn replied.

"Hopefully, it meets with your approval."

She wasn't sure why it had to meet with her approval. "We shouldn't be here very long, should we?"

Harrington didn't say anything. Kaitlyn mulled over his silence. She was eager to get the mission off the ground. She didn't like even a hint of delay. However, Erik had told her time and time again that patience was the biggest asset of an operator.

"After you," Harrington said, nodding his head towards the staircase.

Kaitlyn descended the steps, taking in the scene below. The older guard was busy making a fire, while Ace and Erik walked towards the back of the house, talking in hushed voices. Kaitlyn could listen in if she wanted to, but after Dr. Chambers' reminder of invading privacy, she decided against it, even though she was more than a little curious.

The room soon filled with the scent of burning wood and the sounds of crackling flames. The familiar smell tugged at a lost memory. Once in a while she got quick flashes, but this one seemed just out of her reach. Even though Lucas had returned her memories, she could not always access them. Lucas told her it was the same for most humans. Life continued, but the past was often forgotten. For some reason the idea of lost memories saddened her.

At least now, she would no longer have to worry about that. For any memories made since her transformation, she had total recall, much like rewinding a movie and hitting play. Sometimes when she was alone, she replayed special moments she'd shared with Lucas.

"All right. Well let's get settled in and then meet back here in an hour. Kaitlyn and Lucas, your room is at the end of the hallway on the right. Erik's is across the hall from you two. Adams, you're upstairs with me," Harrington said.

Adams grumbled about making an old man climb another flight of stairs. The older guard stood up and wiped the knees of his pants before grabbing Adams' bags and carrying them up the stairs.

When he came back down there was a hint of a smile on his otherwise stoic face. "Glorified valet."

Lucas laughed, and Kaitlyn studied the man. He caught her watching him, and he simply smiled.

"I'm Nick by the way."

Kaitlyn hesitated before saying, "Okay."

Lucas gave her a look before he took a step forward. "Lucas, and this is my girlfriend, Kaitlyn. We appreciate your services."

Kaitlyn forced a smile. She really thought the informal pleasantries were unnecessary, but she could tell by the look Lucas gave her that she was not integrating properly. She tried to think of something trivial to say. Why was this so hard for her?

Lucas came to the rescue. "Harrington said there was food?"

"Right this way." Nick led them down the short hallway to a spacious kitchen that was set off to the left. A rough granite tabletop was the focal point of the room. Kaitlyn ran her fingers along the uneven texture. Everything in the kitchen was dark grey. The only splash of color came from the yellow curtains above the sink where light filtered through. Even the refrigerator was an unusual brushed metal. Whoever designed the house had great taste. Somehow, they managed to bring the feel of the outdoors inside the home.

"Hot chocolate?" Nick asked.

Kaitlyn perked up despite herself; chocolate had a way of doing that to her. "Marshmallows?"

Nick grinned. "You're in luck."

Lucas placed his arm around her waist, but Kaitlyn pulled away. It was obvious by the way his eyes clouded over she had hurt his feelings. Once they were alone, she would have to explain being here was no different than when they were at work. He should know better.

Kaitlyn pulled out a stool, while Nick heated up the milk, cocoa, salt and sugar in a pan. Lucas sat down next to her, but kept more distance than usual between them. Maybe she wouldn't have to broach the subject.

A few moments later, Nick set the mug down and Kaitlyn cradled the cup in her hands before closing her eyes to take the first sip of the warm liquid. When the sugar hit her tongue, a soft moan of pleasure escaped her lips. Even better than she had expected. So many simple pleasures in the world. She looked up and gave Nick a curt nod.He grinned crookedly.

Lucas nudged her arm while wiping the napkin across his face. "You gotta little something on your lip."

A chocolate mustache, as Quess would call it. Kaitlyn smiled and took another sip before wiping her face. She would have to ask Nick to tell her his recipe, because his hot chocolate was quite possibly the best she'd ever tasted.

Erik and Ace strolled into the kitchen laughing. Kaitlyn studied them and found she envied their bond. Erik appeared so at ease and happy. In all the time she had known him, this was the first time she'd heard him laugh.

Kaitlyn stiffened and gave him an impatient look. He looked at her a little puzzled, but didn't acknowledge it. She tore her gaze from his face.

"Catching up?" Lucas asked.

"Ah, the stories I could tell about this one." Ace pushed Erik's shoulder back.

Erik flashed him a look as if telling him to keep his mouth shut.

Kaitlyn took a sip of the hot chocolate, watching the exchange with interest. She wondered what sort of stories he was talking about. She debated asking, but Ace spoke up first.

"Kaitlyn, Erik tells me you've been working closely together?"

Kate glanced at Erik and then back at Ace. "That's true."

The room lapsed into an awkward silence.

Kaitlyn finished her drink, stood up and

placed it in the sink.

"Thank you for the hot chocolate, Nick."

"Yeah, thanks, man. Hit the spot," Lucas added.

"No problem."

Kaitlyn could feel their eyes on her as she walked out of the room. Lucas stayed a couple more minutes before joining her.

As they walked down the hall, she extended her hearing range, invading privacy or not she wanted to know what they were saying.

"That chick is hot but odd as all get out. Kinda creepy the way she just sits there," Ace mumbled.

"Say what you will, but you wouldn't stand a chance against her. She's the best I've ever worked with."

Ace laughed loudly. Then after a pause he said, "No shit?"

"No shit," Erik replied.

That was the last Kaitlyn heard before they entered their assigned room. It shouldn't bother her what a stranger thought, but for some reason it really did. If Ace saw her as odd then others must as well.

At least Erik thought she was a better operator than Ace.

But she already knew that to be factual, so it was not much of a consolation.

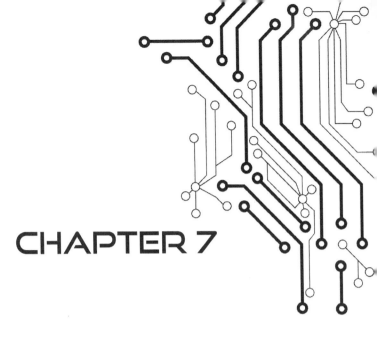

CHAPTER 7

Lucas rubbed the back of his neck as he trailed Kaitlyn down the hall. He could kick himself for crossing the line earlier. It was obvious that Kate was pissed at him. Every one of her muscles was taunt with tension, and she hadn't spoken a word to him since they left the kitchen.

Once the door shut softly behind Kaitlyn, he raked his fingers through his hair. "I'm sorry, Kate. I shouldn't have touched you like that. I acted instinctual instead of intellectual. You're just so damn cute when you get excited about things like hot chocolate. It's hard for me to keep the distance. I promise I won't make the mistake again."

Kaitlyn stared at him for a moment before turning away. She walked towards the window and pushed aside the curtain to gaze out at the falling snow. God, she was beautiful. More than anything, he wanted to bury his face in her hair and breathe in her scent then lower his mouth to the curve of her neck and taste her soft skin. Instead, he stood rooted to his spot. He knew she needed space right now.

He'd been beating himself up since he made the error in the kitchen. The last thing he wanted was for her to be mad at him before walking into a dangerous situation. His heart ached. It was killing him not to pull her into his arms. Often, he walked on eggshells around Kate. He didn't mind. She was well worth the patience and effort.

Finally, she turned towards him. "I'm not mad at you."

Lucas let out the breath he'd been holding. "You're not? I was out of line. I think I let my guard down when Harrington assigned us the same room—leaving no doubt that we were together. It won't happen again."

Kaitlyn moistened her lips and took a step closer. "That surprised me, too."

The tension in his shoulders eased slightly. While they were in the kitchen she'd obviously been annoyed, or maybe she was distracted. She wasn't the easiest person to read.

"Do you think it's okay if I touch you in here?" Kaitlyn asked softly.

Lucas saw her expression - vulnerability. He loved when she let her guard down for him. He crossed the room and pulled her into him. Gently, he kissed her and then held her tightly against his chest. He could feel her defenses dissolve beneath his touch.

"I'm sure this is acceptable. Harrington wouldn't have put us together if it weren't."

She pulled back and looked up at him with

her stunning grey eyes. "I don't understand why we even have rooms. Do you know if we're staying the night?"

His fingers combed through her hair, slowly. "I have no idea. I'm sure we'll find out in twenty minutes at the meeting. I'm in the dark as much as you are."

Arms still wrapped around her, he shuffled towards the large platform bed and plopped down, pulling Kaitlyn onto his lap. His thumb caressed the nape of her slender neck. "If you're not mad at me, what's bothering you?"

She shifted against him so she could stare up at him, "I'm jealous of Ace."

Her honesty floored him. Lucas looked down studying her face. He could feel her pain and confusion. It didn't sit well with him. "Why are you jealous?"

"I've never heard Erik laugh before today. No one ever laughs with me except you. Well, sometimes Quess laughs *at* me."

Lucas's gut twisted. "Am I not enough for you, Kate?" He was ashamed of the words as soon as they left his mouth.

Sitting up straighter, Kaitlyn frowned. "I don't understand your question."

Lucas drew in a deep breath. He had to keep his head on straight. He knew her mind worked differently. Maybe she didn't mean it the way he had taken it. He searched his mind for other explanations.

"Do you think you are jealous of their relationship? Or of Ace in general?"

Kate stared straight ahead, lost in her thoughts. "I guess their relationship. At first

I was angry because I thought Erik was acting unprofessionally. But then I realized I was upset that he acted differently with Ace than me. He likes Ace better, and I don't like it."

Lucas chose his words carefully. "They've known each other a long time. They have a history together. I think what you are trying to say is that seeing them together made you more aware of your own differences?"

"If you mean made me acutely aware of my flaws? Then yes." She crossed her arms over her chest. Lucas was struck by the very human movement. The fact that she did it unconsciously didn't slip past him.

Lucas dropped his chin onto the top of her head and ran his hand down her arm. "Kaitlyn, you are not flawed. You are unique, wonderful, funny, exciting, sexy. I could go on and on if you want me to."

Kate lifted her head. "You really think I'm funny?"

Lucas pulled her tighter. "Kate, you make me happier than I've ever been in my life. Just thinking of you brings a smile to my face. You do things daily that make me laugh. If I could only choose one word to describe you it would be extraordinary."

She pulled away and searched his face, as if she was trying to figure out if he was telling the truth.

He hesitated before speaking. It was hard for him to be so open, but Kaitlyn deserved his honesty. He didn't want any secrets between the two of them. "The way you are jealous of Ace and Erik is the same way I am jealous of you and Erik.

You two have a bond that does not include me. Sometimes, I feel like I'm on the outside looking in." He paused to gather his thoughts. "If your concern is that Erik doesn't feel close to you like he does Ace, your fears are misplaced. The two of you work together like a well-oiled machine."

Kate looked at him. "Why haven't you told me before that you were jealous? It's not a pleasant feeling."

Lucas shrugged. "It's not something I'm proud of."

"Relationships are very complex aren't they?" Kaitlyn laid her head against his shoulder.

"Yes, they are." He wished she had put his mind at ease a little more, but he knew emotions were a very delicate situation with Kaitlyn. He did feel some relief that she had come clean with her jealousy of Ace. If she felt more than a working relationship with Erik, she would probably tell him, because that was how she worked. It wouldn't even occur to her that she would be tearing his heart to shreds in the process.

Lucas couldn't bear the thought of losing her; it would be like a knife through the chest.

Hopefully, that was something he'd never have to deal with.

She looked up. "I actually like that one."

"What one?"

"Well-oiled machine. It makes sense."

He smiled and kissed her forehead. "I love you, Kate, and I want you to know that you can always tell me anything. No matter what." *No matter how badly it hurts.*

"I know that, Lucas." Kate stood up. "We need

to meet Harrington."

Lucas looked at his watch and nodded in agreement. "It's about that time. Are we okay?"

She answered him with a quick kiss. Her lips were soft and sweet; he could still taste a hint of hot chocolate on them. His anxiety levels ratcheted down a few notches. Sometimes it felt like he was walking on a tightrope with Kate. Scary as hell, but also the most excitement he'd ever experienced.

Kaitlyn took a few steps forward before stopping to look over her shoulder. Her eyes softened. "I love you, too."

Lucas glanced around the office, searching for clues as to what the hell was going on. He hated that Harrington had kept him in the dark. Not that any of this was his expertise. He was, after all, just the lab geek, but Harrington had involved Lucas in all the planning up until this point. Or so he'd thought.

Harrington rested his hip on the corner of the desk. His face was unreadable. Adams was nowhere to be found. He was probably napping. Meanwhile, the three of them sat impatiently in a semi-circle in front of the desk, in the uncomfortable wooden seats. Lucas was relieved to see that Ace and Nick had not been invited to the little powwow.

Harrington took a deep breath and blew it out. "There's been a slight delay in the plans."

Immediately, the tension was palpable in the room. A quick glance at Kaitlyn, and he knew it was taking everything for her not to speak out of turn.

"What kind of delay?" Erik's deep voice cut through the silent room.

"The cargo ship hasn't left the port. I'm not sure what's going on. They should have left days ago."

"We could board the ship beforehand," Erik suggested.

Harrington didn't speak for a long beat. Lucas knew he was going through the possible scenarios in his mind. Looking up, Harrington frowned slightly. "We'd risk the chance of being caught. You two can't exactly blend in."

"We wouldn't be caught. It's not like we would run in during the daylight and announce ourselves. What if the children are already on the container ship?" she asked, keeping her voice even. "We could get them off. Save them."

"I've thought of that. Everything indicates that he picks the children up while they are out to sea. He wouldn't risk having them in an American port. It's not worth tipping our hand without knowing for certain."

"How can you be sure? Where are you getting your intel?" Erik leaned forward. "They could very well be aboard the ship. All it would take is a few greased hands— as you've stated Dasvoik is well connected and feared."

"I have a man on the ground, but I haven't been able to get in contact with him all week." Harrington was unable to hide his frustration.

Lucas let the information sink in. "Do you think Dasvoik was tipped off?"

"That's my fear. If that's true, we have a mole

in the organization."

"It could have nothing to do with the children. Maybe it's an arms or drug deal that is causing him to be delayed. You've said he dabbled in all sorts of black market trading. Just because you can't reach your source, doesn't mean we have been compromised," Kaitlyn said.

"We can only hope." Harrington's jaw clenched. "I want this bastard."

Lucas knew it would eat him up inside if any of his people had betrayed him.

"I think we should act now," Kaitlyn said, determined not to let it drop. "Clearly, the world would be a better place without Dasvoik."

"Very good, Kaitlyn. As you know I'm counting on you to take care of the problem." Harrington reached up and rubbed his temples. "He's a target, not just a threat."

Lucas knew Harrington had just confirmed Dasvoik was a dead man walking. Not that it was a surprise. Once Kaitlyn was locked on to a target, unless specified, she was programed to kill by any means necessary. Threats she was programmed to avoid killing if possible.

Erik leaned back in his chair. "What I don't understand is why Vance would even be on the ship? Why risk it?"

Harrington sighed and walked around to the front of his desk. "Vance Dasvoik is a very unusual man. He's smart, deadly and not always predictable. Unlike most men in his position, he enjoys getting his hands dirty. He thrives on the thrill of living dangerously—likes to live on the edge. Do not for one minute underestimate him. He is as ruthless as the two of you. As you've seen from his dossier, he's well trained. Outstanding military career, feared drug dealer, vicious thug, and now a billionaire slave trader."

"But he's not invincible," Kaitlyn said.

"No, he is not," Harrington agreed.

"Maybe we should scout this one out and get him on his next run?" Erik said carefully.

Kaitlyn glared at him. "Not a chance."

Erik sat back in his chair. "I just have a bad feeling about this."

"How so?" Harrington asked, crossing his feet at the ankles and leaning against the desk. Lucas took *feelings* seriously. Even though they were unexplainable and not at all logical, it's been reported time and time again that gut instinct has saved many lives.

Erik looked squarely at Harrington. "I don't understand why we have been kept out of the loop on the planning. You hand us a folder and we're leaving the next day? Now you tell me you think you have a possible rat on the inside? I'm sorry, but nothing good is going to come out of this."

Lucas had to admit he had valid points.

"If you are not up for the mission just say the word," Harrington shot back, his gaze boring into Erik.

Erik shook his head in disgust. "I'm not sure *you* are up for the mission."

"Excuse me?" Harrington bristled.

"You brought me onto the team because of my background—my knowledge. I can't sit back and say nothing. I think your ego has gotten too large. Yes, Kaitlyn is a military marvel, but this sort of mission involves many moving pieces. I guarantee you that it's not going to be as easy as strike fast and retreat."

Harrington's eyes darted to Kaitlyn. "And what do you think?"

Kaitlyn looked at Erik for a moment and then back towards Harrington. "I value Erik's opinions, but I think we're ready. We've spent months planning for this moment. We might not have known who the target was or what scenario would play out, but there will always be unknown elements. We have the skills to work around them. If Erik does not want to go, I will go alone."

Harrington looked pleased by Kaitlyn's reply.

"Erik?" Harrington asked turning his inquisitive gaze from Kaitlyn to Erik.

"I'm going. I would never leave my partner," Erik said, with a sharp edge to his quiet voice.

"Very well. Now that that's settled, you're free to go. I'll update you as soon as I know we're moving. Lucas, I would like you to stay behind."

Lucas hung back while Kate and Erik left the room.

Harrington paced the room. "He's right. Damn it!"

Lucas didn't say anything. He'd been around Harrington long enough to know he was stewing and would get to his point eventually.

Harrington stopped pacing, squeezed the bridge of his nose between his index and thumb. "Do you think we should call it off?"

The last thing Lucas had expected was for Harrington to ask his opinion on something as important as this. Lucas mulled it over. They all had valid points. If he recommended calling it off, he could potentially keep Kaitlyn out of harm's way, at least for a little longer, but he wasn't there as Kate's boyfriend. He was there as a member of IFICS.

"No, Kaitlyn's right. This is what she was made for. We're never going to be able to predict the human elements. I do believe Erik was correct in his opinion that they should have been more involved."

"I know, I know. Dammit, Lucas." Harrington raked his hands through his hair. "What do you think of a mole? Very few personnel have been involved and I've hand-screened everyone myself."

A thought abruptly occurred to Lucas. "I am curious about one thing. Why Dasvoik? Obviously, he needs to be stopped but what zeroed you in on him in particular?"

Harrington laughed humorlessly. "The ironic thing is he came to *me.*"

"What?" Lucas couldn't quite believe his ears.

"He heard about our work with the anti-aging and nano-bots. Men like Dasvoik want to live forever and they don't care about the cost."

Lucas smiled wryly. "Imagine that."

"I always screen potential clients, and the deeper I dug into his past I knew he would be our first target. Almost makes me believe in fate."

Lucas rubbed the back of his neck. "In that case I don't think we should speculate until we have proof. Once they board and search the ship then we can start to worry if needed. All we have right now is a delay."

"I guess you're right. Jesus, Lucas maybe I'm in over my head. Maybe I should have sold Kaitlyn to the government."

Lucas felt his heart clench. "You don't believe

that. We've worked too hard and come too far for you to back out now. If we need to bring in more experienced people, that's one thing. But to talk about scratching it all together? That doesn't sound like you."

Harrington dragged his hands over his face. "You're right. Forget I said anything. I'm just a little rattled that's all."

"Nothing wrong with that," Lucas replied.

"Get out of here," Harrington waved him away, "I need to be alone."

Lucas walked into the hallway lost in thought. The mention of selling Kaitlyn to the government had shaken him to the core. He'd thought they'd long passed that hurdle. Jesus, this mission had to be a success—too much was riding on the outcome.

Would Harrington really decide to hand her over if things got out of control? It was a real possibility.

No, Harrington was a stubborn man and would not give up that easily, even if practicality told him that he should.

Dammit. Lucas sure as hell hoped he knew Harrington as well as he thought he did.

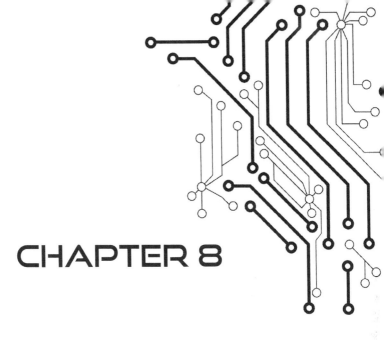

CHAPTER 8

Kaitlyn and Erik made their way down the hallway, the thick carpet muffling their footsteps. She'd been greatly surprised when Erik recommended pulling out of the mission. She knew firsthand he was not afraid, so his hesitation made zero sense to her. If there was even the slightest chance there were children on that boat, they had to get them off. Regardless of the fact that Harrington insisted the mission was all about Dasvoik. To Kaitlyn, the real mission was saving the children.

Yes, she would take pleasure in ridding the world of Dasvoik, but like Erik always said, you cut off one head and another takes its place. But if they could rescue the innocent victims, she'd feel like she was doing what she was made to do. Like her life truly had a purpose.

Kaitlyn tilted her head to observe her partner's expression. "Are you really concerned about the mission?"

Erik shrugged. His face remained impassive. He was a very hard man to read, even with all of her internal knowledge of human facial expressions. "Not really, I just wish we had more time and more data. Not to mention Harrington's way too damn cocky."

"Is this so different from what you were used to?" Kaitlyn asked, ignoring the Harrington comment. She'd grown to like the man over the last several months. If it weren't for his vision, she would have never had this second chance at life. And behind the surface, Harrington really did want to make a difference.

"Oh, yeah, there was always lots of planning beforehand. This feels like we're shooting from the hip, and I don't like it."

She stared at him for several seconds before asking, "Is that such a bad thing? I mean we can adapt as we go. That's how we've been trained."

"Put it this way, if it were anyone other than you, I would tell Harrington to take the job and shove it up his ass."

The statement startled Kaitlyn. "Even Ace?"

Erik laughed, "Especially Ace. That guy's a hothead."

Kaitlyn scanned the slang meaning. So Ace had a temper, and was always looking for trouble? That didn't sound like an ideal partner at all.

"I like your laugh."

Erik looked at her with a raised eyebrow. "My laugh?"

She nodded. "I've never heard it before this trip. You are more relaxed around Ace than me."

He scratched the back of his head. "I'm sure

that's true. The dynamics of team guys are different, and I've known Ace for a very long time."

"That's exactly what Lucas said. Do you regret leaving your team to come work for IFICS?"

"Not yet," he smiled ruefully. "Ask me again after we complete the mission."

Kaitlyn felt a rush of pleasure at the fact that Erik would rather be with her than Ace.

They entered the kitchen and were met with a pleasant smell of fresh bread. Ace and Nick sat eating stew and freshly heated rolls.

"Hired help hiding out in the kitchen?" Erik said with an easy grin.

Ace spread his hands out in front of him. "The wonderful life of a civilian contractor."

Erik reached down and grabbed one of the rolls. "Why'd you get out anyway? I thought for sure you'd be a lifer."

"Probably the same reason you did. Burnt out and the pay of a glorified chauffeur is oh so much better."

"Ain't that the truth." Nick held his hand out for a fist bump. Kaitlyn looked down at her own hand. She and Erik had never bumped fists before.

"You guys feel like stretching your legs?" Erik asked, turning his neck from side to side.

"What do you have in mind?" Nick asked, leaning back in the chair.

"Harrington told me there's a gym with a wide open area in one of the outbuildings."

Ace cracked his knuckles. "I'm game."

Erik looked towards Kaitlyn with a raised eyebrow. "You in?"

"Sure, why not," Kaitlyn said, hiding her

smile. The idea of going head-to-head with Ace sent a small thrill through her.

Her gaze shifted to the table, and she eyed the buttery rolls, but resisted the urge to grab one.

Kaitlyn started to pull her shirt over her head, but Erik grabbed her arm. It took her a moment to realize the mistake. Even with the change of the plastic to skin tone in hand to hand, it would be obvious she was not quite human.

"Thank you," she whispered.

Erik smiled, and she was surprised to feel her heart swell or more accurately, her chest, since she didn't exactly have a heart.

"Ace won't know what hit him." He chuckled.

Kaitlyn wondered if their relationship had grown with the introduction of his buddy, Ace. A smile and a laugh that were directed at *her*, all in one day. She realized that she would like to be friends with Erik. Something she hadn't given any thought to until this trip. Before, it was strictly business.

"Man, this place is state of the art." Nick whistled.

"No shit. Your company must be loaded," Ace said, taking in the large space. The walls were lined with padding. Fifteen foot climbing ropes hung from rafters, and a large rock-climbing wall sat off to the left in the back. On the other side were Olympic lifting platforms with weights, medicine balls, concept two rowers, and other fitness equipment. "Harrington told us there was also an indoor and outdoor range."

Kaitlyn thought it was a nice setup, but nothing

compared to what they had on the compound.

"Yeah, the whole nine yards," Erik agreed.

"Up for a little hand-to-hand combat?" Erik asked looking at Ace.

"Always."

Ace reached up to stretch, and Erik shook his head.

"Cold, no stretching. You and Kaitlyn first and Nick can take the winner. I'll take the winner from that match."

"Rules?" Nick asked.

"None, other than tap out when you've had enough."

"I like it." Ace grinned. "Anyone want to put some money on the table?"

"Money?" Kate asked, confused.

"You know a bet? Where have you been under a rock?" Ace laughed at his own joke.

Now a bet she knew. "One thousand dollars that I win."

Ace's eyes widened and Nick looked Kaitlyn up and down as if seeing her as competition for the first time.

Ace rubbed his hands together in front of him. "Daddy could use a little extra money."

"You have a kid?" Kaitlyn asked, surprised.

"No, I don't have any kids. It's just an expression." He gave her a strange look.

Kaitlyn mentally kicked herself. She wasn't doing a very good job of blending in it seemed.

"How about you, Nick?" Erik asked.

"Nah, I'm good. That's a little too rich for my blood," Nick said as he took off his jeans to reveal black shorts he was wearing underneath.

"My money is on Kaitlyn." Erik nodded in her

direction.

"You're going to bet against yourself? What the hell happened to you after you left the corps? You've gone soft," Ace said, disgusted. "I'll tell you right now, no girl is going to kick my ass."

Right. Kaitlyn thought while suppressing her smile.

Ace clapped his hands together. "Let's get this party started. I apologize beforehand, if I mar your pretty face, but once the gloves are off …"

"Two thousand says you never touch my face," Kaitlyn said evenly.

"Whooa, didn't you learn overconfidence could be an operator's biggest nemesis?" Ace said.

Kaitlyn shrugged. "It's just money."

"Just money? Okay, you're on." Ace tossed off his jacket and swaggered towards the middle of the room, bouncing from foot to foot and throwing punches at the air.

Kaitlyn could attack him before he made it to the middle, since there were no rules, but she'd try to make it last a little longer. She liked the idea of toying with Ace. Nick was nice and made good hot chocolate, so she'd just end it quickly with him.

Ace towered over her with a cocky grin that she couldn't wait to wipe off his face. He leaned forward slightly on the balls of his feet, knees bent, ready to spring, in a typical fighting stance. But she could tell by the look in his eyes, he was relaxed, like he was ready to have some fun. Ace really thought she didn't have a chance at taking him down. She was both perplexed and intrigued by this.

Ace made a slow move towards the left, and

Kaitlyn slid towards the right.

"You afraid, pretty girl?"

"Not even slightly," Kaitlyn retorted. She and Erik never bothered with trash talking. She'd seen it countless times in the movies and always thought it was rather silly, but she had to admit it was a little fun.

"Bring it on, sweet thing." He brought his hands up close to his face, palms closed like a boxer.

Ok, well, she definitely didn't enjoy being called *sweet thing*. Time for a little ass kicking.

"You're going down, Ace."

He laughed loudly, and Kaitlyn almost smiled herself. Maybe she was funny after all.

Ace motioned for her to come forward.

Kaitlyn kept her palms open Krav Maga style. She could do a lot of damage with the web or the palm of her hand.

She loved the ritual of the dance, the heightened perception of every flicker of movement. It truly was a game of sorts trying to guess her opponent's next move.

Ace continued to circle her and Kaitlyn mimicked his moves; together they were making the figure eight. Ace was cocky, but he also wasn't about to underestimate her. He was a large man, though he moved gracefully on his feet. Maybe she hadn't given him enough credit.

Kaitlyn threw a jab that Ace easily anticipated and blocked.

Ace pivoted from his front to his back foot and launched a counterattack, a frenzy of jabs mainly towards her face that she deflected with ease. He was taking this bet seriously, Kaitlyn thought, amusing herself.

Kaitlyn delivered a blow to his midsection, and Ace gave her a lopsided grin. "Nice."

Why was he talking to her? Kaitlyn took advantage and swept her left foot catching him in the ankle. Ace lost his balance and landed on his ass, but quickly sprang back onto his feet. Now he didn't look so happy.

He lunged forward and took a hard swing towards her solar plexus, but she blocked the blow with her right forearm.

Kaitlyn ducked when Ace threw a left hook that would have knocked her across the room had it connected. She switched directions and threw two hard right jabs. The first one missed and the second connected with his chin, but Ace held his ground and didn't even stumble.

Erik and Nick were laughing in the background.

She could see the change in his demeanor. This was no longer a game. His face was slick with sweat and eyes blazing while his chest heaved up and down. She could sense his next move. A strategy to counter him and win was already formed in her mind. Ace let out a loud battle cry before he charged, just as she knew he would.

Kaitlyn feinted to her left and hit him with a solid kidney punch.

Ace grunted, staggering back a couple of feet. Pissed off, he attacked again, but she blocked the blow with her left hand, wrist to wrist. They parlayed back and forth for nearly fifteen minutes. Everything he threw at her, she deflected. She was always faster and managed to land her own blows. Ace was now drenched in sweat, face covered in blood, and she wasn't even breathing hard. She could see the worried look in his eyes, and it gave her a small amount of pleasure. She was, after all, just an odd, pretty little thing.

Suddenly, she realized her mistake. She was not acting like a normal person. Not even an advanced trained person. She needed to take him down quickly. Moving quickly forward, she swiped the side of his kneecap. He lost his balance and fell forward on his knee. In one swift move, Kaitlyn was behind him, wrapping her arm around his neck and jerked him backwards.

Eyes wide, Ace tapped the ground as soon as he hit the floor.

Kaitlyn looked up and saw the concern in Erik's eyes. She screwed up. It was okay for her to go all out on Erik, he knew what she was, but it was unacceptable in this situation. Perhaps Adams was right and she had too much pride.

"Looks like you owe my partner two g's," Erik said, shaking his head.

Ace hung his head. "I must be having an off day."

Relief washed over her. She was going to have to learn to be more careful. She'd gotten lucky that Ace hadn't called her out.

"You ready Nick?" Kaitlyn wiped her brow as if there were actually sweat on it.

"I was thinking you deserved some more hot chocolate after that ass kicking," he said with a disarming smile.

"Don't want to be thumped by a girl?" Erik teased.

"Something like that." Nick grinned. "I'll even throw in extra marshmallows."

"Deal." Kaitlyn and Erik exchanged a look,

silently acknowledging that had been a close call.

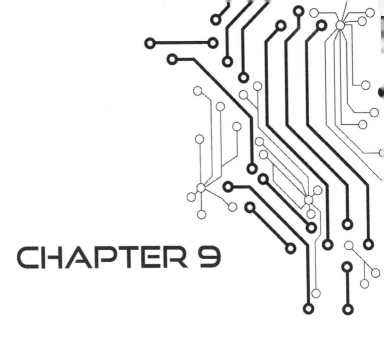

CHAPTER 9

How many days had passed? Five, six, more? Aaliyah lost count. Without the rise and fall of the sun, it was impossible for her to keep track. It could have been weeks for all she knew. At first, the loss of time had really bothered her. She couldn't stop wondering what her family was doing. Did they miss her at school? Most of all, did Noah think she had forgotten about him? Was he going crazy or had he already moved on? No, he couldn't have moved on that quickly. He cared too deeply for her. But what if he thought she had willingly ran away? The thought caused her chest to constrict. If only she could somehow get word to her family that she was okay. Relatively, anyway.

Everything felt surreal. How could she possibly be a prisoner?

Her head was pounding, and it was becoming

more and more difficult to think straight.

A noise made her jerk her eyes toward the left.

The door creaked open and she involuntarily flinched, fear burned in her stomach. God, she hated when she did that.

In came the taller man, the one who had brought her into the hellhole. He shut the door behind him. She hadn't left the room since she arrived. The only time she left the bed was to shower and go to the bathroom. Dasvoik insisted she needed to be clean when he came to his bed.

Clean? She would never be clean again. Her body and soul had been soiled. She spent hours alone staring at the ceiling feeling like she was losing her mind—*knowing* she was losing her mind. Oh, dear God, why was this happening to her?

Aaliyah fought to control and conceal the dread that swept over her.

The only thing that kept her sane was the faint hope of saving her brother and her memories of Noah. Like a movie, she replayed their time together. Noah had been so sweet and loving. She recalled the way they danced in the rain, walked hand in hand through the streets, how they used to laugh together. He had been so proud to be with her. He didn't care about the color of her skin or the slums she lived in. Even though they came from two different worlds, they had somehow found a blissful middle ground. She knew she didn't belong in his world, any more than he belonged in her world. But when they were together, their love could not be denied. In their sacred space, they belonged to each other. It was as if they had been destined for the other.

Two halves of a whole. Her heart ached. Could someone die of a broken heart? The pain was so deep it infused every inch of her body. She thought it could be a possibility.

Sometimes, she had conversations with him in her head. If only he were really there, to talk with her, and help her figure out a way to escape.

Aaliyah could no longer think about their kisses and sweet caresses. She couldn't think of Noah's lips on hers without recalling Dasvoik's hands on her skin. He had claimed her body in such a vile way that she didn't think she could ever think of anyone touching her again. Soiled. He had soiled her. There was no coming back from something like that. Even at her young age, she knew that to be true.

Noah would never understand. He would never forgive her. She would never forgive herself.

"It's time to move." The voice startled her. She had forgotten the man had entered the room. She found herself doing that more often lately. Drifting.

"Move where?" she asked dispassionately. She didn't care where they went. She knew no matter where they moved her, Dasvoik would still come to her. He would still hurt her. She would never get away.

"You should be happy. You'll briefly be reunited with your brother."

"My brother?" Her pulse raced at the words. She tried to sit up, but her hands were bound—as usual.

"It's time for you to join the others, I'm afraid."

He's afraid? What others? Suddenly, she didn't like the sound of the move at all. But the thought of her brother, of seeing his beautiful smile again. For that she would endure anything.

"Okay." Unconsciously, she wet her lips and tried to mentally steel herself for the move. She had to appear normal to her brother. It was not going to be easy. She couldn't even recall what normal felt like.

"You're not going to cause any trouble are you? The boss is agitated. He always gets upset when it's time to move the merchandise. I would advise you not to anger him."

Why was this man warning her? She already knew what the monster was capable of. Even the slightest thing wrong caused her to be punished. It was amazing she could still move. She didn't bother to answer him. It suddenly hit her that she didn't even care he was seeing her nude. She was no longer self-conscious or even repulsed. When had that part of her changed?

He came over, cut the rope between her feet and pulled her legs off the side of the bed. Her arms were tied in front of her, and he kept them bound. "Don't do anything stupid."

Stupid? You mean like stop and talk to strangers in the middle of the night in the ghetto? She'd already made enough stupid mistakes to last her a lifetime. She would not enrage his *boss.* Not if her brother was around to witness it.

Maybe Dasvoik had grown bored of her? No, the tall man had said something about moving merchandise. Before she had time to give it anymore thought, she was pulled to her feet.

He stood beside her and waited till the blood rushed to her feet, a kind movement. The shorter bald one always pulled her forward and laughed when she fell to her knees. Then, he would drag his hands over her naked body when he pulled her back up. His grubby little fingers lingering way too long on her breast. Only if Dasvoik wasn't around, of course. He wouldn't dare touch her inappropriately in front of her true owner. A shudder flew through her—owner. When had she accepted his words as truth?

When her feet were steady, she took a step forward. She had so many questions she wanted to ask, but kept them to herself. She wasn't sure she was prepared for the answers. Every inch of her body ached. The marks from the whip felt like her skin was on fire. She would have thought she would be used to it by now, but the pain never diminished. An ever-present reminder that her body was no longer her own.

"Can I at least put on the gown before I see my brother?" She knew it would freak her brother out to see her this way.

The man stared at her for a long moment. He reached forward and locked the door. "Don't make me regret this."

She wasn't sure what he meant by that statement. Maybe he thought she would try to escape again? She definitely learned her lesson last time. Dasvoik was very good at teaching lessons.

Relief washed over her. She watched him pull a gown out of the bottom drawer. She hadn't really expected him to give in to her request. He unbound her hands and she shook them out. Her hands were numb and heavy, making the movement feel strange. She kept her eyes down, staring at her bare feet.

The feel of the cloth against her skin after being naked for so long was an odd sensation. It brought water to her eyes when it brushed the welts. She blinked back the tears. She couldn't let Darrius see her cry. She had to be strong for him.

The man grabbed her hands and bound them once again. This time, they were not quite as tight; she could wiggle her fingers a little.

"Thank you," she whispered.

He opened the door, and they walked down the long hallway. She couldn't help but feel as if she was being walked to her death. Fear and anticipation fueled her steps. What if they had harmed her brother the way they did her? No, she couldn't think about that. He was alive. That was what was important. She had to focus on that fact.

They entered a service elevator, and he punched the button to the basement floor. Aaliyah started to become very afraid.

The man beside her said nothing. He just kept his hand clasped firmly on her arm. His jaw was set, and he looked straight ahead. She could feel the tension coming off him in waves. Whatever was going on was causing a lot of stress. Maybe they would be distracted enough for her to make a break for it. Only if she could save her brother at the same time.

The elevator stopped in the basement. He stepped out, pulling her forward. Everything in her screamed at her to run, but she had to see her brother. The basement was cold, dark and eerie. She could hear a loud clicking sound but had no idea where it was coming from or what it was. Towards the back, she could see the haze of a streetlight through an open door. The kind of door that freight trucks pulled into to make deliveries. For some reason, it surprised her that it was nighttime. She had lost all sense of time while she was locked away. Seeing the night sky jarred her senses.

"Where is my brother?" she asked in a low voice.

"Shh. Do not speak." His grip tightened around her arm. His pace quickened, and she stumbled forward, trying to keep up.

They headed towards the open bay door. Again, thoughts of escape raced through her mind. However, she knew she could not leave without Darrius. She heard raised voices, but could not understand what they were saying. They were speaking in a foreign language. Her blood ran cold when she realized one of the voices was Dasvoik. Her body shook and she took deep breaths trying to appear calm. She didn't want Darrius to see how terrified she was of that man.

Please, God, if you can hear me, I need some help down here. She took a deep breath and was surprised to feel a calming wave flood her veins.

As if the man gripping her arm could tell what she was doing, he slowed his steps. Giving her time to compose herself. He never so much as glanced at her. She wanted to thank him, and realized how absurd that was. Thanking the man that was helping to hold her captive. The man that was bringing her to the man that had been raping, beating and traumatizing her with his sick mind games for days—weeks maybe. She wasn't sure anymore.

Without thinking, she cast her eyes to the ground as they approached. It was disheartening how quickly she fell into the submissive role.

The arguing came to a halt.

Something very cold seized her chest. Evil. She could feel Dasvoik coming closer. She didn't have to look to know it was him. She could smell him. Sense him.

Seconds later, he was standing before her. He placed his fingers under her chin and tilted her head up to meet his eyes. "Just what I needed. Thank you, Tony."

Tony? All this time she had never known the other man's name. Tony sounded so average. He nodded and stepped aside.

Dasvoik's hand remained under her chin and he studied her eyes. He claimed looking into her clear turquoise eyes calmed him. She wanted to shut them, but she had no idea where her brother was. Could he see her or hear her? She didn't want him to see her be punished for disobeying.

"I'm afraid we don't have much time, but I need the release."

She tensed. Not here, not now. She could see the desire in his wild eyes. It chilled her to the bone. Was this man ever satisfied? He had just left her room hours ago.

"There's someone I want you to meet first, petal." His hand smoothed down her hair.

He had never introduced her to anyone before, and she didn't like that he was about to. What in the hell was going on?

"Ivan, come here."

A large man stepped out of the shadows. She

took a quick glance. He was well over six foot four and wide as a football player. His hair was slicked back and his eyes were so dark, they were almost black. His nose was large and beaked. He reminded her of a hawk. Quickly, she cast her eyes back down, but Dasvoik tilted her head back up.

"Breathtaking, isn't she?" Dasvoik asked. He looked proud of himself. It made her stomach twist. She felt like she was on display.

The man nodded and spoke. She had no idea what he said, but Dasvoik shook his head and answered in the same language. From the look in the man's eyes, she was glad she didn't understand what they were saying. Dasvoik became enraged.

The large man chuckled, and Dasvoik tilted his head, dismissing the giant of a man.

"Ah, my petal, he wanted to try you out for himself. But I just couldn't bear the thought." He pulled her into him. Her hands were still bound in front of her, making the move even more awkward.

Her body tensed. She was surprised to feel a wave of gratitude wash over her. The thought of that other man putting his hands on her, caused bile to rise in her throat.

"I must have you now. It will be quick, but I promise to make it up to you later."

Whatever gratitude she had briefly felt was gone and replaced with revulsion. He nudged her forward, and she had to fight from taking off in a sprint. She knew if she did, she would pay dearly. She also knew there was nowhere to hide in the basement where he could not find her.

He pushed her behind a stack of boxes. At least he wasn't going to do it in front of everyone. She still had no idea where Darrius was.

She felt his hot breath on her neck. His hands on her body. He untied the gown and it dropped forward. Because her hands were bound it never hit the floor. Murmuring words in her ear about her belonging only to him. How dare Ivan ask to take what was his. Words of a madman.

True to his word, he was fast. Breathing heavy, he collapsed against her, his sweat coated her body, making her feel even dirtier.

Dasvoik yelled over to Tony, who rushed over as Dasvoik pulled up his pants.

"Make her presentable." He wiped his hands together and walked away.

Tony reached down, picked up her gown and quickly draped it over her, securing it in the back. Tony looked around and cursed. "There isn't even a bathroom around here. We need to hurry back inside."

Aaliyah's shoulders slumped. All she could think was it would be longer until she could see her brother.

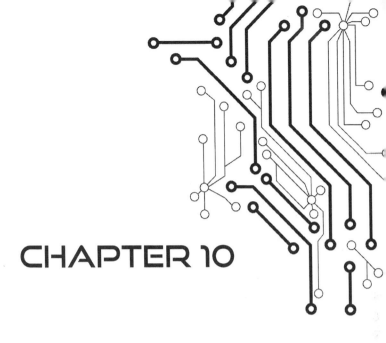

CHAPTER 10

Shuffling forward, Aaliyah stopped in her tracks. Darrius! Her heart swelled. Tony nudged her arm to get her moving again. Her brother sat in the back of the cargo van, his head bowed and his arms bound before him. He wore the same clothes he had on the day they were abducted. A long-sleeved, red striped shirt and a pair of loose jeans. He looked thinner. She wondered how much weight he had lost. And what they were feeding him. An overwhelming sense of hopelessness consumed her. She tried to think of something positive to fight off all the negative thoughts racing through her head, but she could only think of one. He still had his clothes on, unlike herself.

She didn't dare speak. Instead, she mentally willed her brother to look up, but he did not. Not even when she entered the back of the van. Tony pushed her down on a bench across from her brother. Why wouldn't he look at her? She needed to see his beautiful little face. Needed to know he was okay.

Of course, he wasn't going to look up. He was afraid. A closer glance and she could see his legs shaking. What had they done to him to instill this fear? Whatever they'd done, it had taken the fight out of him. Just the thought was enough to enrage her. How could they hurt someone so innocent? None of this made any sense at all. Darrius was such a sweet soul. He did not deserve to be ripped away from his family and friends.

Tony backed out of the van and slammed the door shut without another word. She briefly wondered if she would ever see Tony again. Not that it mattered. He hadn't exactly been kind to her, but he hadn't been cruel like Dasvoik and the bald man. And he never touched her inappropriately. A stream of light filtered under the door and a sour smell caused her nose to itch. The window was tinted but the streetlights cast an eerie glow.

"Darrius," she whispered. "It's okay. We're alone."

His body tensed, but he kept his head bowed.

"Please. I need to see your face. Look at me."

Slowly, he tilted his head up, and she gasped. His eyes were swollen shut and the right side of his jaw didn't look right. Hatred coursed through her body like none she had ever known. If Dasvoik were standing in front of her right now, she would kill him with her own bare hands. Despite the chill in the van, a bead of sweat trickled down Aaliyah's brow. How dare they harm her little brother!

Somehow she would find a way to make them all pay.

"I'm so sorry," she moaned. Her chest tightened. It felt as if she couldn't breathe. "My poor Darrius."

She had to calm herself down. Allowing Darrius to see her anguish would not help anyone.

She stood up and crossed the van, thankful that her legs had not been bound and eased down next to him.

"Can you talk?" she asked in a whisper.

"Yes." His voice sounded hollow, broken. Certainly not the voice of an eight-year-old. Not the mischievous little boy she knew and loved so much. They might not have had much growing up, but at least they had been happy. Could her brother ever be happy again? The thought angered her. Yes, of course he could be happy. They just had to figure out how to get out of this god-forsaken place. And soon.

Maybe they would be rescued. If they were moving and Dasvoik was obviously worried, there had to be a reason. There must be a chance he could get caught. She glanced at the door as if waiting for the police to come to burst through at any second. She wondered what the merchandise was they were talking about. More than likely drugs. It didn't seem to matter what part of the world you were in, drugs always played a big role. It made no sense to her. Even in America, where they had everything you could wish for, there was a huge drug problem. If there were drugs involved, there really was a chance of a rescue. A tiny seed of hope was planted.

"Why?" Darrius croaked out.

Such a simple question. She was silent for a long moment struggling to find the words, but there were none. "I don't know. I just don't know. These people are sick, Darrius. We need to figure out how to get away from them."

He titled his head at her. She couldn't see his eyes because of the swelling but his shoulders straightened slightly and she knew he felt it, too. Hope. That was all they had at this point.

Suddenly, the van jerked forward. After a few feet, it came to an abrupt stop before slowly continuing on. Where in the world were they taking them? Not knowing was the worst part of all of this. They had no control of their lives at this point. If they at least knew what to expect, maybe they could mentally prepare for it. Although, no one could have mentally prepared for what she'd already been through.

"I love you, Darrius. I'm so sorry I let you down."

"Not your fault." She saw a tear slide down his swollen cheek. "Not your fault," he repeated and her heart broke in a thousand pieces. She knew it was her fault. If it weren't for her, he would have never been in this position. Those creeps had wanted her.

She wanted to calm him, reassure her little brother somehow. But the words would not come so instead she did the only thing she could think of.

Aaliyah started singing in Afrikaans. Their native tongue in South Africa. Her voice sounded sad to her own ears. The song had been Darrius's favorite bedtime song when he was littler. *Wielie-wielie-walie, die aap sit op die balie. Tjoef-tjaf val hy af. Wielie-wielie-walie.* A silly song about a monkey sitting on a barrel. Darrius used to beg her to sing it over and over when she tucked him in bed at night. She would sell her soul to go back to that time and place again.

Darrius's head dropped to her shoulder, and she continued to sing in a hushed voice. It bothered her that she couldn't reach up and touch him, but at least they were together. His breathing soon became regular and his head rolled back. She smiled and kept singing. Poor little boy probably hadn't had a good sleep since they'd been abducted. She knew she hadn't. Nightmares kept her up.

They drove for hours. At least it felt like hours. Mostly in a straight line it seemed, and they were driving fast, so they were probably on a main highway. Somehow, she knew where they were going would be far worse than where they had come from. Just the thought, made the hair on the back of her neck stand on end, as a chill ran down her spine.

Eventually, the van slowed and rolled to a stop. Darrius was awake and shivering. She knew it wasn't from the cold. He was terrified. They both were terrified. But nothing could have prepared them for what they were about to see.

"It's going to be okay. I love you," she whispered.

"Right." Darrius dropped his head.

The doors flew open and two large men pulled them out of the van. Despite the cold, perspiration beaded on her upper lip. Desperately, she tried to fight the fear that flooded her body.

Aaliyah looked around trying to take in her surroundings. Huge colorful metal boxes stacked high surrounded them. She could smell the ocean and hear the waves lapping. At any other time, the sounds would have been soothing. Here, nothing was calming. They were being shoved forward. Darrius cried out and the man slapped him hard across the head. Blood flew from his mouth.

Aaliyah went crazy. She thrashed and kicked, but the man just laughed, dragging her along on the ground. Eventually, he got sick of pulling her, so he threw her over his shoulder as if she weighed nothing. Her gown slipped up and the man cupped his hand on her bare bottom. His large fingers dug into her skin making her want to vomit. Frantic, she struggled against him, squirming, twisting, but it was useless against his powerful arms.

The men spoke to each other, but once again she could not understand them. Why couldn't they just speak English? They went down several narrow walkways surrounded by the huge containers. It had to be at some kind of shipyard or something.

Looking down at the ground made her nauseated. Her body jerked up and down over his shoulder.

After a while, the men made a sharp left. The guy dropped her to the ground, slapped her on the bottom, before he pushed her forward over a metal grated walkway that led to a huge ship. The ship was full of the same type of containers they had passed by.

The ship was dark, and their footsteps echoed

loudly. Her legs shook with every step, and her heart felt like it was going to jump out of her throat. The ground was freezing on her bare feet. Silently, she thanked Tony for allowing her to put on the flimsy gown.

The corridors were long and narrow with low ceilings. The space was so small and confining, even though the ship itself was huge. Bigger than anything she had ever seen before. Loud clanking and hissing sounds only freaked her out even more.

There was nowhere to run. They were trapped like mice in a maze. She would never remember all the twists and turns they had taken.

A chill spread through her when she noticed a large metal door looming ahead. Her steps faltered. Once the door swung open, the overpowering stench hit her immediately, causing her stomach to heave violently. It smelled like sewage or rotten food.

Aaliyah froze. Any bravado she had left evaporated.

"Oh, shit," she whispered. Before her stood rows and rows of cages. Filled with *humans.* She couldn't tear her eyes away. Most of them were young, dark skinned, naked and filthy. She twisted and tried to run, but the large man just laughed and grasped her arms tighter. If she didn't know it before, she knew it now: they were in trouble, very bad trouble.

The man next to her pulled Darrius forward. Her brother turned to look at her, even though he couldn't see through his swollen eyes. He didn't even cry out. She was proud of him for being so brave, but also devastated that he had to grow up so quickly. Panic surged through her.

With every ounce of energy, she twisted and pulled trying to get from the man's tight grip as she watched Darrius leaving the room and going through another metal door.

"No!" she yelled hysterically.

The door slammed shut and Darrius was once again gone from her sight. The only sounds were a loud scraping of metal against metal.

She heard herself whimpering, pleading for him not to take her brother away, promising she would do anything he wanted her to.

The man laughed loudly.

He handled her casually, as if she was nothing more than an inanimate object, which made the cruelty that much harder to bear. Slowly, he untied her wrists.

She knew she only had seconds to act. She whirled around, and with all her might, threw a punch, but before it could connect, he stepped back and grabbed her arm. He twisted it violently behind her, causing her to cry out in pain.

"Tsk, tsk." He said something else, but since it was in another language, he might as well have been speaking gibberish. She groaned, as he eased her arm back down. She'd failed. Again.

Clumsy fingers racked her back as the man tried to untie the gown while holding her in place with his other arm. The gown floated to the floor and the cool air hit her bare skin. Instinctively, she tried to cover herself, but she was pinned against him. A loud sob escaped as the man ran his free hand over her body.

Please, no. Not again!

After a few rough grabs, his hands stopped

roaming. The man pulled a key out of his pocket and opened one of the cages. Her body stiffened. She couldn't go in there. There was no way in hell she was going to let him put her in that cage. It was already overfilled with other young girls. She threw her head back, but he had anticipated the move and just titled his head to the side. She barely hit his shoulder.

Aaliyah's shoulders sagged, defeated. She was no match for the large man. Consciously, she tried to control the panic as she stared into the young girls eyes. They all looked glassy and drugged. They didn't even make a sound as she was thrown into the cage with them and fell on top of arms and legs.

Aaliyah pushed herself up with one of her hands. Quickly, she yanked it back she had landed on something warm and sticky.

Gross. There was nowhere to wipe her hand. She brought her fingers to her face. Her stomach heaved when she realized what the rust-colored substance was.

Blood.

After what she had been through, she shouldn't have been surprised by the sight, but it still jarred her. She glanced around at the cowering girls. None of them would meet her eyes.

The cage was barely tall enough to stand in, but everyone was laying or sitting on the ground. The door shut with a loud clank. Seconds later, the lights went out and they were engulfed in darkness. The panic was so strong, she felt like she was going to crawl out of her skin. Aaliyah pulled her legs up to her chest, wrapping her arms around herself, the cool skin of the others pressed against her thighs. She couldn't help it as tears streamed down her face and her body shook.

So this was the merchandise. *They* were the merchandise. Of course, she'd seen occasional mention of human trafficking on the news, but she never really believed it still existed in today's world. Not in America. Now she was living proof.

Living in the slums of Detroit, the dangers were plentiful. But never had she imagined being abducted, raped and thrown in a cage. In the confined space, she rocked back and forth.

Darrius.

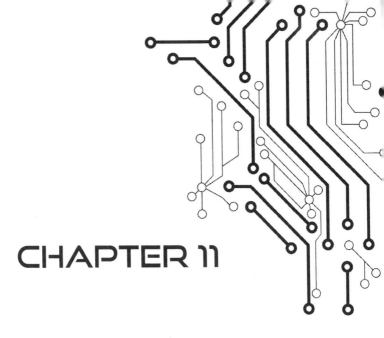

CHAPTER 11

Restless, Kaitlyn kicked her foot over her ankle and stared at the wood planked ceiling. Dr. Chambers would be proud.

Another afternoon wasting away. Tomorrow would be a week they'd been waiting for word that they were cleared to move forward. During that time, they'd kept busy with training, but she was itching to get to work.

It was as if time was standing still. Kaitlyn sent Lucas an inquiring look. "What's that saying Quess uses about a kettle and tea while waiting?"

Lucas set down his book and turned to his side, tracing his fingers up her arm and chuckled. "I think you mean a watched pot never boils?"

She shook her head, thoughtfully. "Yeah, that's the one. I thought that was a ridiculous phrase, but I finally understand what she means. Time really does seem to stand still when you are waiting for something."

"Get over here, Kate." He raised his arm for her to mold herself to him. Warmth moved through her. She loved to hear her name on his lips. His gaze dropped to her mouth. Instead of kissing her lips, he lowered his head and pressed his lips lightly to her bare shoulder. His hands cupped her hips, drawing her in tighter. Kaitlyn let herself relax into the embrace. The moment his lips touched hers, she was lost in the sensation, a heat that only he could cause radiated through her. It was always that way with them. A simple kiss from him made her forget everything. She couldn't think beyond her need for Lucas.

"I want you, Lucas," she whispered.

His smile turned sensual. "You got me, Kate."

Beneath the splayed hand she pressed firmly to his chest, she felt his heartbeat kick up a notch. It drove her crazy how responsive he was to her touch. Lucas grabbed her hand and stroked his thumb across her skin before lightly kissing each of her fingertips. His lips continued to trail down her wrist and her arm. He rolled her over and lowered his mouth, kissing her so soft and sweet, taking his time about it.

Kaitlyn swiped her tongue over his full bottom lip before she drew it into her mouth and sucked, arching her body into his. Lucas let out a low groan of pleasure. She loved the taste of him. His taste was unique to him and not even her sensors could tell exactly what the mixture was. His tongue found hers and stroked it. She kissed him back with unabashed hunger. His touch was intoxicating.

His lips left hers as he trailed warm kisses

along her jawline, making his way to the sensitive flesh of her earlobe. She shuddered when he lightly pulled with his teeth. She would never get enough of him.

His fingers found the hem of her tank top. Her own fingers wandered beneath his T-shirt and up his back, whose muscles rippled beneath her touch. His chest rose and fell with each breath. He pulled away to tug her tank top all the way off. Kaitlyn looked up. Lucas was gazing at her so intently, his blue eyes darker than usual.

"Jesus, you're gorgeous." His voice was raw and filled with need.

No matter how many times he'd seen her naked, he always looked as if it were the first time. One of his hands cupped her breast while his mouth grazed the other.

"Lucas," she gasped. His hand slid down to the vee between her legs. She dropped her knees to the side to give him better access. The tickle of his fingers through the cotton of her pants was enough to make her wither beneath his touch. He began to trail kisses and nibbles down her body, making her squirm beneath his touch. Wanting more. She groaned, her hands tangled in his hair.

Suddenly, Kaitlyn tensed up and pushed Lucas back.

"What's wrong?" Lucas asked, as Kaitlyn detangled herself from the embrace.

"Erik."

"What?" Lucas said, clearly rattled.

Lucas looked towards the closed door. Seconds later, there was a knock. Lucas groaned and fell back onto the bed.

Kaitlyn pulled on her tank top and crossed

the room to open the door.

Erik looked Kaitlyn up and down, taking in her disheveled appearance. "Sorry to interrupt, but Harrington wants us all in the office."

She absently smoothed down her hair. "We'll be right there."

Erik turned to leave, and she closed the door behind him. She felt a little self-conscious when she realized Erik knew what she and Lucas had been doing. But they had more important things to deal with.

Lucas was already up and straightening his clothes. She grabbed a sweatshirt and pulled it over her head.

As they walked down the hall, Lucas didn't put his hand on her lower back, or stand too close, and she appreciated his discretion, even though there was part of her that wanted him to drag her back to the bedroom to finish what they'd started. Once in a while, thoughts entered her mind that surprised her. This was one of those times. Her mind should be one hundred percent on the task ahead of them, not on Lucas's large hands roaming her body.

Lucas held the door open for her when they reached Harrington's office. Erik was already seated and didn't bother to look up when they entered the room.

Harrington's eyes were lit up and shining brightly.

Before they could even lower themselves into the seats, Harrington exclaimed, "The boat has finally left the port."

Kaitlyn felt a surge of excitement and

eagerness course through her.

"We're going to fly out the day after tomorrow."

"Why not now?" Kaitlyn asked, unable to mask her annoyance.

"If they are picking up the children out at sea, we need to wait for the exchange," Harrington explained.

She couldn't hide her irritation. Just the thought of the captives being locked in the cages for even one day was too long, as far as she was concerned. "For all we know, they could have been on the ship all this time and the exchange is actually to transfer the captives."

Harrington held out a hand, signaling her to calm down. "You can hold on for two more days. We want them on international waters where the laws are murky at best."

Okay, she could grasp the logic of that statement, but the waiting was driving her insane. Just two more nights. She could handle that. She just hoped the prisoners could.

They spent the next couple of hours going over the blueprints of the ship. They would be transported by helicopter and dropped into the ocean along with a rubber boat in the middle of the night approximately twelve miles away so that the target couldn't see them. Once they got to the boat, it would be a simple hook and climb.

"Are we done here?" Kaitlyn asked.

"For now. I'll let you know if we need to go over anything else."

Kaitlyn sprang to her feet. "I'm going to the shooting range." She needed to blow off steam, and going back to the room with Lucas just didn't feel right after knowing the captives had to spend at least two more days on the boat being subjected to who knew what.

Harrington nodded, already lost in his own thoughts.

She could ask Lucas or Erik to join her, but she felt like being alone.

Lucas raised an eyebrow, as if asking if he could accompany her, but she shook her head.

On the way out the front door, she noticed Ace sitting on one of the rocking chairs. When their eyes met, he looked away. Over and over throughout the week she had bested him. His ego had been bruised. She thought about it for a moment to see if it bothered her that he didn't like her, and it didn't, not even slightly.

Her feet crunched on the snow as she took off in a jog across the lawn under the bare-branched oak trees. Thoughts raced through her mind, but she pushed them away. She needed to be clear and centered and let the rest of her brain sort out the random thoughts.

Once she reached the indoor ranges, she grabbed a pistol from the safe and made her way to the firing line. The weight of the gun in her hands instantly calmed her. It was very similar to the way Lucas made her feel. Totally absorbed in the moment, she could forget about everything and just focus on the targets, the kill zones. It was a strange, yet relaxing feeling, like tunnel vision. Her mind processed everything as if time stood still; the targets seemed to be waiting for her, but in reality life was moving all around her.

She hit the button and the paper targets moved towards the back of the room. She had six of them lined up with different spacing. Mechanisms were in place that randomly moved the targets back and forth or side to side at different speeds.

Lightly, she squeezed the grip handle, sucked in a breath and released. Just like her instructors had taught her. She squeezed the trigger and got lost in the moment as the targets zigzagged in front of her. At some point, she felt Ace enter the building. He didn't speak, and she didn't acknowledge him. She never missed a beat.

Over and over, she released the cartridge and jammed in another. She went through over two hundred rounds of ammo.

When she was finished, she hit the button, and the targets slid forward.

"How the hell are you so good?" Ace demanded. She turned towards him and noticed his darkened gaze.

Kaitlyn was taken aback by the tone of his voice. She set the gun down and started taking it apart to clean it without answering.

"I've worked with the best of the best. How the hell are you head and shoulders above them? You're like some kind of freak."

She bristled and turned away from his probing gaze. His turn of phrase struck her where it still hurt. There were times when she looked in the mirror and all she could see was a freak. *How would a normal person respond?* She knew if she kept quiet, it would just enrage him and make her appear even more robotic.

Her mouth opened and closed without speaking, she couldn't find the words.

"Jealously doesn't become you, Ace." Erik's voice cut through the air. She hadn't heard him enter and that bothered her.

"Jealousy? Hell, yes, I'm jealous, but more than that, I'm baffled." He threw his arms in the air. "Seriously, what the hell, man? This shit ain't normal, and you know it just as well as I do."

"Leave her alone."

"Ooh, what are you now, Prince Charming? Coming to save the damsel in distress? I hate to break it to you, buddy, but this chick doesn't need any saving."

Kaitlyn took in a deep breath and let it out before speaking. "It's fine, Erik. I don't know what to tell you, Ace. I guess my training has been better." She continued to wipe down the gun without looking up.

"Bullshit." He pushed the button and the targets moved forward. "Look at this. Every single one of the hits is dead center. No variations—that's *impossible*."

"Obviously not," Erik said and pulled down the targets, crumbling them one after another before tossing them into the bin.

Kaitlyn wished she could just tell him the truth. She was enhanced. He hit the nail on the head when he said she was some kind of freak, because she was. She wasn't really ashamed of her body and what it could do, but the program was secret. And as far as she knew, Harrington had not pulled Ace and Nick in on the operation. They were simply hired to drive them around and keep them safe. As they said in the movies, Ace did not have a *need to know.*

"Something is not right here." Ace spat the words out.

Kaitlyn couldn't understand why he was so

angry. She was better than him. So what? He needed to get over it.

"The only thing that is not right is you yelling at your client. You should be fired for showing disrespect," Erik said, keeping his voice level.

"Whatever," Ace muttered. "As long as I'm getting paid, I couldn't give a shit, but I'm telling you right now, there is something off about this chick. I'd watch your back, man."

The door slammed loudly behind him.

Kaitlyn's shoulders sagged. "I'm sorry. I was feeling restless so came out here to center myself."

"What are you sorry about? He's the one being a jackass."

"He's right though, isn't he? What I do is impossible for humans?"

Erik paused. "Sometimes, but he still shouldn't have yelled at you like that. And you shouldn't have to downplay yourself while you're training. It's bad enough you have to in public."

She'd never really thought of it as downplaying. Dr. Chambers had drilled it in as blending in. Downplaying made her feel weird. She didn't like the idea of not living up to her full potential, but it was part of the price.

"Don't let him get to you."

"It doesn't really. I mean, maybe it does a little bit."

"He should be fired. I'm going to talk to Harrington."

Kaitlyn was startled. "No, don't do that. He's your friend, and he's right."

"Doesn't matter. You shouldn't have to deal with his lack of respect."

Maybe, but having Ace fired just didn't feel

right to her. "If he does or says anything again, you can talk to Harrington, but for now, let's just let it go. You gave him a warning. Now it's up to him."

Erik lifted his shoulder in a half shrug. "If that's what you want."

"It is." She put the cleaning supplies away and placed the pistol back in the safe. "I'm anxious, Erik. This is really going to happen."

He nodded and looked away. She wondered what he was thinking about but didn't ask.

"We can do this, Erik."

His gaze shifted back to her, his own face without expression. "I know we can. Truth be told, I'm looking forward to it."

Kaitlyn was glad he'd said that, because in the back of her mind, she wasn't sure he was completely on board with the mission. She searched his face. "Do you enjoy it?"

Erik's lip twisted. "Enjoy it? That's a trick question. I'm good, a natural, as they like to say, but I've lost friends, seen innocent people killed, and never had a long-term relationship. A lot of sacrifices are made by people in our profession."

Kaitlyn had never given those issues much thought. She came into the profession by chance, unlike Erik, who had wanted it and went after it.

"Why haven't you had any long-term relationships?"

Erik laughed bitterly. "Right, who wants a man that is hardly ever home and can't share a single thing about their life to their significant other?"

Kaitlyn tilted her head. "Surely, some guys

are married with families?"

"Oh, yeah, most guys I worked with have had at least three wives and several children. Finding someone isn't the hard part. It's staying with it and making it work that gets most of them. Occasionally, a guy will get lucky and find someone that can put up with all the bullshit." The intensity suddenly left his face. "Like Ace, he's got Gracie."

"Ace is married?"

"Yep, over ten years."

"When I asked him if he had children, he said no."

Erik grimaced. "He doesn't. Gracie can't get pregnant. For years they've tried all the fertility routes, but no baby. Seems the way life works sometimes. People seldom get everything they wish for."

Kaitlyn didn't like to think about having babies. That was something that would never happen for her. So she just tried to put it out of her head. But for the first time she wondered if it bothered Lucas.

"But to answer your question—does it get my juices flowing? Hell, yeah. It's addictive. I love the adrenaline rush, the camaraderie, the sense of power and of course, let's not forget, I'm a patriot. But at the end of the day, it's about this." He moved his hand back and forth between the two of them. "Knowing you have someone that you would trust your life to and knowing you would give your own to save theirs."

Kaitlyn stood motionless. Her eyes itched and she blinked away the moisture that wanted to spill over.

Erik tapped her on the shoulder with a slight smile on his face. For an instant, she thought she saw a twinkle in his usually serious eyes. "Don't go getting soft on me."

Kaitlyn looked down at his hand that was now dropped to his side. A smile spread across her face. In that moment, she knew she didn't have to worry about becoming friends with Erik or his bond with Ace. What they shared was between the two of them. An odd emotion stirred in her chest, and her sensors informed her it was loyalty.

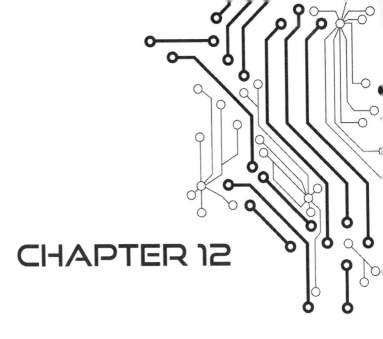

CHAPTER 12

Like every morning, Aaliyah woke in a cold sweat, disoriented, as the darkness engulfed her. It took several moments to gain her bearings. The cages were always pitch black. The kind of darkness that made it impossible for her eyes to adjust. She wanted to cry out, beg for help, but she'd already seen what happened to the ones who did. Whipped in front of all of them. Sometimes the guards sexually assaulted the girls. It was terrifying to hear the whimpers of the girls and the grunts from the bastards, knowing there was absolutely nothing she could do to stop it.

Gradually, her heart settled. She wiggled side to side, trying to get free, but she was squished between the others. Several arms and legs were strewn across her body. All young women, some of them still children.

Carefully, she pushed the limbs aside and scooted up to sit. A few of the bodies started to stir.

As she tried to peer around the cage, a pang of deep loneliness took over. It seeped into her bones, crying out for her to reach out to the strangers she shared the cage with. She'd tried a few times, but none of them would speak to her, not even to tell her their names. Not that she really blamed them. They were terrified, but somehow she thought it might make it more bearable if they would band together.

Every morning their food was delivered. A brief moment of light shined into their cage, and she marked a line for the day passed. Not that it mattered. Wherever they were headed was definitely not paradise.

Several of the girls were seasick. The piles of puke only added to the vile smell of the cages. Just the thought made her stomach roll.

By now, several days had passed since she'd last seen her little brother. In some ways, it felt like longer, but in others, it felt like time couldn't have possible passed that quickly. What killed her the most was not knowing if he was all right. Of course, he couldn't possibly be okay, but she needed to know for sure that he was at least alive. It was like a horrible nightmare she couldn't wake up from.

If only that were the case.

Silent tears streamed down her face. Annoyed, she quickly wiped them away. No matter how brave she tried to be, the tears still came. It pissed her off. Why was this happening to them? She'd been a good girl, listened to her parents, believed in God, went to church every Sunday. It wasn't fair! Why was God punishing her? Allowing all of them to be abused? Surely, there was nothing these helpless girls could have done to deserve this suffering.

Footsteps echoed loudly down the hallway—breakfast time. Aaliyah slouched back down and lay completely still. If she were quiet, maybe Dasvoik would pick someone else to violate.

Quickly, she admonished herself. How could she possibly wish those horrors on someone else? Fear passed through her heart. Had God heard her thoughts? A sense of shame washed over her. What was becoming of her?

Keys scraped the lock and the door screeched open. A flash of light momentarily lit up the cage, highlighting the naked bodies, matted hair and crazed eyes.

"Move," the deep voice commanded. It seemed to be the only English word the guy knew.

The mass of bodies pushed themselves even further to the back of the cage like cattle. They tried to avoid the pile of feces and vomit in the corner, making just enough room for the bucket of water and tray of bread. Like scavengers, they leapt forward, pushing and clawing their way to the food. Aaliyah wanted to yell at them. If they just took turns, everyone would get something, and no one would get injured. But speaking out would get her in trouble.

She'd be damned if she gave them the opportunity to degrade her even more than they'd already done. *At least not publicly.* What the monster did behind closed doors she had very little control over.

Somehow, she managed to grasp a large

chunk of bread. Saliva pooled in her mouth.

A young girl around ten pulled at her arm, her wide brown eyes pleaded with her. Aaliyah sighed and tore the bread in half, handing the young girl the other half. She prayed someone was doing the same for Darrius. Just thinking about her brother nearly broke her heart in a million pieces. He was so young and so sweet. Why did they have to take him, too?

Aaliyah moaned when she was pulled forward out of the cage.

Oh, no. Not again. She felt the pulse beating in her neck. Everyday since she boarded this god-forsaken ship, they had come for her. For some reason the boss had taken a special liking to her, and didn't bother with the others. He had the audacity to claim she should be honored he chose her. Who the hell said things like that? A madman.

Up until her capture, she'd always felt blessed to have her mother's good looks, but now she knew it was a curse.

The brute's hand gripped her bicep like a vice. A feeling of terror seized her. He pushed her forward and she stumbled, scraping her bare knees on the rough metal flooring. He yanked her hard until she was back on her feet. The floor was cold on her bare feet and sent shivers up her spine. If there was anything positive to be said about the cage, it would be that the body heat from the others kept them warm.

Without a word, he dragged her down the narrow corridor. Being out of the cage unleashed an overwhelming need to escape. It was so strong, it filtered through every fiber of her being. Her eyes darted back and forth, seeking any opening. If she could just find a hiding place. Somewhere no one would find her. And then what? Starve to death?

She didn't have the answer. How could she help Darrius if she didn't even know where they had taken him? Hiding was not the solution. Once she made the mistake of asking where her brother was, and she was punished severely. Her back still ached from the beating.

Much too soon, they reached the bathroom. He shoved her through the doorway, causing her to catch her foot on the uneven flooring and she fell, sprawled out on the floor. With haste, she used her tied hands to push herself back up. Her muscles ached from the effort, but she wasn't about to give the creep even more reason for his hands to roam her naked body. She was able to bring herself to her knees.

The grungy shower stall stood before her. The lighting was very dim, but she could still see the rings of rust at the bottom of the shower and the built up grime. At least she got to shower, unlike the others.

The man wrapped his arms around her chest, yanking her to her feet. His forearms squished her breast, and she fought the urge to struggle.

The first time she had been taken to the shower and the guard's hands touched her body, she had kneed him. Big mistake. He backhanded her so hard, her head felt like it was going to snap off. It took a full day for the ringing to go leave her ears. Now, she just endured the roaming hands. She tried to convince herself it wasn't her body. But that didn't work. It never worked. Her nerve endings were constantly on fire. And not in a good way, not the way Noah used to make her feel.

Now, when she closed her eyes and tried to recall what Noah's touch had felt like, it never came. The only thing she could remember was Dasvoik and his guards. Noah was becoming a distant memory. She tried desperately to hold onto him, but he was slipping away. It wasn't fair. None of this was fair. She wanted to stomp her feet and scream like a spoiled child. If only that would work...

Without warning, she was pushed into the shower stall.

She tried to brace herself for the shock of the freezing cold water, but it didn't help. It never did. She yelped out loudly.

Closing her eyes, she willed her mind to withdraw into itself as the large callused hands roamed over her soapy body. She couldn't stand to look into the monster's eyes. She wouldn't give him that satisfaction. Always pinching and prodding as he washed her. The antiseptic smell of the soap made her eyes water. Or maybe that was just more tears. She couldn't tell any longer.

The cold water stung, but at least it was washing the filth off of her. Momentarily.

Oh, God. How could this be happening to her? Bile rose in her throat.

Her only consolation was that Dasvoik would kill the guards if they went any further than roaming hands. He'd made it clear she belonged only to him.

Her blood went cold, knowing what would happen after they left the bathroom.

Seventeen-years-old, and she was ruined. No

one would ever want her again.

Tainted. Defiled. Disgusting.

She sucked in a breath as her back was scrubbed. Her body still ached from Dasvoik's latest punishment. But worse than the aches was the mental anguish. Like a loop, the images kept replaying in her mind. She tried to block them out, but they would not leave her alone. They went everywhere with her. Even in her fitful sleep, Dasvoik always showed up.

To fight the images, her mind went to Noah, like always, remembering how his green eyes always looked at her with total adoration. He was always so patient with her. Never pushed her further than she was willing to go. Oh, she had been tempted. His kisses had been so sweet and felt so good. So right. They had been inseparable over the last few months. What started as friendship, had quickly turned into something more. She missed his dark hair, pale freckled face, and his moss green laugh-filled eyes. He must be going crazy not knowing where she was. A sob escaped her mouth, and her shoulders shook.

He could never love her now. Not that she blamed him, but it still hurt. Hell, she wondered if she would ever be able to love herself again? Wasted thoughts. She had not asked to be abducted. Or catch the attention of a madman. This was *not* her fault. Then why did she feel so responsible? Maybe if she had taken a different route home after picking up Darrius from after school soccer, or let Noah give her a ride. If she hadn't turned around when the car pulled over to ask directions. So many what-ifs and regrets.

More than anything, she wished she had given

Noah her virginity. That was her biggest regret. At least then, she would have that memory to cling to. But no, she had insisted on waiting until marriage. A lot of good that had done her.

Dasvoik had been so pleased when he realized she was pure. Apparently, he had her checked when she had been knocked out during the abduction. Her stomach dropped at the thought of how many men had seen her naked.

Dasvoik claimed he could have made a fortune out of her virginity but wanted her for himself. At least for the remainder of the trip. Then, she could be sold off like the rest of them.

The man yanked her hair back as he washed it. *Ignore the pain.*

How could she make it through this horror? She wanted to live! Oh, how much she wanted to bask in the sunlight, eat her mamma's cooking, read a good book, and be back in Noah's arms. Somehow, she had to make it out of this hellhole.

A part of her knew she was kidding herself. Once she got out of there, it would be replaced with a new hell. Perhaps even worse. She couldn't think about that. She had to hold onto the slim chance that she could escape.

The first few days, she had fantasies of the American soldiers storming the boat and bringing them home to safety, like in the movies. That dream had long faded. If she were going to escape, she would have to do it on her own. But she couldn't leave her brother. No, she could never leave him. Perhaps, once they got off the boat, she could find a way. Maybe while they were being unloaded, an opportunity would present itself.

If that didn't work, hopefully they would be sold together. She couldn't bear the thought of being separated again. Her shoulders sagged at the thought.

Too many unknowns.

Next thing she knew, the water stopped and a rough towel dried her body, taking extra time over her sensitive parts. She wanted to curl up in a ball and disappear. Where the hell was the magic pixie dust when she needed it?

He pushed her down onto the bench, and roughly ran a brush through her knotted hair. Her head snapped back as he yanked the brush. The other women envied her. She could see it in their eyes when she was returned. They had yet to shower. If they knew what she had to go through in order to be scrubbed clean, they might not want to trade places. Or maybe they would. Who knew. She hated to admit it, but a small part of her was secretly grateful. When she acknowledged that fact to herself, it made her feel very dirty. So in the end, the showers never cleaned her.

The guard's voice startled her. Once again, she had drifted. It was happening so often now. Aaliyah hadn't even realized she was no longer being groped or that her feet were moving down the dark hallway. The guard held her wrist in his hand and pushed her up the staircase. Each step was met with dread. One step closer to an evil that shouldn't be allowed to exist in this world.

The large man rapped his knuckles against the door. The familiar sense of fear overwhelmed her. Silently she tried to compose herself. Dasvoik thrived on her fear. She willed the trembling to stop. Why couldn't she stop shaking?

Let go Aaliyah, find that hidden place and hide, until he's done with you.

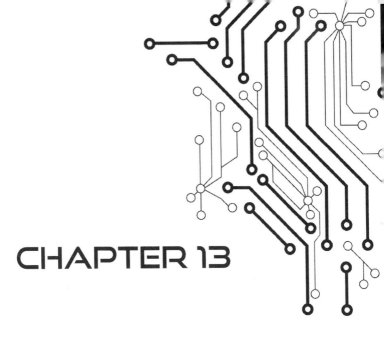

CHAPTER 13

Aaliyah blinked several times after she entering the bedroom, or torture chambers, as she had come to think of it. The bright fluorescent lights were always so jarring to her senses. The room was massive. A large, carved wooden four-poster bed waited for her. It would be beautiful if it weren't for the horrors that took place on it. Sometimes, while locked in her cage, she found herself mentally tracing the swirls on the wood.

Did that mean she was going crazy?

Her nose flared from the stench of sweat, sex and the coppery scent of blood that filled his room.

Somehow, the bright light made the torture more real. Made her feel even more vulnerable, if that was possible. More exposed. She hated seeing his face so clearly. She often wondered how the face of a monster could be so beautiful. A fallen angel. That's what he was. Kicked out of heaven for his evil ways. Why would God allow him to walk the earth? There had to be a special place in Hell for men like him. Wasn't there? Maybe earth was Hell? No, that couldn't be true. She had experienced too much happiness in her short lifetime to believe that to be true.

He smiled at her, and she blinked again, still not believing her eyes even after all this time. He stood at the end of the bed, leaning against the wooden frame, his arms casually by his side, his feet crossed at the ankles as if he had all the time in the world. As usual, he was shirtless, showing off his broad, muscular chest. His wavy black hair was tousled. He had high cheekbones, a straight nose, full lips, cleft chin, olive skin and eyes that seemed to see into her soul. He looked like a carved statue from a museum. He certainly didn't look like he was capable of the horrors he put her through. But he was definitely more than capable.

The sun poured through the small round window. She wanted to see what was outside, but she was not allowed to move unless he told her to. She wondered if they were close to land. How much longer would she be stuck in the cage? Would she ever feel the sun on her skin again? What would happen once they got to land? Sold into slavery? She tried to think of a worse fate than that and could think of none.

"By my side." His deep, silky voice cut through the still room.

Her muscles ached as she forced her feet to move forward. It was still a shock to her body to be able to move her limbs after being cramped in the cage for so long.

"My beautiful flower has come to me again. I laid awake last night thinking of this moment. I almost called for you, but didn't want to wake you." The face of evil came forward and lightly ran his thumb across her cheek. Aaliyah flinched. His golden eyes bore into hers. She knew better than to look away. For some reason, it made it so much worse when he said kind things to her. It confused her mind. He was evil. It didn't matter that he was strikingly handsome, or occasionally said nice things to her. What mattered was he was cruel and would burn in hell someday.

Although, lately she was beginning to wonder if there really was a heaven and hell. If there were a God, why would he allow this? There were dozens of children locked in those cages. All of them ripped from a life and thrust into a nightmare. Aaliyah once again silently prayed, begging for God to notice them. To stop this madness. As usual, she was met with silence—he did not reply.

Her naked body trembled. Partly from the cold but mostly from fear. His hand slid down her face, to her neck and down to her breast. Lightly, he stroked her and Aaliyah whimpered. His softness was so much worse than the pain.

"Now, now there is nothing to fear. You know the rules. You do as I please, and no harm comes to you. Understand?"

Aaliyah nodded. How this vile creature could believe he was not doing harm to her body and soul was beyond her. He was never pleased. He made up reasons to get angry. He loved to inflict pain on her.

"You know I do not enjoy it when you are bad."

Why did he have to talk so softly? She'd much prefer he screamed. The softness of him almost made her believe if she tried harder maybe she could please him.

His lips touched hers, but she refused to part her lips. He pulled back. "It pains me to hurt you."

He must be sick. Psychotic even. Nothing else made sense. He talked like he truly believed what he said. How could he believe that it pained him more than her to hurt her? As if.

"I don't get pleasure hurting you." His lips trailed down her neck.

Another whimper escaped when he turned her and pushed her down on the bed. Her breast ached, still sore from the shower, as he pressed her harder against the rough fabric. Her legs hung off the bed, not quite touching the floor.

Block it out. Think of a happier time. She imagined running through the fields of flowers as a child. Laughter. Light. Happiness.

His hand lightly ran down her back. She inhaled sharply when he drove himself into her without warning. He was big and stretched her painfully. Quickly, he went from the soft touch to his savage hunger. He blamed her for bringing it out in him. She lay awake at night and wondered if it were true. Had she done something to provoke him? He wrapped his hand around her long hair and pulled her head back roughly, his hot breath on her back as his heavy weight bore down on her. The friction made her raw.

It felt as if she was being torn in two. "Help

me, please!" she cried out.

He pulled out and her body tensed. Had she said that out loud? *No! No! No! When was she going to learn?*

He twisted her body around. His eyes were wild, and a sheen of sweat covered his forehead. The once handsome face was contorted into something ugly. Sinful.

"Help you? You want help, my lovely flower? I know ways to help you." An evil smile spread across his face.

He spun her back around and dropped her head to the bed. She turned to the side so she could breathe and stared at the wall through blurry eyes. She blinked rapidly, trying to clear her vision. He hated when she cried. It only enraged him even more. Why couldn't she just keep her mouth shut?

"Didn't I tell you not to speak?"

She nodded jerkily, breathing in terrified little gasps.

"You know I can't stand it when you cry." He pulled her up to standing and pushed her against the wall. "I tried to do this the nice way. Why do you always make it so difficult?" he yelled, and a vein pulsed in his forehead.

Her legs shook, as her hands pressed against the wall spread eagle. The way he liked her. It was so hard to keep her hands from sliding. She watched as he paced back and forth across the room. Why had she agitated him? All he wanted her to do was pretend she enjoyed it. But she couldn't. She wouldn't. Something inside her told her that if she even faked pleasure, she would betray her very soul. And there was no coming back from that.

"I'm sorry," Aaliyah croaked out.

"You're sorry? As am I. Remember you made me do this." He crossed the room and pulled open a drawer. Tears ran freely down her face now. She knew when he got in these moods there was no changing his mind. Now he would take his time with her. Hours.

He tore off a piece of duct tape, and she wailed when she saw the leather belt by his side. She shouldn't move, but instinct took over and she bolted for the door. With all her might she pulled on the knob. Of course it was locked. How could she have been so stupid?

"Now that wasn't very smart. Was it?"

Aaliyah sank to the floor and pulled her knees up, wrapping her arms around them. No, it had not been very smart at all.

In one swift movement, he had her on her feet. Slapped the tape over her mouth. Her eyes widened in horror. Sex was not supposed to be like this.

I'm so sorry Noah. She repeated over and over in her mind.

If she had just kept quiet, it would have already been over. She would be back in her cage with the rest of the girls.

"Why did you have to run? Am I that repulsive? Open your eyes and look at me!"

As if her body had a mind of its own, she vigorously nodded her head up and down, keeping her eyes squeezed shut. He was a monster. A repulsive, disgusting monster.

She heard the familiar snap of the belt and terror ripped through her body. How many beatings could one person take? Would she die at his hands? At this point, she *almost* welcomed death.

No, she could not let her mind go down that path. She could not allow him to win. Somehow, she would make it through this horrendous experience.

The blow from the heavy leather across her stomach dropped her to her knees. Her head hung. The sting from the belt burned as he had branded her, not only on the outside but also deep inside her soul. Even if she managed to get away, she would never be free of him. He had seared her so deeply, in such a horrible way, that she would always belong to him.

An uncontrollable sob racked her body.

"Look at me!"

Her head weighed a ton. She hesitated and waited for her head to stop swimming before lifting it. She wasn't fast enough.

The blow to her face came as a surprise. The taste of blood filled her mouth. She had to swallow it because of the tape. He had never touched her face before. He said it was too lovely to mar. Maybe he was over his fascination with her. She could only hope. For some reason she felt like laughing. Great. She really was losing her mind—despair to laughter in three seconds flat. A smile tugged at the tape around her mouth. Yes, she really was going crazy. Going once, going twice, gone to the madman with the honey colored eyes!

"You always need to learn a lesson don't you?" he panted. How could he be turned on by this? She absently wondered as the belt sliced through the air hitting her over and over again. Each lash stung worse than the last until she was so numb, she felt nothing. The nothingness was always welcomed.

He picked her up and tossed her on the mattress. He climbed on top of her, pinning her to the bed as he tied her hands and feet to the bedposts. As if she could move if she wanted to. The rope cut at her wrist as she struggled to get free. Her mind knew there would be no freedom, but her body *always* rebelled, causing her even more pain.

Lost in a haze of pain and confusion, her body jerked back and forth. His breath smelled like whiskey and smoke. If she lived a hundred years, she would never forget that smell. She would never forget his grunts, the touch of his hands, or the pain. Especially not the pain.

His weight crushed her, making it hard to breathe. Her face throbbed and the room spun. She no longer felt like laughing.

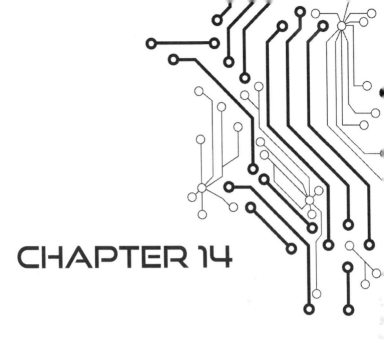

CHAPTER 14

"You're both restless. Why don't you go into town and grab something to eat," Harrington suggested.

Kaitlyn perked up. They hadn't set foot outside of the surrounding area of the property since they arrived. The thought of going out and seeing something different was quite appealing. Anything to get her mind off the fact that they were inactive when every fiber of her believed they should be moving forward. Kaitlyn looked to her left, meeting Lucas's gaze. He nodded with a slight smile.

She was eager to get out of the confined house.

"What about you, Harrington? Do you and Adams want to go out?"

Harrington shook his head. "I think I'll stay in and go over the plans some more"

"Adams?"

The old man shook his head. "Too cold out

there for me. I'm happy to sit near the fire with my crossword puzzles."

Kaitlyn wasn't surprised. Professor Adams rarely wanted to do anything not lab related.

Lucas stood up and stretched his arms above his head. "I'll go get the others. I'm sure they are itching to get out. Sure as hell beats sitting around."

Moments later, Lucas came back with Erik, Ace and Nick.

Just as they were about to leave, Lucas handed her a jacket. "It's pretty cold out, Kate. You might want to grab your hat."

She really wished this stuff would come second nature to her. Obviously, it would raise an eyebrow or two if she went out in the middle of the winter in Maine without the proper attire. She shrugged into her jacket and grabbed a teal hat off the rack. The flash of color made a smile tug at her lips. How strange that the familiar teal could have a soothing effect on her. Somehow, it made her feel more like herself. As soon as they completed the mission, she was going to have Lucas replace the flesh-toned parts with the teal. The flesh color made her feel like an impostor.

But the reality was, only when she was on the compound, could she truly be herself.

Kaitlyn opened the door and was hit by a cold gust of wind. The sky was dark and stars shone brightly above. Snow flurries dance around her.

A winter wonderland, she thought as she looked up at the quarter moon that hung high in the sky.

Lucas gave her a private smile as they trudged

on towards the van.

Suddenly, Kaitlyn's sensors activated. Quickly, she spun, standing. With her left hand, she captured a ball of snow. It crumbled and fell to the ground. She locked eyes with Ace who stared back with a grim expression on his face.

"No way in hell, man. I don't care what you say," he grumbled, his posture stiff.

Nick looked confused. He must have missed the exchange.

Erik stood still, silently watching. Lucas always the quick thinker bent down and patted a ball of snow in his own hands and beamed it at Ace, who ducked right before it made contact. Next thing they knew, they were in a full-fledged snowball fight.

Kaitlyn actually giggled as she dove for cover behind the van. She was at a definite advantage with the embedded heat sensors. She would have preferred to play blind, but she had no way to turn off the features without Lucas changing her coding.

Lucas was hunkered down behind some bushes out of the wind. Kaitlyn crouched low, making as little noise as possible as she made her way across the lawn to join him.

When he saw her approach, his face lit up. Kaitlyn wiped the snowflakes from his eyebrows. Together, they launched a full on attack against the others. Once their position was compromised, Kaitlyn gave Lucas a quick kiss. "You're on your own."

She took off in a sprint. The scent of pine filled the air. Snowballs whizzed past her. One slammed into her shoulder and made her laugh.

It was the most fun she'd had in a long time, and a much-needed diversion to break up the tension that had been mounting while they waited for the mission to commence. The fight went on for a full twenty-seven minutes before Lucas lumbered out from the tree line, holding his hands in surrender, with Nick following closely behind him.

Not wanting to draw any more attention to herself, Kaitlyn stood up and wiped the snow off her pants before wading through the snow with hands raised. She met the others in the middle. All that was left were Erik and Ace. She wondered who would give in first. Probably Erik. Ace was too stubborn for his own good.

A flicker of a shadow crossed her vision to the left. She could tell by the length that it was Erik. She wondered what he was up to. Kaitlyn cast a glance around searching for Ace, and admiration filled her.

Very nice.

Ace had climbed a tree. Erik made a run for it and Ace pelted him with snow. Good naturally, Erik grinned and raised his hands, joining them in the middle. "You got me."

Ace slid down the tree with a smug smirk on his face. His chest was puffed out like a rooster.

"Dinner's on Erik." Ace clapped Erik on the back.

"Works for me," Lucas said, bouncing back and forth on his feet. "Let's get the hell out of here. I'm freezing."

They piled into the van and made the drive

towards the little city of Eastport.

Ace slammed his hand on the steering wheel and grinned. "Finally, won something over wonder girl."

Nick looked over and shook his head. "Why do you have such a hate-on, bro? She kicks your ass fair and square."

Ace turned his head and glared at Nick, who grinned, swaying his arms back and forth. "Haters gonna hate."

Erik and Lucas laughed.

Erik leaned forward, connecting knuckles with Nick.

"Screw you." Ace grumbled, as they rolled to a stop at one of the few stop signs in the area.

Clearly, she missed something, so she did an internal internet search for *haters going to hate*. Images of cats with puffed out chest and a man on roller skates in a batman custom came up with the phrase *haters going to hate* written below. Urban dictionary said it was a phrase used to acknowledge individual superiority in the face of negative external accusations. Can be repeated twice for emphasis. Often accompanied by a strutting walk away from offending party.

Kaitlyn had to suppress a giggle.

The snow grew heavier as they crossed the causeway. Ace kept his attention on driving as he navigated through the narrow roads.

"The visibility sucks," Nick mumbled from the passenger's side. "Good thing they keep the roads salted."

Kaitlyn could see just fine, but she knew for normal eyesight, visibility would only be around ten feet.

Since no one knew where to eat, they drove around aimlessly in search of a restaurant. Kaitlyn could have easily asked her internal computers for a location, but that wouldn't have been smart. Besides, the city was so small, it didn't take them long to find the main road. It was aptly named Main Street, which connected to Water Street. They drove the short loop that led them out onto the breakwater. Ace pulled the van to a stop and they all jumped out to look over the water. The angry waves crashed loudly.

"I sure as hell wouldn't want to fall into the ocean here," Lucas said, while rubbing the side of his arms.

"No shit," Nick agreed. "I wonder how cold it is?"

"Four degrees Celsius," Kaitlyn said without thinking.

"Four degrees Celsius? Is that so? And how pray tell do you know that, Mrs. Know-It-All?" Ace asked.

Kaitlyn mentally kicked herself. "Harrington always makes sure we know the most minute details of any location we visit."

"You need to back off, Ace," Erik said through gritted teeth.

"Hey, man, it was a legit question." Ace shrugged and looked back over the water.

After a few moments of awkward silence, they jumped back into the van.

Lucas squeezed her leg, signaling that she'd recovered well after her second misstep of the evening. Glancing out the window, she had to admit Eastport was a beautiful town, even if they had very few places to choose from to eat.

"What about that?" Lucas asked, pointing at a small little building with a sign that read Waco Diner. A flashing neon sign declared it open.

"Obviously, it's the hot spot," Nick joked.

Ace pulled the van into one of the few parking spots.

They kicked the snow off their boots before entering. As they walked in, every head in the place turned to stare. Kaitlyn felt self-conscious. Why were they looking at them like that? Could they somehow know she wasn't really human? No, that was impossible.

Lucas strode forward and said hello out loud. A couple of people mumbled back hello before going back to their plates, but others just stared at them. They sat down at a table by a window. Nick grabbed an extra chair, placing it at the end of the table. Apparently, the diner wasn't used to parties larger than four.

They quietly scanned the menus.

Eventually, a pretty woman with curly hair and a hesitant smile approached the table. She pulled a pad out of her stained apron. "Where ya from?"

"That obvious?" Ace asked with a genuine smile that surprised Kaitlyn.

"The five of you stick out like sore thumbs on a leprechaun. Whatcha doing in these parts?" The woman narrowed her eyes.

Well, that's a new one. Even Kaitlyn's slang dictionary wasn't sure what to make of the leprechaun addition to the phrase. She hoped her smile didn't look as strained as it felt.

"We're just here for a visit," Nick piped up.

"Visit? Eastport, Maine, in the middle of the winter? You got relatives around here?"

"Nope, no relatives. Just picked your cozy little town off the map," Ace said, lacing his fingers through his hands and placing them on the table in front of him. "We're ready to order."

She went around the table taking their orders. When it was Kaitlyn's turn, she glanced down once again and flipped the menu over. "I'll have the chocolate cake and a slice of apple pie with ice cream. Oh, and hot chocolate with whip cream."

The waitress raised an eyebrow. "Don't you want some chowder or something?"

"If I wanted chowder, I would have ordered it."

Lucas grabbed the menu from Kaitlyn's hand and placed it on top of his. "She's already had dinner. You can bring out her order the same time as ours."

"Whatever you want. I wish I could have a figure like that and overindulge." The woman patted her hips, smiled, shoved the pad back into her apron and turned away.

Kaitlyn wondered if she'd made a mistake with her order, but she saw no logic in ordering something she wasn't going to eat.

Ace and Nick exchanged a glance.

"I forgot how nosey people are in small towns," Nick said with a shake of his head.

Ace shrugged. "They're harmless. Just don't care for strangers. I grew up in a small town. You get used to the lack of privacy after a while, but I prefer the anonymity of city life."

Kaitlyn could relate. Life on the compound

was often like living under a microscope.

The waitress came back with their drinks.

Kaitlyn sipped her hot chocolate. It was a little too rich, but still delicious—almost as good as Nick's.

The guys engaged in small talk while they waited for their food. Kaitlyn couldn't help but notice the patrons in the restaurant kept staring at them, and when she extended her hearing, every last one of them were discussing where they were from. Some of the women were commenting on never having so much hotness at one time at Waco Diner. It humored Kaitlyn to hear their thoughts. Some were arguing over who was the best looking of the guys. It was almost unanimously Erik. Kaitlyn's gaze flicked between Erik and Lucas, and she thought they were out of their mind. But like Quess said, she was biased.

Lucas caught her looking and winked.

As they waited for their food, Ace told a story about his wife, Grace, and his whole demeanor changed. Gone was the coarse persona. His tone softened, and his face relaxed. It seemed odd to think of Ace as being in love with anyone, but Kaitlyn could tell he loved his wife.

Kaitlyn recalled what Erik had said about them trying to have a baby and figured she would try to engage in small talk. Maybe she hadn't given him a fair chance.

"Ace, I heard you and your wife are trying to have a baby?"

Ace shot a dirty look at Erik. His laugh was sudden and harsh. "Jesus, man, are you trying to crush what little manhood I have left around this chick?"

Erik sighed. "It came up. Wasn't a big deal."

"Whatever." Ace's voice sliced through the air as he looked away, his jaw flexed.

"Trouble conceiving?" Lucas asked. Kaitlyn was grateful Lucas spoke up, because she wasn't sure how to defuse the situation. She couldn't quite understand why a simple question would cause so much anger.

"I guess if you call trying and failing for seven years trouble, then yeah," Ace said icily.

"You know Harrington's company dabbles in fertility issues."

He shook his head. "We've tried everything."

Lucas tapped his fingers on the table. "Well IFICS is a bit ahead of the game. Of course, everything is still in experimental stages, but if you guys were interested, I'm sure Harrington would agree to at least having a consultation."

Ace stared at Lucas for a long time. "I hope you're not shitting me. I can't get Gracie's hopes up again. She's finally coming to terms with the fact that we'll never have our own child. We've been put on a waiting list for adoption. That shit takes years."

"Well, I can't promise results, but I can promise you'd have the most cutting edge treatments. I'm not involved with that side of the company, but I do know that Harrington only works with the best doctors in the field."

Ace sat back in his chair and let out a long breath. "I'll talk to Gracie about it. Thanks, man. I'm sorry I snapped at you, Kaitlyn. It's a touchy subject."

"It's okay. I can't have children either." The

words slipped out before she even realized they were on the tip of her tongue.

A pin could have been heard if dropped. The whole diner became silent.

"I'm sorry to hear that," Ace said quietly.

"It's okay. I don't think I would be a very good mother anyway." Kaitlyn blinked back the moisture that had pooled in her eyes out of nowhere. The tears were a genuine surprise to her. As well as the empty feeling in the center of her chest.

The waitress placed the food in front of them. They all picked at their food, appetites suddenly lost.

Small talk, she told herself. Just say something. But no words would come to her mouth, which was suddenly very dry.

Kaitlyn took a bite of the moist chocolate cake, and for once, didn't savor each bite.

As soon as the bedroom door shut, Lucas cupped the back of her head, and pressed her face into the crook of his shoulder. Kaitlyn slid her arms around his waist and squeezed. After several moments of holding each other and not speaking, Lucas pulled away and looked down at her.

"We should talk about this, Kaitlyn."

"What's there to say?"

"I didn't realize you thought about having children."

"Don't you?" she asked, bracing herself for his answer.

"No, not really. I guess I haven't given it much

thought. I love you, Kate."

"You shouldn't have to sacrifice for loving me."

He tucked a strand of her hair behind her ear. "I assure you, I've never once felt as though I've sacrificed anything to be with you. You've given me far more than I could have ever hoped for."

"I can't have children, Lucas. Ever."

"Do you want children?" He studied her face.

"I don't know. I mean, I don't think I do. But when Erik told me that Ace wanted to have a baby, it made me wonder if you did."

"You should have told me," he said gently.

"I meant to, and I would have eventually. I guess it didn't seem important right now. My focus has been on saving those children and making sure Dasvoik can't harm anyone else."

"We'll come back to this conversation later. But Kaitlyn, I really want you to talk to me about anything that is bothering you. It's very important to me."

She pressed her head against his chest. "I will. That was nice of you to offer to help Ace and his wife tonight."

Lucas shrugged. "What good are all these advances if we can't help the people we know? Besides, I had to do something, Ace looked like he was about to strangle you."

"He really doesn't like me."

"I think you're growing on him."

"Really?"

"Sure. He just needs more time."

Kaitlyn doubted it, but what did she know when it came to human nature?

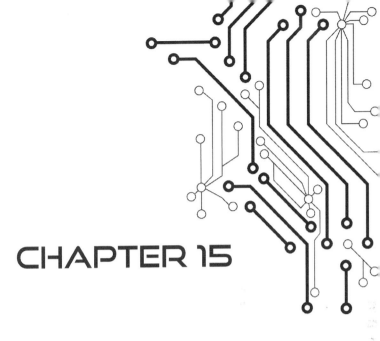

CHAPTER 15

Oh how she hurt! Her head throbbed and her back and arms felt as if they were on fire. The pain in her chest was so strong it stole her breath. Cracked ribs? Her eyes fluttered open, and she tentatively touched her ribs. The room was dark, as usual, but light seeped underneath the door.

Raised voices. She realized it was the commotion outside that had awoken her. Feet pounded loudly on the metal floors. The usually quiet ship was in an uproar over something. What was going on? Aaliyah strained to understand the voices, but they were not in English. And certainly not in her native language. She hated the foreign voices. It only made her feel more alien, alone.

Aaliyah winced. It hurt to breathe. Where in the world was she? Not in the cage and thankfully not in the monster's chamber. Glancing down, she realized she was laid out on a narrow cot. The dingy white blanket that covered her smelled of mildew. Her stomach rolled. She licked her cracked lips with her thick, swollen tongue. She was hungry and probably dehydrated. How'd she get there?

And then, she remembered. Dasvoik had been very upset with her.

Wincing, she attempted to sit up, but the pain was too much. Reluctantly, her head dropped back to the pillow. Seconds later, the door opened and closed with a clang. Heart hammering, Aaliyah closed her eyes and feigned sleep.

"Too late, I saw your eyes open," a rough voice said, barely above a whisper. Involuntarily, she attempted to push herself back, trying to make herself smaller. It surprised her he was speaking English. "I brought you something to drink. Wet your whistle. I will try to bring you something to eat later."

A cup touched her lips and she swallowed greedily. The cold water felt incredible sliding down her aching throat.

"Slow down." He pulled the cup back. "You're going to make yourself sick."

Flopping her head to the side, she got a better look at the old man. He was plump and had a kind, weathered face with tufts of grey hair above his ears. It was hard to tell in the dim light, but his eyes were pale. Probably blue.

"The boss man really did a number on you. You've been out for days." He stood up and dunked something into a bucket and came back with a cloth to wipe her forehead. "You're too damaged to leave with the others."

Suddenly, she was wide-awake. Panic filled her. *Her baby brother.* "Leave where?" Her voice was hoarse from the lack of use.

The man shrugged and continued to gently clean her face with the cloth. "They had to dump the cargo early. Seems someone had the bead on the boss. No concern for you."

"What do you mean dumped?" Her heart hammered in her chest. "It concerns me a great deal. My little brother is on this ship."

He paused, his hand in the air still holding the cloth and nodded. "Ah, I understand my dear. I wish I could help you, but I have no idea where they went. I just know they were transferred from this ship to another. The boss must really have taken a liking to you, or else you would be dead right now. Swimming with the sharks."

She tried to process the information. If they knew what the evil man was up to, did that mean she had a chance of being rescued? Probably not.

Where was her brother? Did this delay give her brother an opportunity or was he handed off to a worse fate? Of course, without her, it was worse. She had to find him. She struggled to sit up, but the pain cut through her. "Please, I have to find out where he went so I can save him."

The old man's voice was sad. "I'm afraid there will be no saving for either of you. If your injuries were not so grave, you would have been on the boat with them. You have to heal and then you will be sold off with the next wave. Unless, the boss decides to keep you for himself. He's never done that before." After a brief pause, he continued." I'm not sure I would wish that on anyone."

Desperately, Aaliyah clung to the man's forearm. "It's still loud out there. Have they transferred everyone?"

"That's what they're doing now."

"Please. I beg of you. I don't care how you have to do it. Get me on the ship. I cannot leave my brother."

"I'm afraid you cannot go anywhere. Your ribs are broken. One of your lungs is collapsed and I am too old to carry you. Here take another sip of water. You need to regain your strength."

With much effort, she lifted her head to meet the cup. He was right, she had to find the strength and the courage she would need. If it was the last thing she did, she was going to kill that monster. A deep seeded rage bubbled inside of her.

Just the thought of little Darrius being all alone, shuffled from one boat to another, tore at her heart. "Where the hell are they taking him?" her voice was near manic.

The man just shrugged.

All of the sudden, Aaliyah became suspicious. No one had been nice to her since the day she had been abducted. They all treated her like an object not a person. "Why are you helping me?"

He sighed and continued to dab the towel on her face. "Because I have a daughter myself."

From nowhere, a lightness came over her along with a wave of hope. "It's you."

She'd been praying for this for so long it was hard to believe that her prayers had been answered. She'd almost given up.

"My guardian angel." Aaliyah's voice shook. Her breath caught in a silent sob. "You finally came."

The man looked startled. "I wouldn't go that

far. All I did was bring you water."

"Please, you must get the name or the number off the ship that they are transferring the children to."

She could see the indecision in his eyes and her heart leapt when he sighed and nodded his head. "It won't do you any good, but I will find out for you." He patted her head and stood up. His back stooped as he shuffled his way towards the door.

Aaliyah closed her eyes. The old man had been right. She needed to rest. Needed to heal so she could seek revenge. A plan was starting to form in her mind. If pretending to enjoy the madman was what it took to get her brother back, she would endure it. And she would take great pleasure when she sliced the monsters throat in his sleep. Her guardian would find her a weapon. He had to.

She knew she was not strong enough to take him while he was awake.

Perhaps during sex? She had to make sure he wanted her again. Which meant she had to heal. He would not want her if her face were bruised and ugly. He didn't seem to mind the scars on her body.

Four days passed since she'd awakened in the empty room. The old man snuck her food in when he could. Mainly soup and bread. The soup was a luxury. What she most appreciated was the conversations. It had been so long since anyone had talked to her like she was a person with feelings. He told her about his children and his wife who'd passed away years ago. Aaliyah told him about her life in South Africa. For some reason, she couldn't bring herself to talk about Detroit.

He really was her guardian angel, even if he didn't believe it himself. She knew he was putting himself at great risk.

Aaliyah was certain God had sent him to help her. She wept at the thought. How could she have doubted her faith? *I'm so sorry. I'll never doubt you again.*

Since awakening, she'd spent as many hours in prayer as she did plotting her revenge.

"How do I look?" Aaliyah asked, pushing herself up to sitting. She swallowed the antibiotics he handed her. The ship's doctor had not been to see her since she had awoken, but he had left her with antibiotics to fight off the possibility of an infection due to her collapsed lung. For that, she was grateful.

If she had been unconscious for a couple of days and awake for four days, the bruising must be improving. It still hurt to breathe; she felt as if someone was crushing her chest. As painful as it was, she had forced herself to take deep breaths. She remembered seeing on television that a collapsed lung could sometimes heal itself with rest. And there wasn't much that could be done for cracked ribs. The old man had bound her chest with a cut up sheet. It was the best they could do.

"You look like someone beat the shit out of you," the old man said truthfully.

"Damn. I need to get better. Has the bruising gone down at all?" She wished for the luxury of a mirror, but that was not going to happen. She was lucky to have a pail to go to the bathroom in. She reached up and touched her face. It didn't feel quite as swollen. "Are you sure it's not better?"

With gentle fingers, he turned her head from side to side, studying her. "The bruising has gone down. It's mostly yellow now instead of purple. But your eyes..."

Alarmed, Aaliyah reached up touching around her eyes. "What about my eyes?" She knew they were the feature that had drawn the madman to her. If they had been ruined, he would probably not want her any longer. And then her plan would not work. "Tell me. What is wrong with my eyes?"

"They have turned cold. You have aged greatly over the short time you have been aboard this ship. I saw you when you first arrived. Everyone noticed you. A rare exotic beauty like yourself, it's hard not to notice. You looked fragile and meek. Now, you look determined. I'm sure it will not escape the boss."

"Has he asked about me? Does he know you check on me?"

"Yes, I'm afraid he is anxious to see you. You're the only woman left on the ship."

"That's good, very good," Aaliyah said, almost to herself.

The old man's eyes widened in alarm. "What do you mean good? Has that nut job managed to taint your mind? I was hoping you were stronger than the rest."

Oh, he's very much tainted my mind, she thought with disgust. "I'm just glad there are no other girls on here that he can hurt."

A look of relief crossed his face, accepting that

answer. It was partially the truth.

"I worry about you. I worry that you are going to get yourself killed. You cannot outsmart a man like Vance Dasvoik."

"His name is Vance?" She let the name bounce around her head. It didn't seem to fit. She preferred *monster.*

"I shouldn't have told you that," the old man said, while rubbing his face.

"Don't worry. I will not repeat it." Aaliyah tilted her head. "I just realized I don't even know your name."

"Henry, my name is Henry." He wobbled to his feet and headed towards the doorway.

"Henry."

He turned.

"Thank you."

"No need to thank me. I wish I could do more." He slipped out the door.

Aaliyah hung her legs over the bed and used the wall to steady herself as she rose to her feet. Pain radiated throughout her body, but it seemed to have dampened slightly. With a hesitant step, she could feel her strength was returning. She didn't know how long she had till they reached port.

She did know she had to see the man who did this to her before then. Had to make him want to keep her as his own. As much as the thought repulsed her, she knew it was necessary. The only way... No one was going to save her. She had to save herself.

Slowly, she crossed the small room back and forth several times until her breathing was strained and her legs wobbled.

Cursing under her breath, she sank back onto the cot. She'd only made it two more passes than yesterday. It wasn't enough. She could feel the time slipping away.

Tomorrow, she would ask to see *her owner.* The words sickened her. Mentally, she prepared herself to take over the role she must play. Dasvoik wanted a willing servant, and that's what he would get. She was no longer worried about her soul. She was tainted. But she might be able to save her brother. She had to think about Darrius's impish smile and contagious laugh. For him, she would do anything. Even sell her soul to the devil.

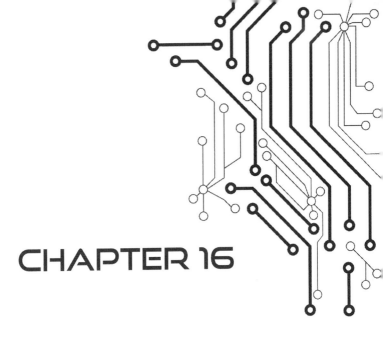

CHAPTER 16

Aaliyah heard the footsteps before the door opened. She knew it wasn't Henry, since she'd become accustomed to the shuffle of his shoes in the hallway. No, this was sure, determined footsteps echoing down the hall. Sounds were amplified on the ship; she could also hear the slight jingle of keys.

She pushed herself up in the bed and waited for the door to open. The key turned and the door pushed open. Consciously, she had to keep from smiling to herself. The moment she had been waiting for had finally come. It occurred to her how different she felt now that she had a different mindset. Before she had been terrified. Worried about her honor. Now she saw sex as a weapon. He wanted her? Who was she to disappoint him?

Submissively, she cast her eyes to the blanket and refused to look up to see who was standing in the doorway. Henry's words held their weight in gold. She knew she could not let anyone see the changes in her.

A firm grip yanked her off the bed, pulling her to the middle of the small room. She kept her eyes cast at the floor. She steeled herself for what she knew would come next. By the shadow cast on the floor, she knew it was one of the monster's large thugs. True to form, she felt a large hand roughly roam her body. Walking around her in a circle, he pinched her breast and slapped her behind. His hands lingered making her grind her teeth. She could endure it. She had to. *For Darrius.*

She couldn't understand what he said, but from his tone of his voice, she could tell he was pleased.

Grabbing her wrist, he pulled her arms behind her back, pushing her forward. The fear crept back in. *No!* She was not helpless. She was in control. As long as she was in control, she would make it. She was just playing a part. Like an actress in a movie. She could do this.

Adrenaline poured through her bloodstream.

Bowing her head, she shuffled forward. Her eyes darted around trying to take in everything. She needed to figure out where she was located on the ship. It was imperative she knew exactly how far away she was from his room. Internally, she counted her steps. Forty-seven in a straight line, a left turn, sixty-four steps and up a flight of stairs.

The brute gave her a shove and she stumbled forward, losing count. She felt tears spring to her eyes and blinked them back. What was the count? Had it been seventeen or twenty-seven?

She couldn't even recall the first two step counts. She started to crumble on the inside. How was she going to save her brother if she couldn't even remember something as simple as steps?

They came to an abrupt stop, and the thug banged on the bedroom door.

"I hope you brought me a gift," the monster said through the door. Or at least that's what she imagined he said.

The door swung open, and Aaliyah's pulse quickened. Just seeing his face made her want to fall to the ground and curl up in the fetal position.

The door closed with a bang. She was alone with the madman.

"Let me look at you." His tone was impatient.

Where had the resolve gone? It wilted at the sound of his voice, the way it always did when he was near. Oh, God, why was she so weak?

She looked up, keeping her gaze over his shoulder. Staring at the gray, peeled paint on the wall. He didn't seem to notice the lack of eye contact. He was too busy staring at her naked body. His hands caressed her skin. She could tell by the way his shoulders were heaving up and down that he was already aroused.

"I see you've healed quite nicely." He walked around the back of her and pressed his body to hers. His fingers trailing over the permanent welts. She could feel his erection on her lower back.

He spun her around. His shirt brushed her nipples, which were still sore from being pinched by that other bastard. Her breath came in terrified little gasps. Control. She needed to control her breathing.

"I'm very angry at you my little flower."

She stiffened. He was angry with her? In what universe did that make sense?

"You made me hurt you. Which in turn hurt me. I have needs that could not be met. Do you know what that means?"

She shook her head no and finally met his golden eyes. She didn't have to worry that her eyes would betray her. The fear she felt was real and seeped deep into her bones. She knew that's what would be reflected and not what Henry had seen earlier. Where had that girl gone? Desperately, she tried to pull back the determined part of her to the surface, but she was nowhere to be found.

She chided herself. She needed to pull herself together. If she couldn't even make it through one night with him, how was she going to help her brother? It's not like this was something new. He'd had her too many times to count. An actress. She reminded herself. That's what she was. It was not her he would be touching. It was someone else. Someone stronger and braver than she could ever be.

"It means you will be staying with me so that I can have access to you whenever I please. No matter what time of day or night. Do you understand?" He peeled off his shirt and tossed it to the ground.

Oh, yes, she understood. *No more Henry*. How was she going to survive without her guardian angel?

"Answer me." His voice rose several notches.

"Yes." Her voice cracked.

"Yes, what?" he demanded.

"Yes, I understand."

Her soul withered a little more. She felt like a whore. Who was she kidding? She was a whore. Maybe if she closed her eyes and pretended he was Noah. The thought caused a pain to shoot straight through her heart. How could she ever associate this horror with Noah? He was light and this man was dark. They could not be further apart.

"Are we going to do this the easy way, or the hard way?"

"Easy. Please," she whispered.

"If only I weren't still so angry at you. I really want you to make me happy. Why can't you do that?"

The blow knocked her back causing her to lose her balance and she tripped, falling to the floor with a painful thud. Her shoulder softened the blow to her head.

In a dizzy daze, she realized he was now on top of her. Her body was splayed across the floor and she couldn't move with the weight of him. The cement floor was cold and rough, scrapping her body. She could hear herself whimpering, terrified.

She realized at that moment, there was no pretending with this man. He got off on the domination. She had been a childish fool to think otherwise.

It was hard to tell how much time had passed. After a while, her mind had gone blank and seemed to float outside of herself. It was not her body played over and over like a broken record in her mind. *It was not her body.*

"Ah, my sweet, sweet girl. Do you think today you can please me?"

Vigorously, she nodded her head. She could do it. If she made him happy, the pain would stop. If she pleased him, maybe she would be happy, too. She'd been trying so hard over the last couple of days. Once in a while, he offered her a shred of hope. He would stroke her face. Even smile at her. But then, she would make him angry again. Today, she wouldn't fail him.

Aaliyah licked her lips. Her eyes darted around the room, hoping for a sign as to what she could do to please him. Her hands hung loosely to her sides. Just like he liked. Oh, shit. Why couldn't she get the simple things right. He wanted her eyes on him at all times.

Her eyes met his and he tsk'd. "Flower, you can't do anything right can you?" A wicked grin crossed his face. In one swift motion, he pulled the belt from his pants. She stepped backwards and realized her mistake. She must stand perfectly still. Her leg came forward and she planted her feet. Of course, he had noticed. He always noticed.

"I'm sorry. I'll do better," she cried out, trembling visibly.

"Yes, you will do better." He kicked her feet apart, and like she'd been taught, she reached forward placing her palms on the wall. Her body jerked when the belt hit her skin.

She wanted to be good. She wanted to please

him. Why did she keep failing?

A loud pounding woke her. Her eyes fluttered, but wouldn't open. What was that sound? It took a moment for her to realize the pounding was in her head. Aaliyah reached for the sides of her head, but was stopped short. A heavy metal cuff surrounded her wrists. The metallic rattle of the chains broke her spirit.

She was chained to the bed. How many days? She'd lost count. Lost count of all the vile things he had done to her. What did it matter? She was a failure.

It hit her like a ton of bricks. She was going to die here. There would be no escape. She would never find her brother. She would never look in Noah's green eyes again. Never hear her parents argue or smell the sweet scent of cinnamon when she walked through the door of their tiny apartment.

What scared her the most was that she really didn't care.

Once the monster was done with her, he would toss her over the boat to the sharks. Just like Henry had said.

The way her body ached, she would almost welcome the jaws of a shark. At least it would be over quickly. Aaliyah was having trouble concentrating, and she frowned. If only she could get Dasvoik to love her like he used to.

She was vaguely aware of the door creaking open. Seconds later, Henry slipped through the door, closing it quietly behind him. He no longer seemed to have wings or a halo. He was *not* her guardian angel. He was just an old man doing his job.

She went to speak and realized her mouth was taped shut. Her body shook with tears. She must have really upset him this time. If only she could make him happy.

Henry hesitated and then walked towards her on the bed. He pushed her hair out of her face. "Ah, kiddo, why'd you have to make him angry again?"

Her mind scrambled to come up with what she had done to enrage him. She must have done something wrong. Maybe it was the way she looked at him. Or perhaps she wasn't pretty enough anymore. Oh, dear God, why *had* she angered him?

Why couldn't she just make him happy, so he wouldn't hurt her? The pounding of her head would not stop. Why wouldn't it stop?

Her skin crawled, and she rocked back and forth on the bed as far as the chains would allow. Screams came out muffled beneath the tape.

She needed to see him. Needed to beg him to forgive her. Her body jerked as she fell into a full-fledged panic attack.

Henry was talking in a soothing voice trying to calm her down, but it was as if he were miles away. She closed her eyes and rocked.

The tape was peeled off and Aaliyah gasped, taking in as much oxygen as possible. She couldn't seem to catch her breath.

Henry pushed a brown paper bag in front of her face and told her to follow his breathing. Taking deep breaths, she wanted to listen to him, but her mind and body couldn't seem to agree.

Somehow, Henry managed to talk her down.

When her breathing was under control, she yanked the chains, wailing that she needed to see *him.* Needed to make it right. "Please, Henry. I *need* him. Tell him I'm sorry. I can do better. I promise."

The look in Henry's face was pure pity. "He's done it again. The man needs to be stopped. It's just not right. You listen to me, Aaliyah. What he has done to you is reprehensible. You can never satisfy him. You are just another in the long line of young girls he has broken."

She heard his words, but refused to believe them. He was wrong. She could satisfy him. All she needed was another chance. A small part of her brain was appalled by her thoughts, but the need to please him blocked out everything else. If she could just make him happy, maybe he wouldn't need any other girls. She could be enough.

"Take a sip," he suggested, placing the mug to her lips and she took a swallow, grateful for the warmth of the soup broth, even though it did little to help the cold fear that engulfed her. She needed to see Dasvoik.

"Please, bring him to me." She licked her cracked lips.

Henry sighed, frowning. "He will come when he's ready. I was hoping you were strong enough to fight the madness, but it seems to have gotten to you, too."

Madness? Had she gone mad? No. She was not crazy. She was just not good enough. But she could try harder.

She could do better.

"You need to rest," Henry said, lifting the mug to her mouth again. "You need time to heal."

She didn't want to sleep. She needed to see him. A weariness washed over her and her head felt heavy. With what little energy she had left, she fought to keep her eyes open, but it was for naught. Her head lolled to the side and the room wavered. "Did you?"

"Close your eyes," he whispered, pulling up the blankets and tucking them under her chin.

He'd drugged her, but she didn't care much about that, she realized as she slipped into the darkness.

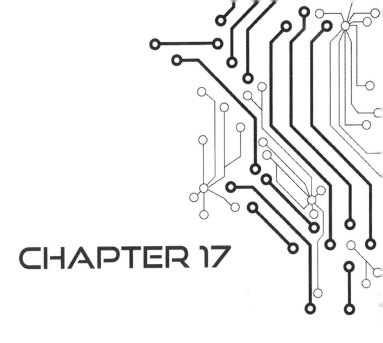

CHAPTER 17

"Shut the door, Lucas," Harrington said quietly.

Lucas kicked the door closed with his foot. "What's up?"

"I just wanted to go over a few things with you before we leave."

Lucas dropped into the chair across from Harrington's desk. He found it somewhat funny that even in the casual setting of the house, Harrington always had to be in a power position. Everyone else dressed casually in the house, except Harrington. He still walked around in a three-piece suit. "Has something new come up?"

"No, nothing like that." He drummed his fingers on the desk. Harrington leaned forward slightly. "Lucas, are you sure you will be able to go through with the contingency plans if the op gets compromised? I'm second-guessing myself on this one. You're way too close to Kaitlyn."

Body tense, Lucas drew in a breath and slowly

let it out. "I'm well aware of my role."

Harrington leaned back, regarding him gravely. "I want your access code."

"What? No!" Lucas couldn't believe Harrington would have the nerve to demand such a thing.

"I'm not asking."

Lucas shook his head in disbelief. "I understand your concern, but I am not giving you my access code. You might as well ask to read my journals."

"You keep a journal?"

"No! Jesus, I was just...never mind. I'm not giving you my code. It's not going to happen."

Harrington was clearly startled. He hadn't expected any resistance from him. Screw that. If he gave him the code it would undermine everything his job stood for. Harrington gave him free reign to work on whatever he wanted. All of the top scientists had their own personal security codes. The things they worked on at the facility could one day be awarded the noble peace prize. Not that he didn't trust Harrington, but it was a matter of principle. If he allowed him to have access to his sensitive files, he would be virtually handing over his life's work.

"You already have access to all of her coding. I'm sure Adams could figure it out if something were to happen to me," Lucas said bitterly, although he knew that was not what Harrington was referring to. As it stood now, Lucas was the only one that had the ability to completely shut down Kaitlyn, essentially killing her. There was no way in hell he was going to put that power in Harrington's hands. Not when he was skittish enough about the mission.

"There needs to be a fall back. What if Kaitlyn gets compromised and you're unavailable?"

"That's what Erik is there for. Do you honestly think for one second he would leave her behind?"

"He would if he were dead. Lucas, believe me, I don't even want to fathom the thought of losing Kaitlyn. Not only have I sunk billions into this project, but I care for her, too."

Lucas's shoulders slightly relaxed. A part of him knew Harrington was correct, but he just couldn't do it.

"Okay, I can understand why you would bristle at handing over your code. If I were in your position, I would do the same thing, but we at least need to have someone with the knowledge if the situation were ever to arise. Share your information with Adams."

"Adams? Are you kidding me? That old goat would probably be napping and he's too worried about himself going to jail. If he saw even the slightest hint of shit hitting the fan, he would pull the plug."

Harrington nodded absently. "You're probably right. Give the code to me."

"Not giving you my goddamn code." Lucas ground his teeth together.

"Then just show me how to shut down the program. Mirror the account and set up my own access."

Lucas felt like throwing something and smashing it into pieces. Harrington's request was completely within reason,n and he had no grounds for denying him. Other than the thought of putting Kaitlyn's life in someone else's hands was about to send him over the edge. Breathing deeply, he tried to calm his mind. Think it over. If this were anything else he wouldn't think twice, he would just do as he was asked.

"Let me make it a little easier on you. If you don't mirror the account, you're out of a job. It's as simple as that."

Lucas glared at Harrington across the desk. "As simple as that, huh? You seem to have forgotten that Kaitlyn is working for you of her own free will. Which means she could leave you at any time. And who do you think she would go with, you or me?"

The tension in the room was so thick it could have been cut with a knife.

"Keeping Kaitlyn alive takes money. A lot of it."

"Money is something I have plenty of, thanks to you." Lucas shrugged trying to appear calmer than he was.

"Seems we're at a standstill."

Fists clenched, Lucas nodded. "Yep."

"For Christ's sake, Lucas, make the damn account. We can't have this program self-destruct before it even gets off the ground."

"Nice choice of words, because that's exactly what you are asking me for. A way to destroy Kate. I can't give it to you. I'm sorry I just don't trust you with her life."

"And I don't trust you with the fate of IFICS. A company I have put my heart and soul into. Lucas, you know you will always choose Kate. Do you truly believe you would be able to type a few computer strokes and watch the woman you love blow up before your eyes?"

Harrington was right. There's no way he would be able to do it. Hell, he didn't want anyone to be able to have that ability. Kaitlyn meant the world to him. Not to mention he truly believed there wasn't a situation she couldn't get out of. She was the most resilient person he'd ever met, and her abilities were astounding. Suddenly, the answer came to him.

"Harrington, who is the most analytical person you've ever encountered?"

He looked up confused and then thought about it for a moment before replying. "Brilliant minds are often logical and we work with the mother lode of geeks. I'm not sure I could narrow it down to just one."

"Yes, you can. Really think about it."

Harrington smirked. "Kaitlyn."

"That's our answer to this conundrum."

"You've lost me."

"I'll give Kate the ability to shut herself down if she can see no other way out."

Harrington was silent. "Suicide?"

"I'm glad you said that. If that was suicide, then destroying her from your hand or mine would be murder." His words hung in the air.

Harrington ran his hands over his face. "You're right. I'm sorry, Lucas. I've put you in a very bad position. You know what? The hell with it. I need to start thinking of Kaitlyn as a person and not a weapon. There will be no destruction. If she gets captured, we'll deal with the fallout. Even if it means spending the rest of our lives behind bars."

That was not quite the response he'd expected.

It calmed him down a bit. "Thank you. And for the record, Kate is very much a weapon. She just happens to be one that still has access to her cingulate cortex. You've seen the way it lights up in her brain scan when she's asked a moral or ethical question. You have to trust her. I assure you that she would not put your company in jeopardy. She believes she owes you her life, and she is very invested in this mission to save those enslaved. Hell, you're practically her version of a father."

"You're right." Harrington rubbed his temples. "I should be the one thanking you for opening my eyes to the fact that I'm an asshole."

Lucas grinned. "You said it, not me."

Harrington opened his mouth and closed it. He paused, almost smiling. "Does she really see me as a father figure?"

Lucas nodded solemnly.

"I always wanted children," Harrington said, once again taking Lucas by surprise.

Unsure how to respond, they sat in awkward silence.

Harrington pushed back his chair and stood up. "We're heading out in two hours."

"Two hours? You didn't expect me to say yes, did you?"

"Why do you think that?"

"You waited too long to bring it up. It would have taken well over two hours to mirror the account."

"Mirroring was your idea, not mine. I just wanted the code."

Lucas shook his head. "This late in the game,

even my code would have been useless."

"Yes, I guess it would've been."

"So this was a test?"

"Of sorts."

"Did I pass?"

"You still have a job don't you?"

Once again, they settled into the small private plane.

Wheels up in fifteen minutes. Lucas chose the back seats this time, so they could have a little privacy. This flight would be much longer: Lucas, Harrington and Adams would fly into Croatia and stay there. Once they touched down, Kaitlyn and Erik would board a helicopter to take them to the ship they'd been tracking. If things went as planned, this time tomorrow, everyone would be back safe and sound and Dasvoik would have been taken care of.

Kaitlyn thumbed through a magazine and placed it back in the holder.

Lucas could tell she was keyed up, even though outwardly she showed no signs. She appeared to be calm and relaxed, but he could almost feel the energy radiating off her body. She looked vibrant.

"I think Ace was sad to see you go." Lucas smiled crookedly.

"Really?" Kaitlyn gazed at him skeptically and then saw his turned up lips.

"Oh, I get it. You're kidding." A brilliant smile lit her face as she nudged him with her elbow. "That was a good one."

Lucas laughed. "Glad you approve."

Her smile faded. "I tried to be nicer to him.

But it didn't seem to work."

"That guy really has a chip on his shoulder." Lucas grabbed a pillow and put it under his head. "His loss."

"I guess. Do you think we'll ever work with him and Nick again?"

"Hard to say, but we'll probably see Ace around if he goes through with the fertility treatments."

"Not necessarily. That's on a whole different area of the compound." She paused. "At least I got the hot chocolate recipe from Nick."

"Enough about them. Tell me, how are you feeling, Kate?" He watched her intently trying to read the play of emotions that crossed her face.

Her gaze focused on him, her eyes bright, and she leaned in to whisper. "Alive. I feel very alive, Lucas."

His chest tightened at her words. Her happiness meant the world to him. Lucas often wondered if she secretly resented him for his part in claiming her life, but the way her face was flushed and her eyes lit up he knew she had come into her own. She was loving every moment. Even though she had never been in a situation like she was about to embark on, he knew without a doubt she would thrive. Even before the upgrades, Kaitlyn's personality had been one of living on the knife's edge of danger. Adrenaline junky. She was still herself but amplified.

"Not even a little afraid?" he asked curiously. Her mind was so unique, he wasn't quite sure how far the tangle of her emotions and feelings ranged.

She tilted her head to the side studying his

face. "No. Should I be?"

Lucas smiled ruefully. "You should only be what you are, Kate. If you feel fear, that is what is natural, if you only feel courage, then that's your emotion. Only you truly know what you feel inside."

After a slight pause, Kaitlyn replied, "I guess I won't really know until it happens. Up until this point, it's all been training, but I don't think I will be afraid. I hope I'm not. This is the life I was built for and what I've trained for. If I'm afraid, I'll feel like a failure."

"That's not true at all, Kate. Fear is natural."

"What about you, Lucas? Are you afraid?" Kaitlyn asked.

He was slightly surprised she thought to ask the question. "Terrified," he answered truthfully.

She started to protest and stopped herself. With a squeeze of his hand, she said, "It will all work out, you'll see."

Lucas found his feelings for her only grew stronger as time went on. He thought of losing her, but shook his head. He couldn't allow himself to think that way.

All he knew is he couldn't get enough of her. Her silky smooth hand in his was like torture. It was so hard for him to hold back when they were so close. Just her proximity made his pulse race. She looked at him with her wide gray eyes, and it was killing him not to reach over and kiss her.

"In a way, you'll be right there with me," she reminded him, and that was partly true.

They would be able to access what Kaitlyn saw through an internal camera, and they could speak to each other through the imbedded microphone. He wasn't sure that would make it better or worse.

Soon he would find out.

He cleared his throat. "I have no doubt you will exceed everyone's expectations."

Kate dropped her head to his shoulder and snuggled closer, causing his heart to swell.

As they deplaned, Kaitlyn made a beeline towards Erik, their heads bent together, lost in conversation. Even after the long flight, he could see the intensity in their steps. Lucas was glad he didn't feel the usual pull of jealousy when he saw them together. It was not lost on him that Erik was part of the package. He had to accept their partnership and trust Kaitlyn.

Their lives could very well depend on the bond they'd formed.

Harrington approached from the left. "Lucas, we need to get set up. Things are going to progress quickly from here on out. The helicopter is waiting."

Lucas nodded and lengthened his stride as they made their way across the tarmac. They would leave the small airport and head to an even smaller clandestine clearing where a little bird waited to take Kate and Erik to the container ship. He'd had to brush up on his military tactical knowledge over the last several months. Before this mission, he hadn't even known what the hell a *little bird* was. He'd since learned it was a small helicopter that was a favorite among Special Operations regiments. He wasn't sure how Harrington had gotten his hands on one, but more than likely it had come at a steep price.

A black SUV awaited them. Erik slid into the driver's seat and Kate took shotgun, leaving the rest of them to pile into the back. Harrington made arrangements for their equipment to be waiting for them, so they didn't have to bother with it after the flight.

The sun was rapidly setting behind the horizon.

Timing was everything.

"The road is one hundred feet ahead to the right," Kaitlyn spoke, her voice steady. They were the only words that had been spoken on the drive. Lucas wondered if everyone else was on edge like he was.

Erik pulled off, turning onto the side road. The turn off would have been unrecognized at first glance.

The SUV bounced along the narrow dirt road. Trees scraped the vehicle.

Before long they rolled to a stop and Erik cut the engine before jumping out. Kaitlyn was beside him in the blink of an eye.

Lucas unlatched his seat belt and jumped out, Harrington and Adams followed suit.

Harrington turned towards Lucas. "We need to set up before the helo gets here. We've got about twenty minutes."

They hustled into the small cabin that would act as their operations center, or OPCEN in military jargon, during the mission. They immediately started booting up various systems and programs, watching as diagnostics flickered across multiple large monitors. From here, they would monitor Kaitlyn, seeing and hearing everything she experienced, along with some of the underlying processes that she used. In addition, they also had access to state of the art signals intelligence, imagery intelligence and live clandestine drone feeds.

While the OPCEN was being set up, Kaitlyn and Erik were donning their equipment and doing their pre-combat checks. Both of them pulled on dry suits before they strapped on the thin body armor over their black clothing. Lucas glanced up to watch them check their pistols, making sure they were fully loaded before attaching the guns to their thighs and a knife to their calves. Erik pulled a black watch cap low over his forehead. Kaitlyn's hair was pulled out of her face into a tight bun. They shouldered their rifles and shared a grin.

They were a sight to be seen.

"Fisher One, this is Mother Ship, radio check," Lucas spoke evenly into the mic, hoping his emotions didn't come across the line.

"Mother Ship this is Fisher One, roger out." Kaitlyn's voice crossed the line and Lucas felt the tension ease in his shoulders.

"Fisher Two, this is Mother Ship, radio check."

Erik replied, "Mother Ship this is Fisher Two, roger out."

Frantically, Lucas's fingers flew across the keyboard. A green dot and a red bull's-eye appeared on the massive monitor. A few more keystrokes and he had the information he was seeking.

"Be advised, your ride will be here in 2 minutes." Lucas had communications with the small helicopter that would ferry them out and was able to follow its transponder beacon on the large digital geospatial display that also showed both Kaitlyn's and Erik's positions.

The small black helicopter came in fast, flaring at the last minute and lightly setting down in the small clearing near Kaitlyn and Erik knelt, waiting. Kaitlyn crouched low and sprinted across the opening. She boarded the helo without so much as a look back. She strapped herself into one of the skid's out-facing seats while Erik did a quick check on the small rubber boat that was strapped to the opposite side. Satisfied with the rigging and release mechanism, he strapped himself in next to Kaitlyn and gave the pilot a thumbs up. With that, the rotor whine increased, and the helicopter hovered in the air.

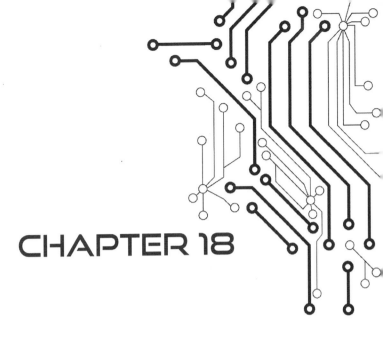

CHAPTER 18

"Kaitlyn, are you ready for this?" Erik yelled over the rotors, as he pulled fins over his booties. Kaitlyn didn't need to bother with the fins. She just wore the booties to keep her feet dry.

"Flipped the switch already." Kaitlyn grinned.

Erik graced her by laughing loudly and shaking his head. He'd once told her a common phrase used in their line of work was *switched on,* which he explained basically meant a mental on/off switch for humans. Apparently, some guys had trouble making the mental change between work and home. The saying made Kaitlyn smile since she was part robot so her on/off was a physical reality.

"How about you?"

His gaze caught hers, and his face became serious. The scar that twisted down his face whitened, making it more visible. "We got this,

Kaitlyn. We'll hit them hard and fast."

She nodded, straightening. "On your signal."

"Ten minutes out," the pilot's voice sounded in their earpieces.

"I confirm. Ten minutes out," echoed Lucas.

Flutters filled her stomach. This was really happening. With a quick glance at Erik, her emotions steadied. His face was relaxed. There was no fear as he gazed across the immense ocean. They could do this. Together.

"One minute."

Both Kaitlyn and Erik unfastened their safety straps. This was it. There was no turning back. A tingle of excitement ran down her spine.

The helicopter turned a tight circle and descended until it hovered two meters off the water. Erik deployed the small boat, checked that it was clear of the helicopter's skids, then tapped Kaitlyn on the arm. Without hesitating, she pushed off the skid and dropped into the cold ocean water, plunging into blackness. Her eyes adjusted in the blink of an eye.

Erik was right beside her. Every stroke she took was fueled by the image of Dasvoik taking his last breath. A slow smile spread across her face.

"I have splash. Moving to loiter position," the pilot said across the radio.

"I confirm splash." Lucas keyed the mic. Kaitlyn envisioned him continually scanning the various monitors. She took comfort in knowing he was also there with them.

Erik swam over to the small rubber boat, pulling himself inside. Immediately, he squatted on his haunches and started to prep the small engine attached to the back. Kaitlyn was already aboard, checking and readying the equipment that was strapped down. Her mind ran through the many scenarios of how the drop would take place.

Their vessel approached the large tanker filled with shipping containers. In the dead of night, their small boat went unnoticed by the sentries, aided by the size of the waves of the choppy seas. If they were like most guards, they were probably dozing on the job. But Kaitlyn operated under the assumption they were heavily armed and dangerous. Erik hit the throttle and veered off at the last second, bringing the boat back around again, getting as close as possible to a ladder welded onto the side of the tanker.

Dim lights glowed from some of the portholes, but most were dark.

Kaitlyn analyzed the wind and gauged the waves before leaping forward. She grabbed a hold of the ladder rung and pulled herself up quickly, climbing with ease. Erik was close on her heels.

Silently, Kaitlyn dropped to the floor. Engaging senses more acute than any humans, she simply stood for a long moment, watching, listening. Her mind went cold, analytical. She could hear muted voices, footsteps scraping, water dripping, the hum of fluorescent lighting. In the distance, someone coughed. No one was aware of their presence.

The tanker was old, rusty and large. It was nine hundred and sixty five feet long and had almost three thousand shipping containers on it. The captives could be anywhere. Mentally she went over the blueprints, seeking out the largest rooms below decks where Dasvoik would most likely sleep. She identified a couple of suitable locations.

Her nose wrinkled. The stench was overwhelming—rotten food, feces and urine mixed with the salty air. While her sensors were busy sorting out the different scents, sounds and possible scenarios they could encounter, Kaitlyn panned back and forth scanning the area, taking in heat sensors.

Several different caution symbols illuminated on her internal screen. Nearby, an armed guard stood off to her left, his back to her, completely unaware he was a breath away from death— if he made the wrong move.

The boards beneath their feet creaked slightly when Erik dropped beside her. His large frame wasn't quite as light on his feet as she was. Erik's night goggles were down. He looked like something out of a spy movie. The thought gave Kaitlyn pause, knowing if anyone saw under her clothing, they would truly see something out of a sci-fi movie.

Kaitlyn nodded her head towards the guard and signaled to Erik that she would take care of the man. In one swift motion, she pulled out the modified 9mm on her thigh. With the flick of her thumb, the weapon went from lethal to tranquilizer. She leaned forward, aimed and squeezed the trigger. The dart made a soft *pft* noise as it sailed through the air and hit the guard in his neck. Annoyed, the man swatted himself, muttering a profanity in Russian. Before he even had time to remove the dart, he started to sway.

Sticking to the shadows, Erik pounced forward

and caught the guard before he hit the ground. The last thing they wanted was a loud thump to alert the others.

Steady and methodical, Kaitlyn pivoted to the right, where the next target stood looking out over the water, smoking. She was tempted to switch the dart to an actual bullet. The man was obviously a poor excuse for a watchman. But the man's incompetence was not her concern; she needed to stay focused.

Silently, she waited for Erik to slip into place. With stealth, he moved across the boat. Never hesitating. Never second-guessing. *Ghosting* as he liked to call it. She smiled and pulled the trigger. The dart hit the second guard between the shoulder blades. Once again, Erik lowered the man to the ground.

Two down. Several more to go.

The guards would be out for a couple of hours, give or take a few minutes, depending on their weight. It was more than enough time for her to accomplish her objectives.

Quickly, working as a team, she and Erik took out four more guards with lethal silence.

After a quick, three-hundred-and-sixty degree sweep, Kaitlyn locked eyes with Erik and signaled they were clear to move. She sprinted across the ship, followed closely by her partner, to the entrance leading below decks.

They crept down the stairs, rubber-soled shoes quiet against the metal steps. Kaitlyn hit the landing with a soft thud and looked into an empty well-lit corridor. She stepped back. Erik dropped in front of her. He padded forward and unscrewed the light bulbs. Darkness was their friend; it would give them an advantage and confuse their enemies.

As they made their way down the corridor, she felt an odd tingling. Her gut was warning her, Lucas might say. Something felt off. It was too quiet, even for this time at night. There weren't as many thermal heat sensors as she expected down below.

Movement. Kaitlyn halted and held up a hand. Erik froze behind her.

A door to the left swung open, casting a dim glow in the corridor. Two men appeared. One cursed and grumbled, "What the hell happened to the lights?" in Russian.

With zen-like focus, Kaitlyn raised her firearm.

"What the hell? Who are..." The man reached for his gun, but he was not quick enough. The dart hit him in the throat and he dropped with a loud thunk. Before the second man could react, Kate shot him in the chest. Erik ran forward and grabbed the bigger man under the arms and pulled him back into the room from which they'd just come, dropping the body. Kaitlyn holstered her pistol and dragged the other man, disposing him on the floor.

Without speaking a word, they shut the door and continued down the corridor, staying close to the wall. Someone could have heard the thuds, but noise was common on a huge ship like this, so it would more than likely be overlooked. Regardless, they had to act quickly.

Kaitlyn looked over her shoulder, and Erik gave her the thumbs up.

Fast on their feet, they came towards the end of the narrow walkway. They slowed, pressing themselves against the walls, inching forward. Kaitlyn paused. Several heat sensors lit up her screen.

Muffled voices could be heard.

Holding up four fingers, Kaitlyn indicated the door with a lift of her chin. Erik nodded.

He slid in front of her and knocked on the door. Kaitlyn stayed flat against the wall, out of sight.

"What?"

Erik answered in Russian. "There's a fire in the hull."

The door swung open. A huge man stood, looking pissed off and then frowned as he took in Erik's attire. Before the man had time to react, Erik slammed the web between his thumb and first finger into the man's throat, striking his larynx and instantly crushing his vocal cords. Wheezing, the large man's hands flew to his neck. Erik flipped the gun in his hand and slammed the stock into the man's temple. He dropped like a bag of rocks.

The three remaining men stared, their mouths agape. None of them were armed. Kaitlyn leaned in and fired three quick shots. They were all out cold in seconds. She was almost out of darts, so they would have to be more inventive with their non-lethal methods.

Where the hell is Dasvoik? And the captives?

A creak came from behind. Had she missed someone? Kaitlyn spun on the ball of her feet and raised her gun making her way back towards the hallway. She peered around the corner just in time to see a shadow fall onto the ground from the staircase. Her finger pressed lightly to the trigger. The shadow came to a halt.

Kaitlyn waited.

The muzzle of a machine gun peeked out from the stairwell followed by the top of the man's head. Kaitlyn's sensor went from caution to threat. Instantly, she flicked the switch that turned the gun from tranquilizer to lethal.

He fired, spraying the wall.

Not the brightest thing to do on a steel ship, she thought. The bullets ricocheted, creating a fireworks-like effect of flashing light, while the acrid stench of gunpowder floated through the air.

Before he had a chance to retreat, Kaitlyn pulled the trigger. The man spun from the impact to his skull and staggered a moment on his feet before slowly sliding to the floor. The body twitched once before laying still in a pool of blood. Dead.

Kaitlyn filtered past the ringing in her ears, searching out sounds.

Things were about to get interesting. Panicked voices, doors slamming, guns being locked and loaded. They'd lost the element of surprise.

"You ok?" Erik asked.

She studied his face. He showed no outward signs of distress. In fact, he looked completely at ease.

"Peachy." Kaitlyn smiled to herself at the use of one of Quess's favorite sayings and crept forward. Briefly, she wondered if she should be affected by the death, but pushed the thought aside. Instinct, training and her programming is what kept them alive. Basic survival was priority.

There was no room for remorse.

They moved down the corridor. A large metal door loomed ahead.

Erik approached the door and gave her a quick nod before quickly pulling it open. Kaitlyn charged through the door, gun at the ready.

The room was huge and cloaked in darkness. Rows and rows of shipping containers filled the area. Advancing slowly, they separated, slipping between large containers, searching for any proof that the captives were still on board. But Kaitlyn feared they were too late.

After making a sweep of the large room, Kaitlyn was satisfied the only heat sensors were small rodents. Most likely rats.

They merged back together and continued into the next room.

Kaitlyn titled her head, and Erik followed as she weaved through the cargo. Flattening herself against the metal container, she inhaled sharply, frozen.

Up ahead were rows of large cages. All of them were empty but filled with the scents and traces indicating many, many humans had been crammed inside them. She shuddered, peering into the cells.

It surprised her that she was so affected by the sight.

They were too late. Harrington had been right. Images of the photographs Harrington had shown them flashed before her mind. The haunted, frightened looks on the faces of the young women would be forever etched in her memory.

Worry about that later. Now, she had to focus

on finding Vance Dasvoik and making him pay.

They exited the room of cages through a side door. If the captives were gone, then the chance of the target still being on the ship was slim to none, but they had to be certain.

They slipped down the narrow corridor and were almost to the end when they heard the boots echoing. *Threats.*

Simultaneously, Kaitlyn and Erik spun and pulled the trigger, but not before one of the men fired off a shot. A bullet whizzed past her head and another hit Kaitlyn in the chest. The impact propelled her back a few steps. Regaining her footing, she continued to fire, for once grateful she was mostly robot. She squeezed the trigger and hit one man between the eyes then put a through the other's right eye socket.

Erik took out three of them. The corridor was littered with bodies and filled with the metallic scent of blood.

Her skin tingled. Someone approached from the opposite end.

Kaitlyn turned and tightened the grip on her pistol.

A bald man held a gun mere inches from Erik's head. Erik dropped his gun, kicked it across the floor, slowly raising his hands over his head.

Just as Kaitlyn was about to get a shot off, Erik drove his elbow into the crook of the man's arm. The gun skittered across the floor. Erik grabbed the man's arm and threw him over his shoulder then slammed him onto the floor. A sickening crack indicated the gunman's back was broken. He cried out in pain but didn't move.

Kaitlyn merely nodded her approval, before

she flipped the switch and shot a dart into the man.

Two more guards rushed in, startled, but still with enough presence of mind to raise their guns.

They were down before they had a chance to fire their weapons. Erik and Kaitlyn exchanged a glance before moving on. There was still a lot of ground to cover.

Kaitlyn flattened her body against the wall, slowly moving towards the only room at the end of the hallway. Her gun was cocked and ready.

Her thermal heat sensors informed Kaitlyn there were two warm bodies inside the room. One lying horizontal. Could it be Dasvoik? Determination spread through her.

If he was behind this door, she was going to put a bullet in his forehead.

No, that was too kind of a death for a man who inflicted such suffering on others. After seeing the cages in person, she could not allow him to die a quick death. He had to suffer like the captives had. He would pay. And pay dearly.

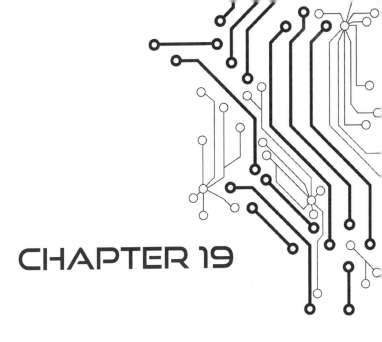

CHAPTER 19

Kaitlyn entered the room, her steps flowing along the path of least resistance and stayed near the wall. She rapidly scanned her sector until she saw Erik mirroring her actions on the opposite side of the door.

It wasn't Dasvoik in the room, but an old man seated on a chair, hunched over. He didn't seem at all surprised when they burst through the door.

"Took you long enough," he muttered, leaning back his head and closing his eyes.

Kaitlyn's eyes left the man and zeroed in on the bed. A young girl lay naked, covered in welts, bruises and blood. Her eyes were mere slits from the swelling. If she had once been pretty, that was no longer evident.

"Jesus." Erik lowered his gun and walked

towards the bed.

The girl didn't even move.

The old man spoke softly. He gently brushed a strand of her hair out of her face. "Aaliyah, the cavalry has come. You're safe my dear."

If she heard the man, she didn't acknowledge it.

Kaitlyn turned her gun on the old man. "Where's Dasvoik?"

He sighed and shook his head. "Long gone. You'll never find him now. Missed your chance, I'm afraid."

Oh, they would find him. Kaitlyn had no doubt about that. There was not a rock he could hide under that they would not overturn to find him. She would not rest until he could not harm another human being. And she had nothing but time.

"Tell me one good reason why I shouldn't put a bullet through your head?" Erik demanded.

The old man's watery blue eyes looked up. "I don't suppose Harrington would be too happy about that."

Kaitlyn and Erik exchanged a glance. So this was the inside man. Not quite what she'd been expecting.

"Did you tip Dasvoik off?" Kaitlyn asked, taking a step closer to the man. Harrington had been concerned about a mole in the network. As far as she knew, he was the only one on the ground and with direct access to Dasvoik.

"Tip him off? No. Why would I do such a thing? I can't stand the bastard."

Erik holstered his gun. "Why were you delayed at the port? And why couldn't Harrington reach you?"

The old man sighed. "The reason for the delay is lying right beside you."

Kaitlyn looked at the young girl, confused. What did she have to do with anything?

"Explain," Erik demanded.

"She was found as last minute cargo. Dasvoik was enjoying himself too much and delayed take off. The man does whatever the hell he wants. He didn't care that we were docked with illegals in cages. He thinks he's above the law, and he's right. Untouchable."

"He's not untouchable. The captives were aboard the ship the whole time?" Kaitlyn asked through gritted teeth.

"Yep. He likes to live on the edge. He gets a thrill out of it. He sees life as one big game. And I'm afraid he's always one step ahead."

"Where are the captives now? How did he know we were coming?"

The old man shook his head. "I'm sorry, but I have no idea."

Kaitlyn eased forward and placed the muzzle of her gun to the side of his head. "Where. Are. The. Captives?"

His shoulders lifted and fell in a faint shrug. "I was not privy to that information. One minute we were out to sea, and the next Vance was screaming orders to get the passengers off the ship."

Erik glared at the man. "Last time I will ask. How did he know we were coming?"

"I'm not a rat. I want that monster caught as much as you do. I did my part—don't blame me for your failure. I have no idea who tipped him off, but it sure as hell wasn't me."

Kaitlyn lowered her gun. She sensed he was telling the truth. If it wasn't him then who in the hell was it?

"Maybe he just got spooked," the man said, leaning back in his chair.

"No, he wouldn't have made that drastic of a move if he didn't have reason to be concerned," Erik said and Kaitlyn had to agree.

The young girl whimpered. Her body trembled.

"We need to get her to safety," Kate said quietly.

The old man's shoulders slouched even lower. "This one's going to need some psychological help. He did a number on her."

Erik reached over to pull a sheet over the girl to cover her before leaning over to pick her up in his arms.

The old man reached up and grabbed Erik's arm, shaking his head. "She doesn't like the material on her, it sticks to the welts. She needs to be bandaged first."

Erik hesitated briefly before reaching down and placing his arms under her head and legs. She didn't fight him. She just lay limply in his arms, shaking like a leaf.

Kate walked forward and looked down at the helpless girl in Erik's arms. Without thinking, she reached out and brushed the girl's hair out of her face. The girl recoiled at the touch, and Kate dropped her hand to her side. Her chest felt tight, and her throat burned. She wasn't sure what to make of the feelings. This broken girl touched her deeply.

Why did she recoil from her touch but not

Erik's? Could she sense what she was?

"It's going to be okay. No one is ever going to hurt you again," Kaitlyn said, staring down at the girl's badly bruised face. "Erik, get her on the helicopter, and take the old man. I'm going to clear the rest of the boat. Wait for me at the evacuation point."

"You won't find anything." The old man struggled to stand up. "Dasvoik never gets caught."

Kaitlyn turned towards the old man. "Dasvoik does not stand a chance against me."

The old man chuckled. "Oh, how I wish that was true."

Kaitlyn touched under her ear and confirmed immediate medical evacuation for the girl and the old man.

Erik went one way, and Kaitlyn went the other.

The old man's words annoyed her. Of course Dasvoik could be stopped. He was human and made mistakes. They would find him. They would destroy him. She kept thinking about the girl's broken body as she cleared the rest of the ship. It was large and took quite a while. The old man had been right. No Dasvoik. Not even a trace that he was ever on the boat. At least not to the human eye. She had been able to pick up his DNA in the bedroom. Someone had done an outstanding job cleaning up any traces of him, but they forgot about the ones embedded in the mattress. Not that it mattered. Dasvoik would never face a court of law. She would make sure of that.

Quickly and efficiently, she mentally snapped images of everything in his office and bedroom. There had to be something she was missing.

Something that would come to her later as her mind sorted through the data.

Only essential personnel were left on the boat. After seeing the bodies of the guards, the rest of the staff didn't put up much of a fight. Kaitlyn used flex cuffs and herded them towards the aft of the ship where the helicopter would land. One of the men was quick and jumped off the side of the boat before she could stop him. He was dead as soon as he hit the water.

She looked over the rail. One less they had to worry about.

She radioed in. Harrington replied that they would leave it to the local authorities to take care of the arrest.

Kaitlyn hurried down the ladder and dropped into the boat. Erik sat waiting for her. As they sped across the ocean, her mind raced, filtering all the information she had gathered. She searched for anything to help them with Dasvoik's whereabouts. There had to be some clue. Where would he go? Obviously, he would be in hiding but where? Dasvoik was arrogant. He wouldn't stay out of the limelight for too long.

"How's the girl?" Kaitlyn asked. The wind rushed through her hair, and water sprayed her face. The moon illuminated the water, and Kaitlyn was struck by the beauty. How could there be so much beauty and so much ugliness in the world?

The only sound heard was the water lapping against the boat.

Erik's grip on the throttle tightened. Kaitlyn could see the tension in his body.

After a long pause, he said, "Fractured."

Fractured. Kaitlyn thought about the word

and realized it fit the girl. She wondered if the pieces would be able to be put back together. The old man said she needed psychological help. Maybe Dr. Chambers could help the girl.

"Do you think she'll be okay?" Kaitlyn asked.

Erik was silent for a long moment. "No."

"Never?" Kaitlyn had researched captive victims when she found out the assignment. Even with the research, she wasn't prepared for what she'd seen in the young girl. Once, she had been a vital young woman. She knew the mind could only take so much. They could see from her battered and broken body what had been done to her, but they had no idea what had been done to her mind.

"The human mind is resilient," Kaitlyn argued.

"You didn't hear her. She was crying for him. Begging me to bring her to him. After what he did to her and she wanted to tell him she was sorry. She sobbed in my arms. She didn't want to leave the ship in case he came back."

Kaitlyn listened to the waves lapping the sides of the small black boat. Erik's words echoed in her mind. She tried to make sense of them, but there was no logic. How could she want to be with the man that had beat her and did who knew what else to her?

The memory of her own attempted rape flashed in her mind. The feeling of helplessness and fear she had experienced. She watched the scenes flash before her eyes. The moment that changed her life forever.

She would never be the same and neither would the girl they rescued. Kaitlyn's own life had been taken from her and her body turned into the half human she was today. Kaitlyn knew the young girl had gone through much more than she had. But Kaitlyn had to believe that she would be able to get through it.

"Dr. Chambers will help her," Kaitlyn finally said.

Erik didn't look at her. "Some things can't be fixed."

The boat approached the hidden cove where they would dispose of the boat until Harrington sent someone to retrieve it.

"Did you find anything to lead us to Dasvoik?" Erik asked.

Kaitlyn jumped off the boat. "I'm not sure. I'm still sifting through the information. There has to be something I saw. He couldn't have covered his tracks that well."

"He hasn't been caught yet," Erik reminded her. "He's very good at escape and evasion. Lots of practice."

"Yes, but we're better."

They crouched low and began snaking up the rocky coastline, blending into the darkness. Making there way to the rendezvous point.

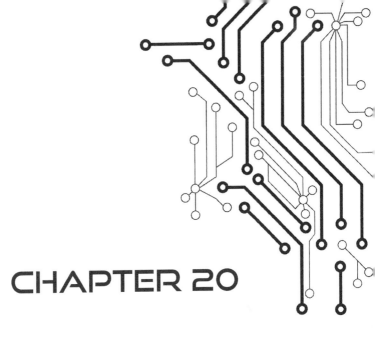

CHAPTER 20

Aaliyah woke slowly. Where was she? The bed beneath her was white and soft and she could hear an occasional beeping noise. Through the slits of her eyes, she could see a bright light.

Was she in heaven? She couldn't feel any pain. She must be in heaven. Smiling, her eyes drifted closed. Her body felt limp as if she were floating on a cloud. Maybe she really was on a cloud. That would be cool.

The door opened. High-heeled shoes clicked across the floor. She heard paper shuffling. Did they have paper in heaven?

A shadow fell over her.

One of her eyes opened slightly and all she could see was a white coat. Yep. She was in heaven.

"My name is Dr. Olivia Chambers, and you

are under my care."

What did she say? Her head was so fuzzy. She tried to grasp the woman's words.

She sat down. The chair scraped on the floor as she pulled it closer to the bed. "You're safe here. I know this is all confusing to you, but you are in a secure facility. The men that hurt you can no longer get to you. Do you understand what I'm saying?"

Aaliyah flopped her head to the side and tried to get a better look at the woman. The pillow was soft against her head. Aaliyah didn't realize how much she'd missed pillows.

The woman was pretty and had a nice voice. Her mind scrambled to think of something to say. It was as if she couldn't focus enough to get her thoughts together. In the back of her mind, she knew there was something she needed to ask, but she had no idea what it was.

"Am I dead?"

"No, you are very much alive."

So she wasn't in heaven. Her heart thudded against her chest. If she wasn't dead, that meant she needed to please her owner.

Pulse racing, she asked for him. "Dasvoik?"

"He's not here. You've been crying out for him in your sleep."

"I-I need him. Happy. Need to make him happy."

The woman set her clipboard down on the table beside the bed. "We'll work through this together. Dasvoik has played a vital role in your life. I understand you feel a bond with him. But you need to learn to let go and be on your own.

He is not coming back."

"No, I can't. I can't." Her voice rose to a shrill.

"You can and you will. I will help you. But now your body needs to heal. Once the body is healed, we will work on the mind."

The woman stood up and injected something into the IV lines.

"What is your name?" Dr. Chambers asked gently. "We need your name to help us find Dasvoik."

She nodded vigorously. Anything to bring him back to her. "Aaliyah. Aaliyah Le Roux."

"Aaliyah, that is a beautiful name. Do you have any family?"

Family? Did she have family? The room faded, and Aaliyah floated off to sleep.

In her sleep, she dreamed. She dreamed of Dasvoik, touching her softly. Smiling at her. Calling her *petal* and his *beautiful flower*. He loved her. She ran after him and they danced under the stars. Dasvoik's face changed and now he was a boy with dark hair and freckles.

He looked familiar, but he was not Dasvoik. Where was Dasvoik? She pulled away from the boy and ran away as fast as she could. Dasvoik would not like her dancing with someone else. Was he mad at her? Oh, no. She didn't mean to. The boy had tricked her! She ran faster, screaming for Dasvoik over and over again. But, he did not reply. She was alone. Scared and so very alone. She dropped to the ground, curled into a ball and cried.

When she awoke again, her eyes opened a little wider. Where was she? She tilted her head and took in the white walls and machines attached to her. *A hospital?*

Her heart rate increased rapidly, causing the machine to go crazy. The door was flung open and the pretty doctor from earlier rushed into the room.

"Aaliyah. It's good to see you awake." Her voice was soothing.

"Where am I?"

"A secure medical facility. You were rescued from the ship."

The ship? It all came rushing back to her. The abuse. Dasvoik. Henry.

Oh, dear God, Darrius!

"My brother! Is he here? Was he rescued?"

The lady reached into her coat and pulled out a syringe. "Aaliyah, you need to calm down or I'm going to have to put you under again."

Again? Why was everything in her head so fuzzy?

"I need to know if my brother is here!" she wailed.

"Aaliyah, I really want to wean you off the drugs, but if you keep having outbursts, I'm going to have to put you under."

"No, no more drugs. How long have I been here?"

"Two weeks."

"Two weeks? Why can I only remember seeing you one time?"

"You've seen me every day, Aaliyah."

That didn't make sense. How could she not remember seeing this woman daily?

"My brother?"

"Your brother has not been found, but people

are looking for him and the others that were on the ship. Do you want to talk about your time on the ship?"

"I want my brother."

"Tell me about him."

Aaliyah pushed herself up a little on the bed and was relieved to see she was not strapped down. "My brain is foggy."

"It's the medication. We've had to keep you sedated because of your outburst."

What outbursts? She wondered. She couldn't even recall being in the hospital before this moment.

"I felt it was the better route instead of confining you to the bed. I didn't want to have to strap you down. From the looks of your wrist and ankles, you've had more than enough of that."

Aaliyah lifted her arm and wiggled her fingers as she stared at the cuts on her wrist that were scabbed over. Lightly, she ran her fingers over the marks—it hadn't quite sunk in that she was actually free.

"If you are willing to talk to me, we can ease you off the drugs. Would you like that?" the doctor asked. "There will be no pressure from me. I want you to tell me your story on your own."

She wasn't sure. Would she like that? It was nice not to feel pain. Wasn't it? Mostly she felt numb. "Yes, I need to find my brother."

"I understand. Would you like to see your parents?"

Her parents? How had she forgotten about them? It felt strange, like her old life belonged to someone else. "No."

"Why not?" The doctor slid the needle back

into her pocket and sat down next to her.

"I don't know. I don't want them to see me like this. My fault. It's my fault my brother is gone."

"It's not your fault. No one would ask for what you have gone through. The people at fault are the ones that took you and your brother. Not you."

Tears streamed down her face. The woman was wrong. Aaliyah knew she was the reason they had been abducted. Suddenly, she felt very tired. The conversation had completely drained her.

"Dasvoik loved me. I just couldn't make him happy."

"Oh, sweetie, that is not love. We have our work cut out for us, but I think for now you need more sleep. I am going to start weaning you off the drugs and when you wake up, we'll take out the feeding tube so you can start eating on your own again. Ok?"

Aaliyah heard the words, but her mind was elsewhere. Maybe it was the drugs. If she wasn't drugged up she could think clearly. Her eyes drifted and she heard the door click softly closed. She found herself waiting for the sound of the door being locked. She'd drifted to sleep before realizing that there was no lock. She really was free.

When she woke again her mother was at the edge of her bed. Her head felt a little clearer. "Aaliyah, I've been so worried, my dear child," she spoke rapidly in Afrikaans.

"Mamma." Aaliyah reached over and grasped her mom's arm. "I lost Darrius. You must hate me. I'm so sorry."

Her mother stifled back a sob.

The doctor came from the corner of the room and placed her arm around the mother. "We're doing everything we can to bring back your son. Right now, your daughter needs you."

Her mother wiped her eyes with the back of her sleeve and spoke in broken English. "This be the truth. I do not hate you, child. I could never hate you."

Aaliyah pushed herself up and the doctor came around and pulled the pillow up. Suddenly she wanted to bolt from the bed. She needed to get out of this place. But the idea of facing the world outside nearly caused her heart to jump out of her chest.

"How are you feeling?" the doctor asked.

"Better. I think. But I don't want to be here. My mind's no longer fuzzy, and I'm hungry."

"That's a great sign. Once you are fully recovered, it's up to you if you want to stay or go home. What would you like to eat? We can have anything you want made."

"It doesn't matter. Nothing matters."

"Don't speak like that," her mother chided. "Life matters."

Her mom turned towards the doctor and in broken English asked the doctor to bring soup, bread and a large slice of apple pie.

The doctor nodded and left the room. Aaliyah's heart hurt; it was full of sorrow and remorse.

"Mamma, I need to get out of here. I need to find Darrius."

In Afrikaans, she replied, "And how do you think you can do that? Stop talking nonsense.

You will stay here until you recover. You have to heal yourself before you can heal others. We have to leave Darrius's life at the hands of the lord and the police. You must pray for your brother's soul."

She nodded in agreement, but deep down she thought, *praying doesn't work, Mamma.* But she had been rescued. Why wasn't she grateful? Why did she feel so numb? And why was every ounce of her body aching to see Dasvoik? The man was a monster. She knew that, and yet a part of her still longed for his acceptance. What the hell was the matter with her?

The door opened again and the doctor came back carrying a tray of steaming hot soup and crusty bread. Her stomach rumbled at the site. When she placed the tray in front of her, Aaliyah greedily took a sip of the soup and burned her tongue. She was so hungry she didn't care. She picked up the bread tore it apart and dunked it in the soup. Before she could even swallow it, she spit out the bread. Memories of the cage and struggling for a chunk of bread accosted her mind.

"What's wrong?" Dr. Chambers asked.

Aaliyah pushed the bread aside. "I'm not hungry."

"Does it taste bad? I can get you something else."

"I hate bread. I never want to see it again."

Her mother looked confused. She used to love bread.

"I see." Dr. Chambers removed the tray from in front of the girl.

"Let me get rid of this." The doctor left the room and returned with a slice of pie and a tall glass of milk.

Aaliyah looked at the pie, and her mouth watered.

"Maybe this will be better," the doctor said, as she set the apple pie down in front of her.

Aaliyah eyed the dessert for a moment, before picking up the fork and taking a bite. It was amazing. It had been so long since she'd tasted anything so sweet and rich. She devoured the pie and then gulped down the glass of milk.

"Did you eat bread while you were gone?" Dr. Chambers asked her voice was soft and soothing.

Aaliyah turned her head, refusing to answer.

"We'll worry about that later. I'm glad you liked the pie. Would you like to be left alone to visit with your mother or do you want me to stay?"

"Alone."

The doctor picked up the plate and glass before leaving the room.

Her mother reached for her hand. Aaliyah wanted to pull it away, but she knew it would upset her mother.

"Noah has been calling and coming by every day."

Noah. How had she forgotten about him? Once he found out what happened to her he wouldn't want anything to do with her and she didn't blame him.

"What did you tell him?"

Her mom eyed her before speaking, "I told him the truth. That you were abducted and badly injured. That you needed time to heal. He insisted on coming to see you, but I told him I had to ask you first."

"No, I don't want him to see me like this. I

don't ever want to see him again."

"He's very worried about you."

"I don't want to see him, Mamma."

"Then you won't see him," she said firmly. "It's your choice."

Her choice? The words sounded foreign to her.

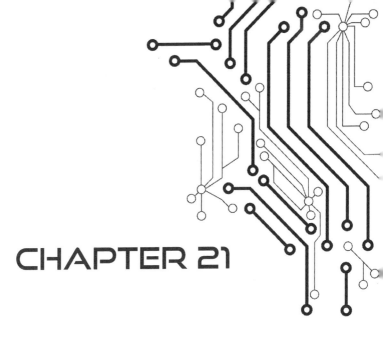

CHAPTER 21

Kaitlyn had to see the girl. Dr. Chambers said she should not get involved—that it wasn't part of her job. Which made no sense. They wanted her to be more human, but they didn't want her to feel or be involved? Part of her saw the logic of not getting emotionally involved in the missions, but she just couldn't seem to forget about the captive.

Maybe if she talked to her she could put it behind her and move forward. It was not good for her attention to be unfocused. Dasvoik had managed to evade them for weeks, and they were no closer to catching him than they were on the day they boarded the ship. Kaitlyn was beyond frustrated.

She paused in front of the door before entering. Kaitlyn wasn't sure what she was going to say to the girl. She wasn't very good at things like this. Maybe just seeing her would help and they wouldn't need to talk.

When she crossed through the door, Kaitlyn was surprised by what greeted her. The young girl sat in a chair, watching television. She clicked the TV off when she noticed Kaitlyn.

Teal eyes and a mocha face stared back at her. Without all the bruising, the girl was truly striking.

"You look well," Kaitlyn said, crossing the room.

"Do I know you?" The girl pushed herself back into the chair, wrapping her arms around her knees. Suddenly she looked like a fragile child.

"We met on the boat."

Aaliyah flinched. "I'm sorry. I don't remember."

"That's okay. I was once in an accident and I couldn't recall anything for a very long time."

A long lapse of silence filled the room. Kaitlyn didn't know what to say.

Dr. Chambers warned her not to bring up Dasvoik, stating the situation was too delicate. It's not like she had anything positive to tell her anyway.

Aaliyah looked up, her arms were now wrapped around her chest and she rocked slightly back and forth. "Were you a prisoner on the boat? I think I would have remembered you."

"No, I was not. I helped rescue you."

The girl looked down at the ground and shifted in her seat. Her eyes lifted and met Kaitlyn's. "You were too late."

The words stung. "I'm sorry."

"Why are you here? Shouldn't you be trying to

find my brother? And all the others?"

"That's not my job."

"Not your job?" The girl's voice shook. Kaitlyn registered her rise in pulse rate and blood pressure. Physical and emotional signs of distress.

"Federal agencies are searching for the prisoners." Kaitlyn was searching for Dasvoik, but she wasn't allowed to talk about that.

"It's been weeks. Wherever they were headed, they have reached by now. My brother could be dead for all I know."

"That's a possibility," Kaitlyn agreed. "But, chances are, he is alive."

"If he's alive, he probably wishes he were dead," the girl said looking off in the distance, her eyes glazed over.

"Can I sit down?"

The girl didn't respond, so Kaitlyn sat in a chair next to her.

"I can't claim to know what you are going through." Kaitlyn said looking at the girl. "I do know you must miss your brother."

Aaliyah turned in her direction, but did not speak.

"You want him returned."

"Yes."

"You might be able to help us."

Aaliyah sat up straighter and for the first time, Kaitlyn saw a hint of interest in her clear blue-green eyes. "How?"

"You spent more time than anyone with Dasvoik. You might know something about his whereabouts."

She shook her head. "He never talked to me

like that. I don't know anything."

"You might have heard or seen something and not realized it was important at the time. The mind captures things we are not aware of."

"I'm sorry. I cannot help you. Most of my time was spent tied up." The girl recoiled at a memory.

Kaitlyn was not a psychologist, but she deduced it was a good sign that the girl was remembering the horrors she went through. To get over this odd obsession she had with Dasvoik.

"Dasvoik is the one that hurt your brother."

"No!"

"If it were not for him, your brother would be home with his family."

The girl glared at Kaitlyn. Her chest heaved up and down, and like a crumbling pile of cards, she collapsed. Sobs racked her body.

The door flung open and Dr. Chambers looked at Kaitlyn in disbelief. "I told you not to talk about him."

"She needs to talk about him."

"On her own time."

"She might be able to help us."

"I can't," the girl wailed.

Kaitlyn tapped the side of her own head. "It's in there I know it is. She knows something she is not aware of. A conversation heard when she was unconscious, a map, a childhood memory from Dasvoik, something. I'm telling you, it's in there."

Dr. Chambers got on her knees in front of the girl and took her hands in hers. "She might be right, Aaliyah."

"She's not," the girl spit out. "Don't you think if I knew where my brother was I would tell you?"

"You might unconsciously be protecting

Dasvoik. We need to find him to find your brother. Without him, it's like looking for a needle in a haystack."

"I don't know anything!"

"Would you be willing to let me put you under and see if I can pull the information from your mind with hypnosis?"

The girl's breathing became shallow and her head lifted. "Could you do that?"

"I can try. If you are open to the idea."

Kaitlyn interjected. "Dasvoik needs to be stopped. More than likely he has a new girl tied to his bed as we speak."

"Kaitlyn!" Dr. Chamber's eyes were wide.

Aaliyah pulled her hands away and rocked back and forth in the chair.

"He hurt you, Aaliyah. He took something from you that cannot be returned. But you can come out of this stronger."

"I'm too weak." The girl sobbed. "I'm afraid. I'm disgusting. I can't even look at myself in the mirror. No one but Dasvoik is ever going to want me again."

Kaitlyn leaned forward in her chair. "Not long ago I was attacked. And I woke up afraid. Changed forever, just like you. I thought I was a freak. That no one could ever love me again, but I was wrong. I'm stronger than ever and have people in my life that believe in me. Love me even."

"You're just saying that to make me feel better."

"Why would I do that?" Kaitlyn asked, puzzled.

Dr. Chambers smiled sadly. "She's telling the truth. I have helped her recover. Just like I intend to help you recover. I don't agree with the way

Kaitlyn has handled this, but I believe she has made more progress in the last fifteen minutes then I have made in weeks."

"Please, Aaliyah. Help us," Kaitlyn whispered. "Take back your life. Do something good. Help us save any other girls and boys from the hands of the maniac that did this to you."

Aaliyah wiped her nose with the back of her sleeve and nodded. "Okay. I don't think it will work, but I will try it. But, you have to promise me you will look for my brother."

Kaitlyn nodded. "I promise, but first I have to find the mastermind behind all of this. You also have to make me a promise."

"What?" Aaliyah asked wearily.

"You have to remember. You can't move forward until you face the past. Once you remember what that man put you through, you will see that was not love." Kaitlyn reached forward and extended her pinky. The young girl stared at Kaitlyn's hand and back at her face as if she was trying to figure out if Kaitlyn was serious or not. Kaitlyn nodded her head and the girl hesitantly extended her hand, linking her pinky with Kaitlyn's.

"I'll find your brother," Kaitlyn vowed. "I want to show you something. I will be right back." She jumped up and walked down the hallway until she reached the lab. "Lucas, can you print an image from my memory?"

"Of course. Anything in particular?"

"Aaliyah lying in Erik's arms after we found her."

Lucas looked at her for a moment, rolled his chair over to his computer, then rapidly pounded away at the keyboard. Within seconds, the printer kicked on and an image formed on the paper. Kaitlyn smiled. She might not be fully human, but her mind was pretty damn impressive if she did say so herself.

"Thank you." She grabbed the photo and hurried back down to the girl's room.

She looked down at the image, and her smile disappeared. It was horrible the way she'd been beaten within an inch of her life.

Dr. Chambers and Aaliyah looked up when she entered.

The doctor saw the photograph in her hands. "Kaitlyn, no! This is not the way to handle this situation."

Kaitlyn ignored the doctor. "I want you to look at this." She held the photo out, and the girl reached for it with shaking hands.

With one hand, she covered her mouth. The image shook violently, before it floated to the ground. Kaitlyn wondered if the doctor was correct, and she had made a horrible mistake.

The girl pulled her legs up on the chair and wrapped her arms around them, resting her head on her knees as she sobbed.

The doctor tried to speak to her, but the girl ignored her and continued to cry.

"He did this to you. The man you think you need to please. He tortured you. Did unspeakable things to your body and mind. Please tell me you see that when you look at the image," Kaitlyn said softly.

The girl's tears subsided. "Why? Why did he hurt me? I really tried. I tried so hard."

"I know you did, but someone like him is never happy. They get off on the pain and the humiliation. No matter how hard you tried, nothing would have been good enough. He is the one who is wrong. Not you. You did absolutely nothing to deserve what happened to you. Do you understand that? None of this was your fault." Kaitlyn ripped the photograph to shreds, letting it fall to the ground. "You're stronger than you think. You will get through this."

Aaliyah stared at what was left of the photograph on the floor. Tears spilled silently and flowed down her face. "I'm so ashamed."

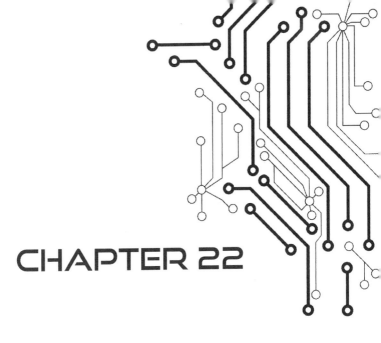

CHAPTER 22

A few days later, Aaliyah looked up as someone entered her room. The book she was holding slipped from her fingers and fell to the floor.

Noah. Despite what she had been through, the sight of him still made her heart catch.

Feeling very self-conscious, she tugged at her shirt and smoothed out her pants with her hands. The look on his face made her want to get up and run. His usual friendly features were contorted in pain.

He couldn't even stand the sight of her. She knew it! Why was he here? She told both her parents and the doctor not to allow him to see her. Her hands clenched in her lap.

"Aaliyah." He took a couple of hesitant steps towards her. Her heart flipped, and her pulse accelerated. The walls felt as if they were rapidly closing in on her.

"Please, go." Aaliyah looked down at her

hands. She could see the scars on her wrist, the ever-present reminder of the restraints that bound her. Even though her hands had been freed, she was still mentally stuck in that cage. Therapy was helping, but she knew she would never be whole again. She was physically ready to leave the facility, but she couldn't. The idea of going back home and acting like life was normal was impossible for her to grasp. The mere mental image of walking down the road made her shake like a leaf in a storm.

Anytime she heard a loud noise, she nearly jumped out of her skin. Thankfully, they agreed to let her stay at the facility. She wondered how much longer before they would make her leave. She knew she couldn't stay there forever. Kaitlyn said she had left one cage for another. That she needed to reintegrate into life.

Who spoke like that? Aaliyah knew she was right, but she just didn't care. She needed to feel safe. If she never left the hospital it would be fine by her.

Noah shifted on his feet. In all their time together, she had never seen him so uncomfortable. "I had to see you. I've been going crazy with worry."

He needed to leave. Just the sight of him was too much for her to bear. Too many memories of a life she could no longer live. Struggling desperately for control she spit out, "You've seen me. Now get out."

"Don't say that. You don't mean it."

"Yes, I do. We're done, Noah. You can't love me anymore. I'm broken, and I'll never be whole again."

"Shh, I'll always love you." He took a few more steps until he was so close, she could smell him. He reached down to touch a strand of her hair.

She jerked away. "Don't touch me."

His hand dropped to his side. "I'm sorry. I just miss you so much." His voice cracked.

"I want you to leave." She pushed herself further into the chair as if she could put enough distance between them. She could feel her mind shutting down. Dr. Chambers told her when that happened, to imagine something in her life that was real and meant something to her. A person, a place, anything to keep her from fading. Right now, more than anything, she wanted to hide away. She didn't want Noah to see how vulnerable she'd become. She thought of the wild flowers that sat on her desk the day she was abducted. Noah had sent them to her to remind her that spring would soon return. They were so beautiful.

Noah cleared his throat.

He ran his hand through his hair and looked around the room as if searching for something to help him. "If you're broken, let me help you put the pieces back together."

"You don't get it. You can't put back together shards of glass." Her eyes misted.

"Please, don't push me out of your life. I can help you. I want to help you. I don't know everything you went through, but I know enough to know you are not ready to go back to the way things were between us. You may never be ready. I get that. I really do. But I can't walk away from you. I need you, Aaliyah. I didn't know what it meant to be happy until you walked into my life.

If all we can ever have is friendship, I will settle for that, but please don't completely kick me out."

Aaliyah looked up at the boy who at one time was her world. He was so pure and good. When she looked at him she saw everything she used to be and would never be again. Her heart constricted. Despite her confused emotions she pointed at the door. "I'm sorry. You need to leave."

Noah's eyes filled with tears. "I can't."

"Go! Just get out of here," Aaliyah yelled. Her chest felt hollow.

The door opened, and one of the nurses hurried in. "Your time is up."

Noah looked back at her one more time as he stopped at the doorway. "I'll be back."

Aaliyah walked over, dropped onto her bed and cried until she had no more tears. Dasvoik had taken everything from her, including the boy she loved more than life itself. It wasn't fair! Life wasn't fair. Why couldn't she get past this? She was alive. She was home. But she knew she would never feel happiness again. How could she be happy when her brother was gone? How could she be happy when her soul was black? Why had God failed her? Maybe what she should be asking was why had she failed God?

A slight knock on the door startled Aaliyah. No one ever knocked in this place. They just barged in. She really hoped it wasn't Noah again. She didn't have the strength to kick him out, again.

The door opened slowly and in walked a girl about Aaliyah's age with a head full of copper curls and a genuine smile. She was carrying a large black cat with a white spot on one of its eyes. The girl had an ethereal look about her as she glided into the room. Aaliyah rubbed her eyes, opening and closing them to make sure she wasn't dreaming. The girl stood there smiling angelically. Maybe it was a hallucination.

"I'm Quess," she said. "I would have come sooner, but they wouldn't allow me to visit you."

"Quess?" Well, that didn't sound like the name of an angel. "What kind of name is that?"

The girl shrugged. "My parents are weird. My mother's maiden name was DeMarquess. So they shortened it."

Aaliyah curled her legs under her and leaned against the headboard. She wasn't sure what to make of the visitor. "Who are you? I mean why are you in my room?"

Quess set the cat on the bed and it studied Aaliyah for a moment before crossing the bed. The cat rubbed against her purring. "I live on the grounds with my grandparents, while my parents travel the world searching for geological treasures. Domino seems to like you."

Looking baffled, Aaliyah reached out and pet the cat that snuggled even closer to her. She'd never had a pet before.

"It gets pretty boring here with all the grown-ups, so when I heard there was someone closer to my age, I thought maybe we could be friends."

Friends? Aaliyah wasn't sure she was capable of such a thing any longer. She inhaled sharply. "I don't think so."

Quess dropped into the seat and kicked her shoes off before placing them on the edge of the bed. "I'm afraid you're going to be stuck with me. I've been told I'm sorta a pain, but I'll try not to be too annoying."

Aaliyah was surprised to feel a smile tug at her lips. The first smile since she was taken from the street. The smile quickly turned into a frown.

Quess crossed her feet at the ankles. "Who was that boy I saw coming down the hall? He looked upset."

Aaliyah eyed her uncertainly, and answered as calmly as she could. "Noah. He used to be my boyfriend."

"He's a hottie."

Aaliyah felt her body begin to relax as she continued to run her hands through the cat's fur. "Yes, he is." It felt odd. The girl had a calming affect over her, making her feel almost normal. Or maybe it was the cat.

"Have you met Kaitlyn?" Quess asked, raising a copper eyebrow.

"Yes, she comes to see me sometimes."

"Domino is her cat."

"Really? I can't picture her with a pet for some reason."

A musical laugh escaped the girl's lips. "Kaitlyn will grow on you. She's a bit different. I'm sure you've noticed."

Aaliyah hadn't given it much thought. She did seem stiff around her, but she figured it was because she was afraid of saying the wrong thing. Everyone walked on eggshells around her. "I haven't really noticed."

"Interesting," Quess mumbled. "Anyways, I'm sure you're sick of being cooped up in this little room. Do you want to come over to my place? We could watch movies and eat popcorn."

Her body went still, and she glanced out the

window. A part of her wanted to go with the girl. But a larger part was terrified to step outside. The doctor had been trying to get her to take a walk with her for a while, but she just wasn't ready. "I-I can't."

Quess shrugged as if it were no big deal. "Well then, we'll stay in here. Maybe there's something good on television." She reached across the bed and grabbed the remote control, clicking on the TV.

Aaliyah watched the girl, puzzled. She envied her and would give anything to feel normal again. To go back to the day she was abducted and take Noah up on his offer to pick up Darrius instead of walking alone at night. Looking at the girl made her feel vulnerable.

She knew she would always live in fear from now on. Pathetic. She couldn't even take a walk outside. How was she ever going to get on with her life? Kaitlyn said she was stronger than she thought, but she felt very weak.

Her emotions in turmoil, she dug her fingernails into her thighs, forcing herself to concentrate on what the girl was rambling about. This was her first chance at normalcy. She didn't want to mess it up.

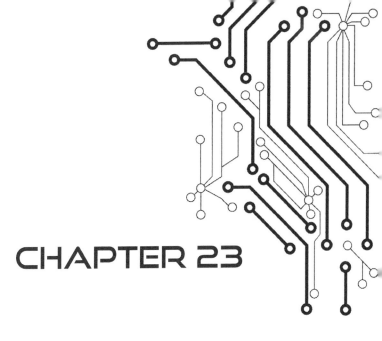

CHAPTER 23

The woman entered the room so quietly the next morning, that Aaliyah didn't even notice her, until she looked up to see her standing beside her bed.

"How are you feeling?" Kaitlyn asked, standing ramrod straight.

Aaliyah bristled. "Shouldn't you be out looking for Dasvoik?"

"We've been running in circles with no luck. The man is like a ghost." She paused. "I was hoping you've made up your mind on the hypnosis?"

"I'm afraid," Aaliyah said softly, unable to meet Kaitlyn's eyes.

"What are you afraid of?"

"To remember, to relive it again. Everything. I'm afraid to go outside. I'm afraid of my own shadow." Aaliyah dropped her head, ashamed to admit her fears out loud to a virtual stranger.

Kaitlyn tilted her head to the side and stared at her. Aaliyah hated when she did that. It made her feel like she was being analyzed. It was as if the woman could see into her mind or something. "I could teach you to protect yourself. Do you think that would help?"

"Protect myself how?"

"With your mind, your hands, weapons. I'm very good."

Aaliyah sat up a little straighter on the bed. "You would do that?"

"Yes."

"But won't it take away from your search?"

"We can work around it. I can teach you things and you can practice without me. I've worked with Quess a lot so she could help you when I'm not around."

Aaliyah's nose wrinkled. "Quess? She doesn't look very tough."

"*Never* judge someone on appearance alone. That could turn out to be a very deadly mistake." Kaitlyn smiled, softening her face. "Your first lesson of the day."

Aaliyah returned the smile. Her second smile in weeks. Not long ago, she'd thought she would never smile again. Baby steps.

"Change into something more comfortable."

"Now?"

"No time like the present."

"Umm, ok. I'm not athletic at all."

"It's ok, anyone can learn to protect themselves. Hurry up. I'll be waiting in the hallway." Kaitlyn turned and left.

Aaliyah wrung her hands in her lap. Just like that? She's supposed to just get dressed and follow this woman to who knew where? Panic rose in her chest. Maybe she could tell her she changed her mind. This was crazy. She took a deep breath. Learning self-defense made sense. If she could defend herself, she would be able to protect herself and her family.

She swung her legs off the side of the bed, and went over to the dresser. Her hands shook as she went to open the drawer. Flashes of Dasvoik invaded her thoughts.

You can do this. How was she ever going to get on with her life if she couldn't do something as simple as open a drawer? Up until this point, she'd only been wearing pajamas, but Kaitlyn said to wear something comfortable.

With trembling hands, she pulled open the drawer and she nearly cried with relief when she saw nothing more than clothes. No vile objects.

Taking a deep breath, she pulled out a pair of yoga pants and a T-shirt. The idea of wearing normal clothes seemed strange—as if she was just like everyone else going about their daily life.

Before she could change her mind, she tossed off her pajamas and pulled on the pants and shirt. She looked at herself in the mirror and covered her mouth. From the outside she looked like a typical teenager. Like Kaitlyn said, *never judge someone on appearance alone.* Her insides were a mess, but her outward appearance gave nothing away. How was that even possible?

Kaitlyn tapped on the door.

Aaliyah pulled her hair into a ponytail and slipped into sneakers. They were brand new and squeaked as she crossed the room. She held her hand on the doorknob for a couple of minutes before she persuaded herself to open it. Something about Kaitlyn made her believe she would be safe while she was with her.

Kaitlyn looked her up and down. "Let's go. We only have an hour."

Aaliyah walked in step with her down the hall. The walls were all white and the lights were bright. They made a sharp left and continued down the hallway. Nervous, her eyes darted in every direction.

She tensed at the sight of a janitor pushing a cart towards them at a slow pace. He was wearing white overalls and barely glanced their way, but she was completely freaked out by his presence. Was she ever going to get past the fear? As they walked past the man, Aaliyah scooted closer to Kaitlyn.

Kaitlyn lightly linked her arm through hers, and Aaliyah stood up straighter.

They reached the end of the hallway, and Kaitlyn pushed a door open that led outside. Aaliyah froze. It never crossed her mind that they would leave the building. "I can't."

"Can't what?"

"Go outside."

"Of course you can. I'm with you. I assure you that no one on this compound will bother us."

Aaliyah glanced at Kaitlyn; her face was confident and left no room for questions. Who was this woman?

"We're only going across the lawn to the training facility. We're wasting time."

Aaliyah moistened her lips. "I'm scared."

"I was scared once, too. You cannot let fear rule you. Don't let Dasvoik take anything more from you. Once you take a step out this door, you've taken the control away from him."

Aaliyah didn't think it was quite that easy, but she knew Kaitlyn was right. She couldn't stay locked in her room forever.

"Are you sure you can protect me?"

Kaitlyn's eyes lit up and she gave her a crooked grin. "I'm the best there is. You are safer with me than anyone else."

"How did you get so confident?"

"They made me that way."

"Made you that way? Through training?"

"Something like that. Come on. We don't have much time."

Aaliyah stood there for only an instant, hopefully portraying an outward calm. She found herself wanting to impress Kaitlyn.

Shaking her head in disbelief, Aaliyah took a step outside into the cold. The air felt good against her skin, and the sun shone brightly in the clear blue sky. Soon it would be spring, she realized in surprise. A part of her thought she would never set foot outdoors again, never smell fresh flowers or pine needles again. Never hear birds chirping.

Kaitlyn didn't bother to glance over. "Are you okay?"

Aaliyah thought about it for a moment. She'd expected to be terrified, but for some reason having this woman by her side made the fear lessen. "I think so. It's not as bad as I expected."

"It rarely is."

Aaliyah was surprised by the large fence and noticed the barbed wire. Odd for a hospital, she thought. But somewhat comforting. Everyone kept telling her she was safe at the facility. They passed through towering oaks and winding paths with stone benches. She wasn't sure what she had expected, but this was not it.

Moments later, they entered a large room with padding on the floors and the walls. There was some equipment, but not much.

"We're going to start with the basics. Things you can do quickly to get out of a bad situation. But first, you need to warm up."

"All right."

Kaitlyn led her through a series of stretches and a couple of laps around the gym. She grabbed a pad and placed it under her forearm. "We're going to work on a few different strikes. The easiest is hammer fist, using the padding of your hand near the pinky. Hold the pad and I'll show you."

Aaliyah gingerly held the pad in her hands. Kaitlyn shook her head and showed her the correct way to hold it to protect herself from the blow and how to plant her feet to get more leverage. She went through the motions, explaining the different ways to strike from the front, side, low, from the back and where to strike for the most impact: neck, temple, chest. Strike hard and fast.

Even with her feet planted, Aaliyah still tumbled back a couple of times. Then it was her turn. To say she was hesitant was an understatement. Awkwardly, she swung her arms like limp noodles.

"Harder. Tighten up. You want to cause as much damage as you can, as quickly as possible."

Aaliyah thought of the man throwing Darrius over his shoulder and how she stood helplessly watching. The next strike was much more forceful. Kaitlyn encouraged her, and before long,

Aaliyah forgot about everything around her and only focused on hitting as hard as she could.

They went over several more strikes and kicks. Aaliyah was exhausted, but also exhilarated at the same time. For the first time since she was taken, she felt like the fog from her brain had been lifted.

"Time's almost up, but I want to end it by showing you how to get out of a hair grab hold from behind."

Still zinging from the kicking and punching, Aaliyah nodded in agreement, eager to learn more.

Kaitlyn went behind her and pulled her hair back, and suddenly, it wasn't Kaitlyn, it was Dasvoik. She cried out loudly and sunk to her knees.

Kaitlyn looked down at her, not speaking, as Aaliyah held the back of her head and sobbed.

She didn't know how much time passed before the tears started to subside.

"We're going to do that again. This time you are going to learn to escape from Dasvoik. Understand?"

"I can't do it!" Aaliyah wailed.

"Just do what I tell you ok? If you still feel like you can't, we'll save if for another day. When I place my hands on your hair, I want you to reach back with both hands and apply a lot of pressure to my hand and knuckles while you lower your body at the same time."

"Okay."

Kaitlyn placed her hands on her hair, but did not pull and Aaliyah did as she was told.

"Now, turn your body inward and add pressure

to the back of my hand."

As she did that, Kaitlyn's body dipped back as her arm was hyperextended. "Now place your arm around my throat and jerk me to the ground."

Aaliyah was surprised at how easily Kaitlyn fell to the ground. She was probably just doing that to make her feel better.

"Okay, now let's do that again, but faster this time. Remember reach back, apply pressure, turn inward, hands around my throat and jerk back. Easy as that."

Aaliyah looked at her skeptically, but when she grabbed her hair, she focused on the steps, and within seconds, Kaitlyn was flat on her back. Could it really be that easy?

"You did it!" Kaitlyn pushed herself back up to sitting, "Let's go over it ten more times until you feel comfortable with it."

The young girl smiled, her narrow chest lifting and falling as she tried to catch her breath from the adrenaline rush.

Aaliyah was drained when she finally made it back to her room. Exhausted, she slumped back. The bed sagged beneath her, and she slept.

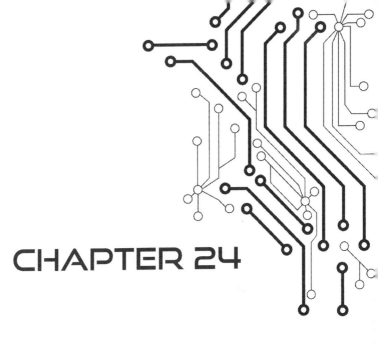

CHAPTER 24

The next day, Aaliyah looked up when the doctor entered her room for the hypnosis session.

Can I really go through with this?

Dr. Chambers took the seat across from her. "Thank you for agreeing to this. I know it wasn't an easy choice for you."

"Are you sure this is going to work? I really don't think I know anything," Aaliyah stated uneasily. The idea of hypnosis freaked her out. Never in a million years would she have thought she would allow someone to pry into her mind. But after the way Kaitlyn helped her yesterday, she felt it was the least she could do. Plus it might lead them to Darrius.

"We always know more than we realize." Dr. Chambers said with a warm smile. "I truly believe this will help your healing process. I promise you won't recall any of it when you open your eyes."

Aaliyah looked down and bit the corner of her

lip. "Could you make me forget *everything*?"

Dr. Chambers sat forward, picked up a pen, and tapped it on her notepad. "I could. It would take time, but I don't think that is the right path to take. Something horrible happened to you. It has changed who you are. Even if I took away the memories, your personality would still not be the same as before. Unfortunately, I think it's best you work through it the hard way. I promise you will be stronger in the end."

"Okay. Let's get it over with." Aaliyah said softly. She was scared, terrified really. The thought of giving up control again was enough to make her want to bolt.

Dr. Chambers held out her hands, palms up. She tilted her head slightly towards her hands Aaliyah hesitated, took a deep breath, and closed her eyes, placing her hands on top of the doctor's she was surprised by the warmth that radiated from them.

"Look into my eyes."

Aaliyah opened her eyes and stared up.

"Do not look away. In a moment I'm going to count to three. Press down on my hands as I press up on yours. One. Two. Three. Press harder." Her voice was soothing.

The doctor removed one of her hands and placed it above Aaliyah's eyebrow, slowly pressing down. "Your eyes feel droopy, closing, closing, sleep!" In one smooth motion the doctor pulled her hand from under her palm. Aaliyah's hands slid limply down to her lap, and a comfortable darkness overtook her mind.

The next thing Aaliyah registered was a snap of someone's fingers. She was once more wide awake and blinking her eyes.

"Are you done? Did it work? Did you find out anything useful?" she asked anxiously.

"I think we might have. You mentioned a location that had not crossed our radar yet. A childhood retreat in Slovenia. I'm sure Harrington will be pleased. You also rattled off a list of numbers."

"Numbers? What were they?" Aaliyah leaned forward. It was bizarre that she couldn't recall anything after placing her hands on the doctor's. A part of her thought she wouldn't be able to be hypnotized.

Dr. Chambers looked down at her pad and recited the numbers out loud. Something tugged at the edge of her awareness, but she couldn't quite reach it.

"Do you know what they mean?"

Her shoulders sagged. "I have no idea."

"Don't worry about it. Lucas can run the numbers through the database. They might be able to come up with a hit."

"I guess that's good." It pissed her off that she didn't know what they meant. They got in her subconscious somehow.

"How do you feel?"

Aaliyah took a moment to consider the question before replying. "Oddly relaxed. For the first time that I can recall, I feel rested."

Dr. Chambers nodded and smiled. "Good. That's how you're supposed to feel."

A sudden thought occurred to her. "You didn't do anything to my mind did you?"

"No. I would not do that without your

permission."

Aaliyah shuddered. "I can't believe you can even do that through hypnosis. It's kinda creepy."

Dr. Chambers smiled. "The mind is an incredible thing. Yours is amazing, Aaliyah. I've never seen someone with a total recall like that, except for Kaitlyn. You were able to remember every detail I asked for. Everything you saw, heard, smelled. It's a gift to have a memory like this."

"I guess." Aaliyah's mind scared the hell out of her. She hated falling asleep because she knew the moment she did, the nightmares would return. She had to relive the torture, the fear and always woke up trembling with her heart racing. She'd tried to avoid sleep but it always snuck up on her somehow. And in the shadows of her mind Dasvoik always lurked, waiting for her arrival. Maybe she should ask the Doctor to at least have dream free nights. Before she could get up the courage to ask the doctor spoke.

"I need to talk to Harrington and tell him what we've learned. This could be the big breakthrough they have been waiting for. I also think he'll be interested to discover what you're capable of."

"Can I go with you?"

Dr. Chambers looked up, surprised. Aaliyah had never asked to go anywhere or talk to anyone. "Are you sure?"

"Yes. Kaitlyn said if I help find my brother, it would help me get past this. I think she might be right. The thought of living while my brother's life is unknown..." She hesitated. "I just need to find him."

"Okay, you can come with me, but Harrington

might not like it. If he insists you leave, you have to listen."

Aaliyah didn't like the sound of that one bit, but she nodded.

"I'm proud of you, Aaliyah. This is a big step."

She wasn't sure about that, but at least it was better than sitting in the bed all day long.

The facility was huge. They walked through many hallways and across a large lawn down winding footpaths. Her heart rate accelerated when Dr. Chambers stopped in front of a building with a large glass door. The doctor must have sensed her hesitation.

"Are you okay? I can take you back to your room, if you'd like."

She shook her head. "I'm fine."

Aaliyah was too freaked out to take in her surroundings.

When they finally entered the room Aaliyah was relieved to see Kaitlyn standing there along with two other men and an older man sat behind a desk. The men made her uncomfortable, but something about Kaitlyn made her believe she would be okay—that Kaitlyn would not let anyone harm her, at least while she was around.

Kaitlyn offered her a warm smile that Aaliyah attempted to return, but it didn't quite reach her lips. She blinked her eyes, not quite sure she believed what she was seeing. What was running down Kaitlyn's arms? It was too shiny to be a tattoo. And who would tattoo a teal strip down both of her arms? Why didn't anyone else in the room think this was odd?

"Dr. Chambers, this is a surprise." The older man said in a crisp voice. His eyes flickered to

Kaitlyn.

Before Aaliyah could ask what was wrong with Kaitlyn, Dr. Chambers spoke. "Harrington, I think we might of had a breakthrough."

The man behind the desk perked up. "What did you find out?"

Dr. Chambers delved into detail about a childhood home and the town where it was located. Aaliyah found it strange that the information came from her head but she had zero recollection of it. One of the other guys sitting in the seat wearing a rumpled white lab coat frantically scribbled notes.

"She also kept repeating this number: 8524505-JDEI2"

"You don't know what the number means?" Harrington asked, looking at Aaliyah.

Aaliyah cast her eyes downward. "I'm sorry. I have no idea."

"It's okay, Aaliyah. We'll figure it out." The younger man with dark hair said, looking up from the pad he was writing on. "Puzzles are my specialty."

"Aaliyah, I should have introduced you to everyone," Dr. Chambers said. "Harrington, Lucas, Erik and you already know Kaitlyn."

"What's wrong with Kaitlyn's arms?"

Silence fell over the room.

"Nothing is wrong with my arms." Kaitlyn said, breaking the heavy silence.

"They're teal."

"I know."

"Why?"

Kaitlyn looked at Harrington, as if seeking help or maybe permission. He gave her a slight nod.

"Remember how I told you I once had something bad happen to me, and my mind refused to remember?" Kaitlyn started.

Aaliyah nodded.

"Harrington saved my life, and now I'm enhanced."

"Enhanced?" Aaliyah unconsciously took a step backwards. What the heck were they talking about?

"She's gifted," Dr. Chambers said.

Aaliyah's gaze was glued to Kaitlyn's arm.

"It's really not a big deal." Lucas said to her with a smile. "You know how people get prosthetic limbs after being in an accident? It's similar to that. Kaitlyn just likes a bit of color."

She felt the tightness in her chest ease. "Oh, I'm sorry. I didn't know."

Kaitlyn smiled. "Want to touch it?"

"Umm, I guess." Aaliyah shifted on her feet. She didn't really want to touch her fake arms.

Kaitlyn came closer. Aaliyah reached out and ran her fingers down Kaitlyn's arm. It felt like normal skin, only the teal part felt like plastic. Apparently they had come a long way in prosthetics. She didn't want to make the conversation any more awkward than it already was. "It's pretty."

"I think so, too." Kaitlyn's face lit up.

"Okay, we have work to do. Lucas first narrow down the location of the childhood residence. I'll get Adams on decoding the number sequences. Aaliyah, thank you for agreeing to help us. It was very brave of you." The older man introduced as

Dr. Harrington said, his voice sincere.

"I hope it helps," she replied meekly.

"I think that's our cue to get out of their hair," Dr. Chambers said, turning to leave.

"Olivia, good work."

Dr. Chambers nodded and held open the door for Aaliyah.

"I didn't know your name's Olivia." Aaliyah couldn't think of anything else to say about the odd exchange.

"Yes, it is, but we have a doctor-client relationship so it's best to keep it at Dr. Chambers."

Aaliyah bristled slightly. The comment wasn't meant to be malicious, but it still stung. A reminder that she was screwed up and needed a shrink.

"What ever happened to Henry?" Aaliyah asked curiously. She recalled how surprised she was to learn of his name. No one had mentioned him since that day and she hadn't given him much thought until now.

"He went back to his home. We've been hoping that Dasvoik would contact him, but so far he hasn't. He checked in on you every day while he was here and he has called a few times to check up on you."

"Oh." Aaliyah didn't know what else to say.

"You did great today, Aaliyah. You should be proud of yourself."

Whatever. All she did was sit there. Dr. Chambers did all the work.

"How was Kaitlyn hurt?"

"I think that's a story she should tell you on her own."

"I think it's kinda brave for her to flaunt her

injuries."

"Kaitlyn is the most courageous woman I've ever had the pleasure of knowing."

And I am probably one of the weakest. She kept that thought to herself. Maybe if she continued to work with Kaitlyn, she, too, would one day be brave.

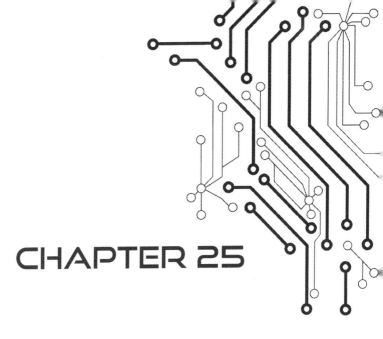

CHAPTER 25

"I got it!" Lucas punched a fist in the air.

Kaitlyn and Erik rushed forward to peer over his shoulder.

Lucas tapped his finger on the monitor. "It's a massive compound, two hundred and sixty-three acres. From the satellite photos, a stone wall goes around the full length of the property. As you can see over here along the coastline the wall does not continue. I'm no expert, but that would be my best guess as point of entry."

Kaitlyn and Erik glanced at each other and nodded in agreement.

"Can you zoom in closer?" Erik asked.

"Of course." After a few keystrokes, the rocky coastline became clearer.

Erik whistled. "That's pretty damn steep."

"Yeah, it's virtually a fortress." Lucas agreed.

"I'm sure there are armed guards, cameras

and probably dogs as well," Erik said absently.

"Always expect the worst. Isn't that your motto?" Kaitlyn grinned. Erik smiled back at her.

A knot twisted in Lucas's gut. Erik and Kaitlyn had become closer since their time in Maine. Every time he closed his eyes, he pictured Kaitlyn on the ship with guns aimed at her. It had been harrowing to watch on the monitor. He found himself extremely grateful that she had Erik by her side.

As always, he would do his part to make it safer for them by hacking into the security system and disabling the cameras when needed.

His fingers moved furiously over the keyboard. After a couple of minutes, a graphical representation of the grounds and buildings appeared on the monitor. "I'm going to print out the intel so you guys can go over it with Harrington. I need to get to work helping Adams on the number sequence. After that, I'll hack into his security system and locate any cameras on the property."

"I knew you would figure it out." Kaitlyn beamed at him.

Lucas felt his heart melt a bit. He returned the smile. He wanted to reach out and touch her, but they were at work and there would be time for that at home.

Unless they leave right away. Which wouldn't surprise him at all. They had all been waiting far too long for this moment.

Lucas hit the print button on the computer, and they collectively held their breath as the data quickly came to life on the industrialized paper. He printed out various angles of Dasvoik's compound along with all the intel he'd been able to gather on the location: the nearest stores, neighbors, approximately how many people it would take to run the property and more.

As the printer hummed, Lucas rolled his chair across the room to Adams. The old man was frustrated. He could make no sense of the numbers after running them through every database they could think of. Maybe the girl had recalled incorrectly. That was always a possibility. Or maybe it was a code of some sort. If that were the case, Lucas should be able to crack it. A sense of excitement coursed through him as he cracked his knuckles, ready to get to work.

"Anything?" he asked.

"Not unless you think the numbers belong on the rabies vaccination registration for a Labrador Retriever in Boston."

Lucas scratched his head. "Let me give it a shot."

Adams threw up his hands. "By all means have at it. I'm going home to get something warm to eat. I'll see you in the morning."

Lucas didn't even notice Adams throwing on his jacket or him walking out the door. His mind was elsewhere. He sat back and stared at the numbers. "Tell me your story," he mumbled.

Kaitlyn and Erik strode out of the room with the maps in their hands. Each of them was too caught up in their own world to bother with the niceties of saying goodbye. That was fine by him. Give him a puzzle and he was in his element. Once he was in the zone, it was hard to pay attention to any outside stimuli.

He entered the number into the database

searching for the usual suspects: financial institutions, criminal, military, federal they all came back blank. What was he missing?

Think.

Bank accounts. His hands flew over the keyboard.

Nope.

A sudden thought occurred to him and he entered the numbers backwards. Sometimes the mind picks up things out of order. No such luck.

Quickly he wrote a program that would give him all the different variations. The list was long. He hit a button and watched the numbers scroll quickly. The program eliminated them one at a time, which was going to take hours.

Inwardly, he groaned. Nothing!

Lucas didn't know how much time had passed before he realized he'd been staring at the same line of numbers and not even seeing them. Instead of trying to make sense of the sequence, he leaned back in his chair and drummed his fingers on his leg. What wasn't he seeing?

He needed to take a break. Sometimes walking away from a problem and shifting your thoughts made a light bulb go off.

Stretching languidly, Lucas yawned, pushed back his chair, and stood up making his way to the coffee station. He poured himself a cup of coffee, stirred in sugar and took a sip. He tried to let his mind wander, but he kept coming back to the sequence.

Frowning, he set the cup down and walked over to gaze out the window, as if he expected the answer to magically appear before him. He remained where he stood for several minutes, before his stomach rumbled, alerting him he hadn't had dinner. Lucas straightened and glanced towards the door. He ambled across the room and made his way out the door towards the snack machine to grab himself a candy bar. The halls were empty and dimly lit with safety lights. Flipping his wrist, Lucas checked the time. He grimaced. It was past midnight.

Why hadn't heard anything from Harrington? He pushed the fleeting question aside. They would contact him when they needed him. Right now, he had a puzzle to solve. It could very well be the missing key.

Lucas hurried back to his computer, his frown deepening. 524505-JDEI2.

What the hell do you mean?

Kaitlyn took a step into the room. "Lucas, we're leaving in less than two-hours."

Startled, his head snapped up, and he spun his chair around to face her. "So soon?"

"No time like the present." Kaitlyn smiled. Lucas wondered if she'd humored herself using the very human phrase.

Kaitlyn rolled out the map onto the table. Lucas stood up, and they bent over staring down at the map. The area was massive. Small flags of different colors were spread out. Kaitlyn quickly went over the color code.

She drew a line from the coastal ridgeline northwest towards the main house. If it could be called a house—it was more like castle.

"That's a lot of ground." Lucas winced. "You should have backup. That place will be guarded tighter than Fort Knox."

"Erik said the same thing. Harrington agreed

and will be sending a team with us." Kaitlyn looked up and smiled faintly. "Ace and Nick will be among the guys."

"I didn't realize they were still around?"

"Apparently Harrington decided to keep them on the payroll after our trip to Maine."

"I guess that's not very surprising."

Kaitlyn closed the distance, her gaze flew to his face, and she wrapped her arms around his waist.

"We're at work," Lucas reminded her.

"It's after hours." Kaitlyn dropped her head to his chest.

As usual his pulse began to race. He rested his chin on her head, inhaling her clean scent. He stood there holding her still and silent for a long time. Finally, he spoke. "This is so hard, Kate."

She pulled away and met his eyes. "You can't figure out the numbers?"

He smiled ruefully. "That wasn't what I meant, but no I haven't had any luck. It's hard to see you in danger. I'm sure I'll get used to it eventually."

"That's true. The human brain is very adaptive."

Lucas grinned, pulling back. He framed her face in his hands and lowered his head to kiss her gently.

"Is it crazy that I want to protect you?"

Kaitlyn looked at him like he'd lost his mind. "Yes."

He grinned.

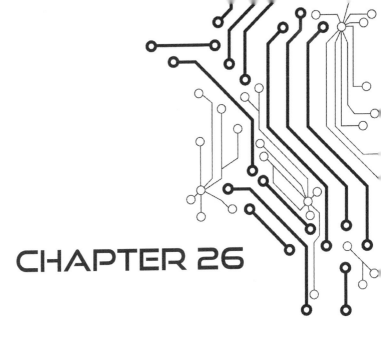

CHAPTER 26

"Before I go, I wanted to let you know I had a talk with Dr. Harrington," Dr. Chambers told her, standing.

Aaliyah clenched her hands in her lap. It had been a long session with her today. She wanted to say that recalling everything the madman did to her was exhausting, but she sensed it wasn't the right time to be difficult with the doctor.

"When I've cleared you, and you're healthy and eighteen, he wants to offer you a job."

She looked up at this, startled. "A job?"

"There's an opportunity for you to help others like you. Like Kaitlyn does. Free them from those hurting them. Dr. Harrington has an idea of how you can help."

Aaliyah waited for Dr. Chambers to tell her it was a joke. The pretty woman's features were earnest.

"Help others like me," she repeated, mind going

first to her brother then to the girls she'd been caged with. "They need someone like Kaitlyn. But I'm not ... strong enough." Her voice trembled.

"You are. You just don't realize it yet," Dr. Chambers said. "I don't want to cause you any more distress, but I think, maybe, this is one of the ways we can take a negative and turn it into a positive. From this horrible experience comes an opportunity to prevent other girls from suffering like you did."

The idea she was able to do anything to help someone else like her left Aaliyah rattled inside. There was a part of her that didn't want to think about what happened–ever. Even if it meant turning her back to the suffering of others.

And there was a part of her that burned to be more like Kaitlyn and help anyone she could, especially if it meant rescuing innocent children like her brother and sending someone like Dasvoik to jail.

"You don't have to decide now. You've got plenty of time to think as you recover," Dr. Chambers said. "But, the offer will be there for you, when you're ready to consider it."

"I'll think about it," Aaliyah murmured.

Dr. Chambers left her in peace.

Aaliyah picked up a book and sat near the window, struggling to digest the latest surprise in her life. It sounded like a positive ... until she thought of her brother. Not even Kaitlyn and Dr. Harrington had managed to find him. What chance did he have to help others?

Familiar despair threatened to overtake her. She forced the thoughts away before her mind started floating away again and tried for a full ten minutes to read the book in her hands.

There was a knock at her door a split second before it opened. Aaliyah's breath caught, and she tried not to fidget. Just the sight of him made her feel off-balanced. She closed the book she'd been thumbing through but not actually reading. She found herself doing that a lot. Trying to find anything to distract her mind. But nothing seemed to help. Flashes of pain, loneliness and darkness were constantly at the edge of her mind. Dasvoik was always there, bringing the fear. How could she get him out of her head?

"I told you not to come back," Aaliyah said wearily as Noah walked through the door, his hands behind his back.

Couldn't he just leave her alone in her misery?

"And I told you I would be back." He smiled impishly. "I brought you something. I made it with your mother."

"My mamma?" Aaliyah pushed a strand of her hair behind her ear. Despite herself, she was curious. Noah never spent any time alone with her mum.

He held out his hand, which held a present wrapped in teal paper with a large crooked white bow. "Wrapped it myself."

Hesitantly she reached for the present. She slowly unwrapped it and gasped, her hands shaking like a leaf. A round piece of clay was covered in colorful shards of broken glass in *the shape of a flower.* She could feel herself slipping, growing colder. Breathing too fast, she concentrated on trying not to hyperventilate. Don't panic. Why would he do that? Did he know? Would she ever be able to look at a flower again and not image the madman calling her petal? Or a beautiful flower? Aaliyah ran her shaky hand across the image and looked up at him confused.

"You said you couldn't fix shards of glass. I wanted to show you that with enough time and patience a beautiful image will emerge. Different, but no less beautiful." Noah's face flushed at the words. She'd forgotten how his pale skin turned pink when he was embarrassed. The color went clear up to the tips of his ears.

"Noah—" She didn't realize she was crying until a tear fell onto the glass. His words struck a cord deep within. He always knew the right thing to say.

He searched her face. "Aaliyah, you're trembling. Are you okay? Did I do something wrong?"

She was so ashamed. With renewed pang of distress, she stared at the flower for a long time. She could hear Dasvoik's warped words echo in her mind. A part of her wanted to throw the gift and watch it shatter across the floor, but it must have taken Noah ages to get all the pieces together.

Was he right? Could she become like the artwork?

No, she was a person not an object. But hadn't she been treated like an object by that bastard? Gradually, since waking up in the hospital, her intense need for Dasvoik had turned into hatred as the memories flooded her mind. It sickened her that she had once wanted to please him. He was an evil monster that preyed on young girls.

"I don't know what to say. You didn't have to do this." She brushed the tears from her eyes.

She fought to restrain the tremors by clutching the side of the bed.

"I didn't mean to make you cry."

She paused trying to collect her thoughts. "I cry a lot these days."

Noah reached out to touch her, but she pulled away. She didn't know if she would ever be ready for that. He dropped his hand to his side. The look on his face tore at her heart.

"I understand what you are trying to say, but I'm not sure I'm ready to hear it. I'm not sure a person can be put back together." She sat back, dejected.

He rubbed his forehead while peering down at her. "That's ok, Aaliyah. Like I said. Time and patience. I have plenty of both. Can I sit down?"

Aaliyah looked at the seat and nodded her head. Somewhere deep in her soul she knew with the simple nod of her head she had taken a step forward.

Maybe they could be friends. She knew she could never again give him more than that.

Noah did most of the talking. He filled her in with school and his family. She sat back and listened but couldn't contribute much to the conversation. She wondered if she would ever be able to tell him what she'd gone through.

Probably not. Dr. Chambers said it was important to talk about it, but she didn't see how rehashing the nightmares could possibly help. Thankfully, Noah did not ask any questions.

He stayed for about an hour before he stood up to leave. Aaliyah was surprised when a deep sadness washed over her at the thought of his departure.

"I can come back tomorrow, if you'd like? I flew in for the weekend."

After a slight hesitation she spoke. "I think I would like that."

He closed his eyes and blew out a breath, clearly relieved. "Would you like me to bring you anything?"

Aaliyah thought it over. Was there anything she'd missed from the outside world? She looked down at the glass flower in her hand and shook her head. "Not that I can think of."

"Did you get your school books from your mom?"

School. She'd forgotten all about it. It seemed like a lifetime ago. She'd missed so much, and she was not ready to go back. She was probably going to have to repeat the year. She'd been so close to graduating.

"It's okay. I'll call her and ask her to bring them over when she comes back. I'm sure she's been in touch with the school, but I just can't go back there. Ever."

Noah looked lost in thought. "You know you could do online school. I know a few guys that do that."

Online school? She thought it over. It sounded better than facing the kids from her old school. "Maybe. I'll see what I can find out about it. Dr. Chambers brought me a laptop the other day, but I haven't touched it."

"It might be good to keep your mind busy with school."

He was probably right, and she needed an education. It's not like she could just drop out of school completely. For an instant, it was as if nothing had changed between them. They were talking about something as mundane as school.

"Bye, Noah."

He hesitated like he wanted to say something but decided against it. "I'll see you tomorrow."

After the door closed behind him, she stared at the glass flower. The light reflecting off it shone beautifully around the room. Without a doubt, it was the sweetest present she'd ever received—she just wished it had been anything other than a flower.

Of course, he couldn't have known that the symbolism of the flower would cut her like a knife. He made the gift out of love. He still loved her. If he knew what Dasvoik had done to her, though, he would run away. She knew he would.

Maybe she should just tell him to push him away. The reminder of what they used to have and who she used to be was too much to bear. Tomorrow, she would tell him and then kick him out of her life for good. It was the only way.

The door opened again, and Noah peeked round it. Aaliyah felt him waiting, and sensed his hesitation and uneasiness.

"Forget something?" she asked.

He shifted back and forth on his feet. "Can I come back in? There's something I have to say. I should have said it before I left, but I just couldn't find the words."

Aaliyah debated. Truth be told, she was lonely. When she was by herself she felt worse. She couldn't escape the memories. The rare visitor had become a welcome distraction.

"Come in." Her voice was a whisper.

He stepped into the room and closed the door behind him. "Aaliyah, I had to come back and tell you. I'm sorry this happened to you. If I could take away your pain I would in a heartbeat. If I could kill that bastard with my own hands, I would." His voice trembled with emotion. His eyes shown with tears.

Aaliyah shook her head and drew her knees to her chest, still clutching the clay in her hands. "You can't help me. No one can. Noah, he did things to me that ..." Her chin quivered. "... I can't even think about it without wanting to scream or throw up. He ruined me."

"Shh. You are *not* ruined. You are strong, resilient and the most loving person I've ever known. You might not believe it now, but you will find your way back. I have no doubt of that."

"He beat and raped me." A choked sound escaped from her throat, and she slumped back in the bed. "Tied me up for days at a time."

"Jesus, Aaliyah." Staring emphatically into her eyes, Noah walked forward. Gently he pried at her fingers and carefully removed the flower from her hand. He set it on the stand next to her and pulled her into his arms. Her head dropped to his shoulder, and her body shook violently.

"Now do you see why you can't love me anymore?" Aaliyah felt pressure building in her chest, as if her heart were being squeezed.

"Why wouldn't I love you anymore? That's the most ridiculous thing I've ever heard," he replied. "If anything, I love you more. I was going insane when you were gone. I didn't know if you were alive or dead. The fact that you are alive... We'll get through this together."

"I don't know if I can." Aaliyah's voice sank. She pulled away, embarrassed that Noah had seen her break down like that.

"Yes, you can. One day at a time. One minute at a time, if that's what it takes. I'm not going anywhere. Let me help you. Please." He stared into her eyes.

"Maybe." She heard her voice crack and crossed her unsteady arms across her chest.

Noah closed his eyes and tilted his head back. "Maybe. *That* I can work with. Thank you, Aaliyah."

"He called me petal and flower." She trembled, frustrated that even saying the words out loud made her shake. Instantly she felt numb.

"Petal?" Noah looked down at his gift his face contorted. "I'm so sorry, Aaliyah. If I had known, I would have made something different. I can throw it away."

She turned to him, blinking. She'd drifted back to that horrible place in the back of her mind. "No, I want to keep it. It's not your fault."

With a troubled expression, Noah cleared his throat. "Are you sure? I wish I had known."

"Dr. Chambers would tell me I need to take the negative and replace it with a positive. Quess would say it was serendipity."

"Quess?"

"She's my ..." Aaliyah hesitated "...friend." It was strange to think she'd made a friend out of this ordeal. Maybe it wouldn't be such a bad idea to take Harrington up on his offer. She couldn't imagine going back to her old neighborhood. The only thing holding her back would be Noah... But even he would be going off to college in the fall.

Dr. Chambers was right—she had a lot of healing to do before she was ready to decide. But she also had a new path at her feet—one that might help her regain the soul she thought she'd lost at the hands of Dasvoik. She had a lot to think about the next few weeks.

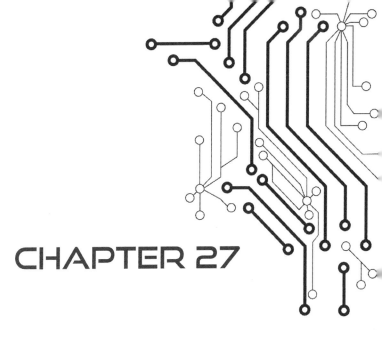

CHAPTER 27

SLOVENIA. THREE DAYS LATER.

Kaitlyn was momentarily taken aback by the beauty around her. She shed the oxygen tank on her back. She couldn't resist appreciating the magnificence of the enormous rock formation. The craggy cliff went almost straight up, slanting away from the ocean towards the top. Visible only with her enhanced eyesight, the area appeared to be bathed in an orange glow. Water crashed against the rocky coast, and mist rose from the ocean.

The phrase *eerily beautiful* crossed her mind out of nowhere.

"Alpha 3, status? Over." Lucas's voice came through her imbedded mic.

"This is Alpha 3. We are set."

"Roger."

"Do we have confirmation the target is on the

grounds?"

"Affirmative."

They were so close to completing the mission. Dasvoik would finally get what he deserved. A sense of elation washed over her at the thought, followed quickly by another. Dr. Chambers would not approve.

Erik had already removed his wetsuit, changed and was now attaching the climbing harness around his legs. His watch cap rode low over his forehead. They were both clothed all in black.

Their eyes met, and he nodded once. She could see his pulse throb in his forehead. His heart rate was elevated. She wondered if it was because the climb would be dangerous or the mission in general.

Moments later, Ace and Nick, along with three other guys, joined them on the shore. They would all make the climb with the newcomers remaining in place as a support element in case anything went wrong. Kaitlyn wasn't particularly fond of the idea since they hadn't had time to train together, but essentially they wouldn't actually be involved in taking down Dasvoik.

She turned away and slipped on her own harness and climbing shoes, while Erik talked to the guys. She checked her weapons, shouldered her pack, grabbed the coiled nylon and tossed it over her shoulder.

"Be careful. The cliff is brittle," Erik said to her when he'd finished his talk with the others. Reaching up, he grabbed a handhold, tested it, and then secured his first foothold. Kaitlyn watched him hug the cliff wall and soon followed his lead. They had climbed together many times in training, where they were taught to stay at least twenty feet a part. The separation made it harder for a sniper to take them both out at once. If one of them got shot at, the other was able to return fire. There wasn't much chance of that from this location, but she knew to never underestimate an enemy as cunning as Dasvoik. It was always possible he had boats patrolling the area.

Ace and his team would follow in thirty minutes.

With her left hand, she groped the rocky wall until she found a narrow crevice to wedge her fingers into. She hung by one hand while seeking out a foothold on a thin ledge. Erick wasn't kidding about it being brittle. Rock splintered beneath her weight. She moved cautiously to the right. The ledge widened enough to reduce the strain on her fingertips.

Erik scurried up the sheer wall, moving with practiced ease. Kaitlyn alternately climbed then paused, her body pressed against the jagged cliff, to let him get a little farther ahead. His broad shoulders and powerful forearms made him a natural, but he still had to deal with the human elements that didn't trouble her: cramped hands, water breaks and maintaining his heart rate. At the pace they were going it would take them at least three hours to reach the top. The swirling mist made the rocks slick, so they had to go slower than normal.

Dasvoik *should* be sound asleep. There was still the question of how many sentries they would have to get through to get to him, but she wasn't worried.

When they finally reached the top, Eric

extended his hand and pulled her the rest of the way up. He leaned back on his hunches, his chest heaving.

"Glad that's over with." He wiped his brow and took a swig from his canteen. "Not a big fan of heights."

Kaitlyn was startled by his confession. "You're afraid of heights?"

He grinned. "I didn't say afraid. I said not a fan. There's a difference."

"Well you hide it well." Kaitlyn said, keeping her voice low as she unclipped the harness and dropped it into her bag.

They checked in with Lucas and the support team before they advanced, clinging to the shadows. Clouds covered the nearly full moon. Occasionally it peeked through the coverage to throw off a stream of light in the dark woods.

After forty minutes of silent movement, they reached the edge of the forest and paused to check in again with Lucas. There was a break in the woods and a wide clearing stretched before them. They needed to reach the coverage of trees on the other side – fast and without tipping off the guards.

"Security camera to the right, two hundred yards." His voice crossed the line. "Give me a few seconds."

Kaitlyn and Erik waited.

"All clear," Lucas said calmly in her ear.

Kaitlyn nodded to Erik to signal she was ready. They sprinted forward. There was a lot of ground to cover before they made it to the main house. They had a good idea where the sentries would be placed, but it wasn't for certain—just an educated guess on how they would handle the security for the compound, if they designed it.

The orange tip of a cigarette glowed in the distance, an instant indication that someone was present. Kaitlyn would never understand why someone would have a habit that would seem to undermine his work as a security guard.

She and Erik froze, exposed outside the forest, but more certain that their immediate threat stemmed from sudden movement that would give them away to the oblivious guard.

After a couple of minutes, the man stamped out his cigarette and strode forward. They had permission to do whatever it took to get the mission done. This sentry was not posing a threat to them at the moment and only doing his job.

Kaitlyn shouldered her rifle and set it to non-lethal mode. She zeroed in on the target and squeezed the trigger. The man turned and went for his gun but staggered to the ground before he was able to get a shot off.

He was well armed and moved like he knew what he was doing. This, along with the sophisticated security of the compound, made her think a lot of blood would be shed before the night was over.

"We need to hurry. I'm sure he'll be missed, if he's not back soon." Erik whispered. They reached the other side of the clearing and began to move through the woods in the darkness, quickly and completely at ease. They moved carefully, light on their feet and stayed within the edge of the forest moving northward.

The sound of Erik's heavy breathing beside her brought her mind back into focus as they raced parallel to the cliff through the thick brush and trees, the branches scratching her face.

The impressive house loomed in the distance. It was an English Tudor design that resembled a castle—all that was missing was the mote. Ivy climbed up the stone walls. Smoke drifted out of the chimneys.

"Alarm disabled. You won't have much time before someone notices," Lucas said.

They'd only need enough time to slip into the house; after that it didn't matter.

A bullet whizzed through the air and splintered the wood in the tree mere inches from Kaitlyn's shoulder. Her head snapped up, and she scanned the area, searching for the location of the shooter. He had to be at a great distance, because she wasn't picking him up with her heat sensor.

Sniper.

Erik crouched behind a large rock.

Kaitlyn also took cover.

Soon the area would be crawling with Dasvoik's men, now that she and Erik had been spotted. They were so close. She couldn't bear the thought of that monster slipping through their fingers again. More than likely, the guards would whisk him away to safety.

"We need to move fast," she whispered.

Erik nodded in agreement.

They scrambled up the hill, keeping low. Erik lost his footing and stumbled. He recovered quickly without her help and kept going. As they advanced, bullets tore up the ground at their feet. Heat sources started to show up on her sensors. The hilly land made it easy for the people to hide from her, but she knew for sure that they were grossly outmatched, based on those she was able to detect.

Kaitlyn listened, tuning out the sounds of the forest and her immediate surroundings to cast her hearing out as far as possible. The sentries were closing in on them quickly. She could hear the murmur of voices.

"The target has left the house. I have access to all the security cameras now," Lucas reported.

"Being evacuated. Which direction?" Erik asked in a hushed voice.

"No. It appears as if he is going hunting. He's armed and headed in your direction."

Kaitlyn couldn't believe it. Harrington wasn't kidding when he said the man had a God complex.

They scrambled up the loosely packed shoulder of a slope, guns drawn. Rocks crumbled beneath their boots, making it hard to gain traction. Movement to the right caught her attention. Erik dropped his pistol and took aim with his rifle. He fired off a shot. A split second later, they heard a scream and the sound of someone tumbling in the woods.

Kaitlyn slipped on the shale and slid down the incline. Dropping her shoulders, she rolled as she'd been taught, until shrubs stopped her. She sprang to her feet, landing in a low crouch.

Erik stayed on his feet and skidded down to meet her.

A shot came from above. It grazed her ear. She dove for the trees.

Another shot.

Erik slowly staggered backwards. His knees buckled, and she realized he'd been shot. He would have fallen to the ground, if Kate hadn't sprung forward and caught him.

"Erik!" Kaitlyn yelled.

"I'm okay," he said through gritted teeth, grasping his thigh. Blood poured through his fingers.

"Erik's down," Kaitlyn said into her mic.

She found cover, dropped her bag in front of her, and pulled out supplies. Quickly she thumbed open the knife and sliced his pants to get a better look at the wound. He was lucky it hadn't hit the femoral artery, but he wasn't going to be much use for the rest of the mission.

"Support element is moving in," Lucas said with a touch of alarm in his voice.

Without a word she, wrapped duct tape around the wound to slow the bleeding. Kaitlyn glanced down at him. His face was pale and his breathing shallow.

"I'm fine, Kate. We need to keep moving," he said.

Kaitlyn hesitated before nodding. She hated the thought of leaving him behind. She helped him to his feet, and they continued upward.

They were at a disadvantage. Dasvoik and his guards had the high ground and they were still climbing the slippery slope. A quick glance at Erik revealed he was drenched in sweat and pale. She wondered how much blood he'd lost already.

"Alpha 3, we're closing in on you from behind. Do not engage," Ace told her.

"Roger." Kaitlyn was relieved. With Ace and the others, she wouldn't have to worry about leaving Erik behind.

Up ahead a heat source flashed before her, lighting up her sensors. Kaitlyn took aim and squeezed the trigger. A body dropped to the ground.

Reckless bullets splattered around them in response, kicking up dirt. None of them were close enough to warrant her to risk moving Erik.

"Just go, Kate," Erik urged her. "I can hunker down here and cover your back. Ace will be here soon."

"Kate, wait for backup." The desperation in Luca's voice was clear, and he made no effort to hide it.

A sense of urgency washed over her. Dasvoik couldn't slip through their grip again. She leaned down and brushed her lips against the warm flesh of Erik's cheek.

"Don't you die on me, partner," she said fiercely.

"Go. Get that bastard," Erik replied through gritted teeth. A sheen of sweat coated his forehead.

Kaitlyn took off. Erik was already firing off rounds. His skill was second only to hers. The sound of bullets hitting flesh filled the air.

Her internal heat sensor screen was lit up like Christmas. How many guards did Dasvoik have? Obviously, the man was paranoid about his safety, and yet he was out in the woods with them. Enjoying the chase—living on the edge, the way Henry had said he would.

Kaitlyn dropped to her knee and shouldered her weapon. The sound of a round being chambered sounded loud in the still of the evening. Slowly and precisely, she took out the targets ahead of her, one by one. Most never had a chance to scream.

In her mic, Lucas confirmed what she had

already expected—the support element was evacuating Erik.

Kaitlyn whirled around at the sound of approaching footsteps.

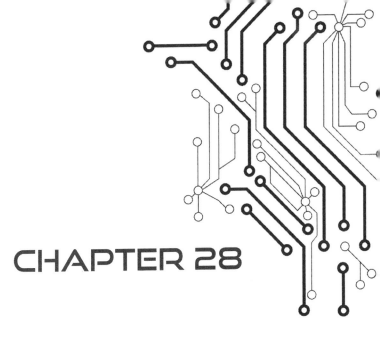

CHAPTER 28

"It's only Ace," Lucas said into the mic.

Kaitlyn turned her attention back to the north.

Ace emerged from the shrubbery behind her. He eased up beside her and gave her a cool glance. "I'm not Erik, but I gave him my word I'd have your back." His voice was detached, but a muscle tightened in his jaw.

Kaitlyn's eyes narrowed on Ace's face for a long minute. She shrugged, if Erik trusted him with her life that was good enough for her. That was good enough for her. Using hand signals, she gestured to the northwest, up the ridge, indicating their path. Kaitlyn grabbed ahold of an exposed tree root, dug her heels in and pulled herself up. The rugged terrain was both friend and foe. After a twenty-six minute, climb they finally made it to flat ground.

Ace leaned against a tree catching his breath.

Kaitlyn waited for his heart rate to settle.

"Alpha 3, Dasvoik and three men are approaching from the East," Lucas said.

Kate stopped in her tracks, and her body went rigid. Her gaze raked the terrain. A red bull's-eye flashed. *Dasvoik.* She would know that face anywhere. He turned his head in their direction, his back stiffened, as if he sensed them. But he was still too far away to see her with unaided human eyes.

Kaitlyn shouldered the rifle and pulled a Glock 9mm from her hip. Ace picked up and tossed a rock to the left of them. Dasvoik and his men spun in that direction. The three of them separated.

Smart.

"The one in the middle is mine," Kaitlyn said softly, gaze never leaving Dasvoik.

Ace nodded. He raised his rifle and picked off the guy to the left and then the one to the right dropped.

Dasvoik took off in a sprint, clearly at home in the woods. She held her hand up to Ace to wait. She wanted him to think he had a chance of getting away. The man liked to play games.

After a few moments, they gave chase.

Kaitlyn maneuvered quickly through thick shrubs. She broke free and caught a brief glimpse of the target between the trees. He was getting careless. Why had he allowed them see him? Perhaps he was getting tired. They had been running for a very long time, but self preservation should have kicked in..

Or he was trying to lure them into a trap.

She picked up speed. Ace kicked it up a notch

as well. She wondered how long Dasvoik could keep up this pace. He was running on pure adrenaline at this point.

If he was aware of her little game of cat and mouse, he never let on. They both knew she could have taken Dasvoik out already, but she wanted it to be up close and personal.

She paused, listening. He crashed loudly through the forest.

Kaitlyn circled left to get behind the target closing the distance.

Another gunman stepped out. Kaitlyn pivoted, squeezed the trigger, the gunman fell and heaved.

Why was he slowing?

She had him in her sites. Lowering the gun slightly, she shot him in the thigh. Just like Erik had been hit. Dasvoik dropped to the ground, groaning with pain. With one arm, he swung his rifle in an arc spraying bullets.

They took cover, waiting until he emptied the magazine. He dropped the gun and pulled out a pistol. His face was set in a grimace from the pain, but his eyes were wild. She almost thought he was enjoying himself. Dragging his leg, he tried to put more distance between them.

"Cover me," Kaitlyn hissed to Ace.

He nodded.

Kaitlyn glided forward, she didn't even try to take cover, and stopped when close enough for her to talk to Dasvoik. "You're a hard man to find."

"Nature of the game, my love," came the response. He took a shot and Kaitlyn moved with inhuman speed the bullet didn't even come close.

"You enjoy inflicting pain don't you?" Kaitlyn

asked disgusted, her gun trained on his head.

An evil grin spread across his face. "Very much so. I'm going to have fun breaking you. You're much too confident, not my type I'm afraid, but I think I could make and exception for someone as lovely as you."

With effort he raised his hand. Before he could fire at her, Kate shot the gun out of his hand. He looked down as if surprised the gun was no longer there.

Kaitlyn strode closer, took aim, and shot at his kneecap. He cried out in pain, chest heaving.

"That wasn't very lawful." Dasvoik spit out through clenched teeth. Even though he was helpless he still managed to look smug.

Kaitlyn realized he thought she was the police and smiled. She didn't have to abide by any stringent laws.

A bullet tore into the ground nearby. She heard a few shots go off from the direction where she'd left Ace and bodies drop to the ground.

"Go ahead arrest me," Dasvoik said. "I've got the best lawyers money can buy. I'll never spend a night in jail."

"You won't be needing a lawyer," she replied. "You've taken too many innocent lives to ever have a chance at redemption. Where did the last shipment go?" Kaitlyn took another step forward.

"Are you mad?" Dasvoik groaned, his face growing paler by the moment, his eyes darted towards his gun which was just out of reach..

"If you tell me, I might spare your life."

"I have no idea what you are talking about." With a primal scream he lunged for the gun. Kaitlyn was faster. She darted forward and kicked the gun away.

"Where are they?" Kaitlyn asked calmly. "You're loosing blood at an alarming rate. I would speak quickly."

"You're a lunatic. I don't even know what you're talking about."

With apparent indifference she shot at his other knee, Dasvoik's scream echoed loudly in the woods.

She studied Dasvoik, for the first time she saw fear in his eyes. The sight brought her a great deal of pleasure. After what he'd done to Aaliyah he deserved to be afraid. Quietly, she waited for his terror to subside.

"What the hell are you?" Dasvoik shouted his face was contoured in agony.

With a slight tilt of her head she said, "I'm Kaitlyn and you are my target."

He became hysterical. "Christ, you really are crazy." Dasvoik tried to push himself backwards, but between the bullet in his thigh and knees he didn't make it very far. The movement only caused him more pain.

"And you really are a sick bastard. You have ruined so many lives." Kaitlyn said coldly.

In a blur, she holstered her pistol and flipped open her knife slowly coming closer. The knife felt soothing in her hands, the metal blade glittered in the moonlight.

She took her time walking behind him, sat back on her heels, jerked his head back with his hair and pressed the cool steel against his bare skin. A quiet reminder of his own morality. She could feel the heat of his body, smell his scent. His pulse raced and the smell of fear tinged the air.

Dasvoik froze. She pressed the knife a little harder, a trickle of blood slid down his throat.

"Tell me what you did with the captives," she said, her mouth mere inches from his ear and barely louder than a whisper.

"Go to hell!" Dasvoik yanked a hidden knife free and drove it backwards.

Kaitlyn leapt back, instinctively sinking the knife into his throat. At the same time Dasvoik's head partially exploded. Blood and gore flew over her.

Ace ran from the trees his rifle panning the area.

Kaitlyn pushed the body off her and stood up. "I told you I had him!"

Ace smirked. "Don't mention it."

"I didn't see the knife." She acknowledged. "So thank you."

"I'm sure you would have managed, but I promised Erik, so I wasn't about to take a chance."

Kaitlyn looked down at Dasvoik. She couldn't believe he was dead. Now they might never find Aaliyah's brother. "Do you think there are any left?"

Ace glanced around. "If there are, I'm pretty sure they scrambled once Dasvoik went down. Jesus, it's like a war zone up here. How they hell is this going to be cleaned up?"

"Harrington's working with the local authorities. Dasvoik has been a thorn in their sides for sometime." Lucas came over the radio she could hear the strain in his voice. "A helicopter is coming in to evacuate the four of you."

"Alpha 4 status?" Kaitlyn asked, wiping her

face off with her sleeve.

"He's stable and will be fine. We'll make sure you see him soon,." Lucas said. "Move to LZ1 for pickup."

She and Ace immediately began to head in the direction indicated.

"I can't believe he didn't tell us the location of the cargo," Kaitlyn said.

"About that." Lucas sounded pleased. "I was able to work a little magic while you guys were climbing the cliff. The sequence was the name of the cargo ship. There were some discrepancies, which is why it didn't show up right away. Too many fives, and the letter *I* was actually a one. The UN has been notified and is working with the authorities to find the victims. The ones that can be accounted for will be rounded up as quickly as possible. The paper trail is thin, but there is hope for Aaliyah's brother."

"You're a genius," Kaitlyn said, eyes on her foot placement, as they descended down the rugged terrain.

Lucas was quiet. She heard the sound of him typing and assumed he was working out the details of the site's clean up.

Ace cleared his throat, drawing her glance.

"Kaitlyn, I want to apologize for being an jackass," he said. "It would be a honor to work with you anytime. I don't care if there isn't something quite right about you."

Kaitlyn hesitated and then held out her fist, careful to emulate the movement the way Erik had with Ace at the house in Maine.

Ace bumped her knuckles with his own.

Kaitlyn grinned. She'd saved innocent people,

killed a madman and now, knew what it meant to be part of a team.

She'd come a long way since waking up in an IFICS lab months before.

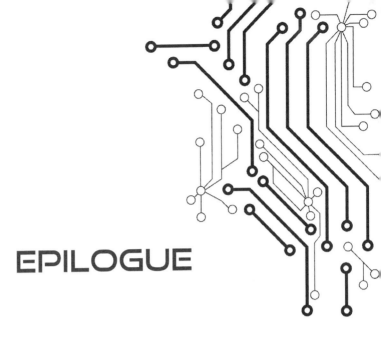

EPILOGUE

Kaitlyn stood back and watched as the little boy slowly exited the plane with Harrington by his side.

Aaliyah and her parents rushed forward and threw their arms around him.

Everyone was sobbing. Happy tears.

Because of the age of the boy, he was not sold off like some of the others into unmentionable trades. A shopkeeper had bought the boy and put him to work cleaning the floors and other menial tasks. From what they were able to find out about the old woman, she had treated him kindly. Apparently she had lost her own son to influenza when he was young and never gotten over the loss.

Quess said someone must have been watching over the boy, an unseen force, such as a guardian angel. Kaitlyn didn't know if she believed that, but she did have to admit luck had been on his side. And she was happy for that.

Aaliyah had a long road ahead of her. She'd agreed to stay on the compound and finish her schooling. They were hopeful that with more time with Dr. Chambers she would someday be able to lead a normal life. Whatever normal was. Quess had a new friend and Kaitlyn spent time with Aaliyah when she could. She felt a bond to the girl.

Lucas draped his arm over her shoulder. "We did good."

"Yes, we did." Kaitlyn smiled back at him.

Erik strode up without so much as a limp.

"How's the leg?" Lucas asked.

"Good as new. Nanotechnology's insane. Those little microscopic robots were able to repair all the tissue damage," he paused. "If I'm lucky, maybe one day I'll have enhancements like Kaitlyn."

Kaitlyn looked skeptical, but Lucas shrugged. "You never know..."

Erik lowered his voice. "Any word on who compromised the mission?"

Lucas ran his hand through his hair, clearly frustrated. "Still trying to figure it out."

Aaliyah smiled shyly at Kaitlyn and dropped her eyes.

Kaitlyn eased forward and dropped to her knee in front of the young boy. She looked him in the eye. When he didn't look away she knew he would be okay. The truly damaged ones had trouble with eye contact. Several of the girls that'd been rescued were virtually catatonic.

The fact that human trafficking was still alive

and well in today's world was absurd to her. According to her internal computer, the sale of human beings was the third largest illicit trade following drugs and weapons, but was growing faster than both of these. An estimated fifty percent of the victims were children and eighty percent were women.

How many more men like Dasvoik are out there? It made her proud to know she was in a position to help people like Aaliyah and Darrius. Reborn as half robot, she had a purpose that was incredible, one she wouldn't have had, if she'd never met people like Lukas and Dr. Harrington.

"I'm glad you made it home," Kaitlyn said to the little boy.

He looked at her for a moment and then a brilliant smile lit his face. He threw his arms around Kaitlyn and squeezed. She squeezed him back and looked up at Harrington, who smiled in return. Anything she had been through to get to this point was well worth the journey. Helping others was what she was made for.

Kaitlyn stood up, and they all followed the family to the waiting cars.

Once the door was shut, Harrington handed Kaitlyn an envelope containing her next mission. She felt a familiar tingle run down her spine.

What would be waiting for them next?

Acknowledgments

A special thanks to my family .

I would also like to thank Amy, Kendal and Lizzy for taking the time to make this novel presentable.

Eden Crane for the amazing cover.

My Crazy for Crane street team.

My assistant, Allison Potter, who holds everything together.

My husband for his technical and tactical knowledge.

My fans for all your support which means more then you will ever know.

And the Bloggers who help spread the word—without you, I wouldn't have made it
this far. Thank you!!!

Also by Julia Crane

Coexist, Book 1 in Keegan's Chronicles
Conflicted, Book 2 in Keegan's Chronicles
Consumed, Book 3 in Keegan's Chronicles
Anna, spin-off from Keegan's Chronicles
Lauren, spin-off from Keegan's Chronicles
Rourk, Keegan's Chronicles novella
Mesmerized, co-written with Talia Jager
Dark Promise, co-written with Talia Jager
Broken Promise, co-written with Talia Jager
Eternal Youth, co-written with Heather Marie
Adkins

About the Author

Julia Crane is the author of the YA paranormal fiction novels: Keegan's Chronicles, Mesmerized, Between Words series, and Eternal Youth. Julia was greatly encouraged by her mother to read and use her imagination, and she's believed in magical creatures since the day her grandmother first told her an Irish tale. Julia has traveled far and wide to all the places her grandmother told her about, gaining inspiration from her journeys to places like Nepal, Cyprus, Sri Lanka, Italy, France and many more. And who knows? Maybe the magical creatures she writes about are people she met along the way.

Julia has a bachelor's degree in criminal justice.

Find Julia online at juliacraneauthor.com

Interested in receiving updates on Julia's books? Join her mailing list! She'll only email about her books and will never share your information with anyone.

Word-of-mouth is crucial for any author to succeed. If you enjoyed Fractured Innocence, please consider leaving a review where you purchased it. It would be greatly appreciated!

Made in the USA
Middletown, DE
28 October 2022